WAITING TO PLAY

LAKE SPARK OFF-SEASON

BOOK 3

EVEY LYON

LAKE SPARK OFF-SEASON SERIES

Waiting to Score

Waiting to Win

Waiting to Play

1

VAUGHN

Oh no.

My sober state is doing absolutely zero to deter my wandering eyes.

I was stuck wondering about this curiosity last night at the wedding of my buddy Connor. And it seems that I'm doing it again at this brunch for out-of-town guests.

It might be a cliché, but damn, the maid of honor is hot... and single. Couldn't tear my sight away if I tried.

I kind of ignore the tiny detail that she's also the sister of my nemesis on the ice, but maybe I get my kicks out of the idea that Briggs Chase would flip.

Isla is beautiful and has natural blonde hair that has a bounce when she swivels her hips on the dance floor, because, yeah, I noticed. I'm sure she's been to plenty of her brother's hockey games, but I never really got a chance to notice because we only play the Spinners up here in Illinois so many times a season. And even though they're technically a Chicago team, the owner just moved them to Lake Spark. I'm based down in Florida where the weather is warm and winter's a dream.

Connor and Hadley had a Vegas wedding a few months ago that they didn't quite remember, so they had a redo in Lake Spark, and now we are all thrown together for this over-the-top wedding weekend. The last few days have been kind of unreal considering Connor's dad is a hockey legend, it's his Uncle Declan who owns the Spinners, and Connor himself is making waves as a hockey star. This meant that the guest list was nothing less than the best of our league.

Then there is his teammate who wants to kill me on a normal day. I guess it's fair, as I've thrown Briggs down in a few scuffles, including a penalty that cost him an important game. Which is why his glare is strong when I'm around.

His sister, Isla, doesn't give me a glare, though. Instead, I was picking up flirty vibes from across the room. Unfortunately, she was on maid-of-honor duty most of the time, so I didn't really get a chance to talk to her. My effort to take her back to my hotel room last night was thwarted when I heard her mention that she was going to stay at Hadley's parents' house to be up early to help prepare brunch. What kind of maid of honor does that? Shouldn't she be partying into the early hours, drinking a tequila too many, and walking barefoot as she carries her heels, preferable back to my room?

I have three hours before I need to head to the airport because I have training tomorrow. This morning is my only chance to talk to the woman whose name is Isla, like an island. An island I would love to be deserted on… with her.

A hand lands on my shoulder, drawing me out of staring at Isla helping the bride's mother adjust a few trays of coffee cake.

"How is Lake Spark treating you, Vaughn?" Declan asks as he hands me a mimosa. I'm sure he would want me on their team if I'm looking for a career change.

A knowing smirk hitches on the corner of my mouth.

"You mean, would I be tempted to make this small little town a permanent spot?"

He grins. For the most part, he's a good guy. Another hockey legend who retired young then bought a team because he was already worth probably billions from his family. "While I could tell you that you have a spot on my team whether you retire this season or not, we both know it wouldn't be appropriate. Although, before you dive into that ridiculous table-sized charcuterie board, I should mention that in the event that you retire, if you're interested, our general manager isn't very popular according to the media."

The thought does create a mental note that I stick in the back of my head. I know my hockey career is dying down. I'm in my mid-thirties, and maybe I have one or two seasons left, but it depends on how I play this coming season. Still, I don't want to think about it now. I examine the over-the-top charcuterie table, complete with fruit, cheese, meats, breads, and nuts, and that's not even including the dessert table. My gaze darts back to Declan. "Oh, look at that, they have a quiche section." I do my best to deter him. "You made your point."

He smiles tightly. "I came to say hi and because I wanted to check in with you. I merely meant to ask if everyone has been hospitable." Only partly a lie, I think.

"Sure, you did." Okay, I sound skeptical, while my eyes scan the room to find the woman with a bright smile that could get me in trouble, but she disappeared.

"Isla went to check on Ace." The man read my mind. My eyes sideline to him, and he shrugs. "It's okay, your secret is safe with me."

"Ace?"

"The dog. Connor and Hadley's dog. My family has a

thing for ensuring our Labradors dress for the occasion." He shakes his head, as he seems to find it ridiculous.

"Right." I spot my exit at the sliding door.

"Isla's brother is helping Ford with something, so go quickly. It's your window of opportunity, which is good because I need Briggs in tip-top shape for pre-season games, so I'd rather he doesn't catch you within a ten-foot radius of his sister," Declan gives me a warning, yet a smile is hinted on his lips.

"I'm going to get some fresh air," I say and walk away.

"I'm sure," Declan mumbles.

I make my way outside to find Isla grumbling at the Lab-mix dog that just wants to play.

"Come on, Ace. Can't you do this for like one hour?" She's talking to the dog as she tries to tie on his bandana that has the date of the wedding and Connor and Hadley's names. Isla is oblivious that I'm approaching.

I wait for her to notice, and I soak in the view of Lake Spark, with pristine dark blue water and pine trees outlining the lake. The dock looks like it gets good use. I can't imagine that the small power boat at the end of the dock stays out all year, as they actually have four seasons in Illinois.

Isla grumbles once more as she kneels down because the dog lies on his back with his paws in the air. "This shouldn't be part of maid-of-honor duty."

Clearing my throat, her head perks up, and an awkward smile graces her mouth. "Oh, hey, you don't happen to have some magic skill to get this dog to cooperate, do you?"

"Sorry, Isla. I left my dog-whisperer talents at home."

It earns me a laugh, and she stands up, abandoning her efforts. Isla doesn't seem shy around me, and her face lightens when I'm here. A cute kind of bashful.

"It's okay." She steps closer to me, scans the area, then

pretends to whisper. "I'm kind of hoping when the dog catches sight of that ridiculous cold-meat section inside that he will make a rookie move and land himself in the doghouse."

I rumble a laugh. "That sounds like a plan we need to initiate."

Isla brings her hand to her hip and tips her nose up. "We?"

I gently roll my shoulder back, relaxing, because I'm liking the ease of our conversation so far. "I didn't get much chance to talk to you last night. All I know is that your Briggs's sister, best friend of the bride, and you work in marketing at the Spinners training facility. For all I know, you actually hate hockey."

She tilts her head slightly with a hum that drills straight to my groin. "Well, you know I can't hate hockey considering that's my brother's career. You know, the brother who I'm positive would like to rip you into shreds, and that's when he's having a great day. The brother who will lose it if he glances outside to see we're talking."

I forgot I had a mimosa in my hand and use this opportunity to take a sip. "You're just being polite to an out-of-town guest." I'm unfazed.

"Fair enough." A gleam flares in her eyes before she takes the mimosa from my hand, with her fingers briefly sweeping across my knuckles, and her touch has far more impact on my body than I should want. Then her lips purse against the rim and she drinks from my glass. I love how the shyness I thought she had seems to have been obliterated into a sexiness that I don't even think she means to be transmitting. "Ready for your new season?"

"I am. After a trip to the Turks and Caicos back in June, I've been developing my skills all summer."

"On or off the ice?" Now, now, that was 100% a playful inuendo that I fully support.

My grin stretches. "Are you this forward with all out-of-town guests or do I get special treatment?"

"I don't know what you're thinking, but I meant did you try cooking or sewing over the summer?" She's coy, and her smirk doesn't fade.

"Is that what you did this summer?"

She scoffs. "My summer was enjoying the lake, coffees at Jolly Joe's with jellybeans with an obscure food coloring that means you get a surprise at the end of every coffee, and calming down my friend because she accidentally married a guy. Typical Lake Spark shenanigans."

"Sounds tranquil." I take back my glass of spiked orange juice.

We both watch the dog run to the other Labrador that I think belongs to Connor's parents. "Not my problem anymore." She seems relieved the dog is gone and drops the bandana to the ground. "Connor and Hadley stayed at the Dizzy Duck Inn last night to have a wedding night, even though they've already had one or three. It meant their furbaby stayed here."

"That makes sense. You didn't get much chance to party last night," I comment.

A beaming smile spreads on her face. "I enjoyed last night, just didn't hit the dance floor too often. I really wanted to help the happy couple's parents with everything, not to mention Hadley's dress required assistance once or twice. But I don't mind, they are all family to me, the closest thing except for Briggs. I mean, I got to talk to a lot of people."

I admire her selflessness wrapped in every word. "You talked to everyone except me."

She holds her finger up. "Wrong. I talked to everyone

except any hockey player who doesn't play on the Spinners and happens to be single, and my deep study of the guest list and table arrangements meant there were four men who fell into that category. Those are the ones I didn't get to talk to, including you, Vaughn Madden."

"Ouch. Unlucky for them, good news for me." We both glance out across the lake and seem to find a peaceful moment. "I've only been here a few times. I volunteered once at the summer camp and partook in a developmental skills camp. But that was a few years ago. A shame my trip is short this time around."

"Probably for the best. Winter is fast approaching."

My face turns puzzled. "It's only early September."

A deep rumble of a laugh escapes her lips. "It's Illinois, it could be flurries of snow or beach weather come October. We are not graced with Florida weather."

"Are you ever in Florida?" I'm a winger, which means being forward is natural.

She laughs, and it vibrates down my spine again and my attraction spikes. "Funny you should ask. I'm actually going down to Tampa in November for a conference." That's my city, and this must be a sign.

"November is a good time. You can escape the temperatures beginning to change here, in exchange for warm weather down there. The chance for hurricanes is not very likely either."

Isla doesn't say anything, instead keeping her wry smile as she studies me. "A shame we weren't sitting at the same table last night so you could give me some tips on places to go to, as I'm staying a few extra days, but there was a clear instruction for the seating chart that you and my brother were not to be at the same table."

"You seem to have a different view of me than your brother," I point out.

"It takes a lot for me to dislike someone. You haven't given me any reason, because I know what happens on the ice is all part of a game," she explains.

"Give me your phone." I hold out my hand, curling my fingers, indicating that she should hand it over.

Isla winces. "Sorry, I left it inside."

I dig into my pocket to grab my cell to type in her number, but we are interrupted by the sound of cheers, as it seems Connor and Hadley have arrived.

"That's our cue to head back in and discover if the smoked cheese is better than the Swiss in the cheese section. Besides… I might have forgotten my number." Isla smirks before she begins to step away, and instantly I reach out to touch her elbow and stop her.

For a moment, her gaze flicks up and I can't form words. But then it spits out. "When you're down in Florida, we should try and meet up."

Isla chortles and her jaw moves side to side. "Not a good idea."

"Why? Don't trust yourself around me?" I wonder.

"Something like that."

She leaves my grasp, but I'm still drawn to her like a magnet, even when she strides away. Isla's right, she shouldn't trust herself around me. I'm the guy who isn't searching for much except gratification that hopefully involves her dress on the floor and good conversation.

By the time I follow her back inside, Isla's vanished into the room of people. It's a solid half-hour later when Connor is talking to me that I spot Isla again.

"It really means a lot that you came out for the wedding." Connor hands me a new champagne flute.

"No problem. A bit smug, though, don't you think? I sent a wedding present after your Vegas nuptials, and now I need to do it all over again because you decided to remember it this time?" I smirk at him.

He smiles. "Give a donation to charity instead and you'll get over it. You shouldn't be sending me any gifts at all, considering in a few weeks when the season starts, I'm going to conquer you on the ice when we eventually have a game together on the roster."

My brows pinch together. "Wishful thinking, buddy."

His response is to chuckle then pat my shoulder before heading to the next guest. I inspect my watch and realize I should be heading out of here to make my flight. However, my feet don't move when I catch sight of Isla holding a small plate of food, and she approaches me with caution, probably searching for her brother.

"The Swiss cheese is the winner, and did you remember your number yet?" I tell her, and her gorgeous lips are getting harassed by her tongue swiping to the corner of her mouth.

"Really having memory problems today. Who are you again?" She's teasing me, and I laugh at her humor. "And duly noted about the cheese. Have a safe flight, Vaughn." Is that a sultry look she's giving me? It's a fine way to end the morning.

A shame I don't get more. It's okay, though, there is always next time. I'm an athlete for a reason; I'm determined to win.

EARLY NOVEMBER

Well, this is just not what I planned.

Not by what's about to go down, but by the fact our home

game has been postponed and rescheduled for later in the season due to a late-season hurricane that's approaching.

However, this situation also means I got lucky. Really lucky.

My thumb traces the text message on the screen.

CONNOR

Saw the game highlights. You holding up with the hurricane approaching? Hadley is losing her cool because her best friend is down there for a conference and didn't get a flight back. Tell me something that can calm my wife down?

ME

The hurricane? Yeah, well, it's only a category one. People were buying hurricane cakes at the grocery store earlier. Hadley's friend will be okay. Most hotels are prepared for this, or maybe she's somewhere out of the flood zone. Do you know which hotel?

CONNOR

I think Isla is staying at the Pelican Blue. I'll tell Hadley to relax. Good luck!

I smirk to myself, because my buddy casually mentioning the intel on Isla was exactly what I needed to perk up my current state that landed me in this hotel a few hours later. He may have been thinking about the maid of honor's safety, but in reality, he unknowingly handed me the information I needed to get me here, sitting with a bottle of beer in hand, waiting for the prize that I wanted to claim already weeks ago.

Normally, I don't really drink much during the season, but a beer is perfectly fine right now. I focus on my drink, yet I feel her sit down at the bar, unaware of my presence.

The gripe that escapes her lips is my undoing, I swear.

"Dry white, please. Of course, this is my life. The one time I decide to mix work with a few vacation days in the sun, a hurricane decides to trap me in a hotel," she grumbles to the barman.

I bite my lip, as I'm entertained while I listen to her complain. I wasn't lying to Connor, this hotel is hurricane-proof, has a great generator, and a hurricane doesn't seem to faze the staff either. We're safe.

Is Isla safe from me? Not so much.

Rotating on my barstool, I face her, and she's sporting hot-as-hell yoga pants and a cute sweatshirt.

"It could be worse. You could be trapped in a hotel with me, because we just didn't get enough time during our last stint."

Her eyes whip to me and shock hits her that I'm sitting in front of her, before her lips curl into a smirk that spells trouble for the both of us.

ISLA

Why is Vaughn Madden sitting next to me in a hotel bar during a hurricane? And why do my instincts feel as though being trapped suddenly doesn't seem so bad?

I stare at him, intrigued or impressed by this twist of fate. However, his devilish grin and the glint in his blue eyes inform me that there is no fate involved. In fact, he hinted with persistence back at the wedding that it wouldn't be the last time we saw one another. Damn, his dirty blond hair is a length that is short, but I could still comb my fingers through that wave on top.

"Isn't this a coincidence," I state as my head lolls to the side gently, with zero conviction in my voice.

"Hardly," he says bluntly. "Your concerned friends let it slip that you were staying here, they don't know that I'm seeing you, though. And lucky for you, the league has postponed our upcoming home game. Mother Nature just conspired with me, clearly angry that you never gave me your number, Isla," he chides before he takes a sip of his drink.

"Hurricane-sized angry?" Doubt casts over my face

before I quickly nod a thanks to the barman for my wine that he sets in front of me.

Vaughn leans against the bar, very confident with whatever he has up his sleeve. "You know, a late-season hurricane in November is extremely rare. Only a handful have hit Florida. But it might pass us and hit south or could stall, which would prolong our presence with one another."

I scoff a sound. "Tell that to the airport that closed, and now I'm stuck here because of Hurricane Nora."

"With me," he points out.

I play with the stem of my wine glass. "How convenient." I try to suppress the smile itching to escape my lips, but I can't.

The tips of his fingers touch near my elbow, catching me by surprise, and my eyes dart to see the proof that our skin is touching, yet I already feel a flutter in my belly.

It's not that I was playing hard to get or not very interested back during the wedding weekend. My gut was just telling me that it wouldn't really go anywhere, not to mention I was so busy with everything. But in truth, I'm attracted to him, far too much.

"It is *very* convenient. Wasn't planning on this occurrence at all." Vaughn's voice sounds playful, yet there seems to be an underlying truth.

"Neither was I. However, now would be the time to highlight what plan you conspired and is floating in your head."

"Dirty things." He's direct.

I have to chortle because he won't even try to hide it. "I figured." A silence overtakes us, and we both glance to the television mounted on the wall, with a weather report on display. "I've never been in a hurricane before," I mention.

"You know, they used to only give hurricanes female

names, but then they stopped. However, it's a historical fact that female hurricanes are by far more dangerous."

I snicker. "Maybe I should be scared then."

His fingers gently brush just below my elbow. "Don't be scared. It's really a minor one, won't even hit during high tide. Tomorrow it will probably be sunny with no wind," he explains, and I appreciate that it seems he is trying to ease my concerns. He ends our touch so he can lean back on his barstool and get comfortable, as neither one of us can go anywhere.

"I'm not scared at all, so I won't need your strong arms to hold me. I'm from the Midwest, I've been through plenty of tornadoes."

Vaughn lifts his finger. "Now, a tornado and a hurricane are not the same thing, and once you realize that, then I'll be here with my strong arms, willing to hold you."

Warm heat hits my face, and I glance up to attempt to read his eyes, but my cheeks feel so tight from the wry smile I'm trying to keep tame. "You've been through a tornado? Where are you actually from? You've only played for Tampa for a short while, right?" I take a sip of my wine, hoping to ease my curiosity of where this will all lead.

"I'm from Colorado, and I've been down here for nearly seven years. Hence, my expertise on weather."

"Maybe I'll appreciate it when the lights go out."

He leans in. "Hurricane or not, the lights will be going out." It's a low gravelly husk that makes my body tingle.

Again, I have to laugh. "What is this, really? It's not like you've been thinking about me for two months, so if you found out I'm here and thought what the hell, let's have some fun, then you are…" My lips quirk out, debating what to say, but I love honesty. "Not exactly mistaken." I have no qualms about enjoying sex.

Now he chuckles. "Thought so."

We look at one another with ridiculous smiles, a connection that feels far too natural. To some, he may appear way too cocky, but I can tell it's all in good jest.

"Why aren't you at your home? You do live here," I point out.

"Well, as much as this is probably going to be an easy hurricane, the only anticipation that I have is in regards to you, when I discovered that you were here." He grabs a handful of nuts from the bowl on the bar. "And by chance, you're staying in the hotel that a buddy of mine invested in."

Lines form on my forehead. "Did he help you land a room here then?"

Vaughn shakes his head. "Nah, me sitting before you about to blow your mind is all thanks to your friends freaking out about you being safe and my determined ability to nab a room using my celebrity status."

A fond smile takes over me. "Hadley and Connor are great people. All of them are. Their parents, uncles and aunts, even the dogs. They're family to me."

A shade of interest and care hits his face while his gorgeous eyes narrow. "You don't come from a big family?"

I tuck a few strands of hair behind my ear and look down at the floor then back up. "No, not at all. It's me and Briggs. Our dad took off before I was born, and our mom, well, decided she didn't want to be a mom and left when I was five, so we lived with our grandmother who passed a few years back. Never heard from either of our parents again, and truthfully, never want to." Wow, I just laid it all out there, and it feels like a relieving whoosh.

Vaughn reaches out to touch my shoulder gently in a comforting manner. "Sorry to hear. I understand you completely. Our dad wasn't around at all, except for the random times he would float in and out of our lives, always in trouble. Our mom really did it all as a single mom, but now she lives in New Mexico with a new husband, so we don't see her much, as she is more occupied with her new marriage, and to be honest, has kind of forgotten us, as though we don't exist."

"We?"

"My older brother, Stone. He used to play hockey too, actually. We have a sports gene or something. Now, he lives in Chicago. We're pretty close."

"Older brothers can be great. Briggs and I are close, as you've figured out."

He chuckles again, this time deeper and at the back of his throat. "Oh, I know. But I don't particularly care about his opinions."

I grab some peanuts. "That was always clear."

"What is it you do exactly at the sports complex?" Vaughn wonders, and I like that we are, in a way, getting to know one another.

"I work in marketing. At first, it was for the summer camps that Ford runs, mostly for kids and charity events. Then it was the development summer training for young pro athletes. However, since the Spinners moved to Lake Spark to train, I liaison often with the team marketing department. I'm super lucky that Ford is my boss, as he is a good one, laid back and lets me come up with my own ideas. Trusts me until I have the end product," I explain.

Vaughn's lips purse out as he thinks about something. "Sounds kind of fun. I wanted to study sports management in college, but I was drafted at twenty so couldn't finish. A shame, because I have only a few years, if at all, playing before I need to shift gears."

"Well, you're not the first guy to be in that situation."

It's darker than it should be in here because the hurricane shutters are closed as a precaution, but I think it's late afternoon. I'm losing track of time because we're picking up right where we left off two months ago.

"I wouldn't have figured that you would manage to get yourself here, with determination flooding your eyes," I note.

"You know, many people stress before a storm, but I always felt rest is key."

I raise a brow at him. "You need rest, yet here you are."

A suave grin appears to curl on the corner of his lips that look soft, and his dimples are my downfall, causing my inner walls to tighten. "Ah, so you're saying I won't be getting rest?"

Swirling on the stool to face me head-on, he plants his hands down on the edges of my seat to ensure I have no escape.

"Truthfully, I'm still kind of thrown by the fact you appeared here during a storm," I admit.

"Shall I lay it out for you?"

I nod once purely to play along.

"I think you're more than gorgeous, and your flirting game is strong. I'm not looking for serious, not now. Not even casual. But a night is something I can do, and I enjoy that it's a little more than that. Talking to you is easy."

I study Vaughn for a solid few seconds. "I don't want you to think that I do this all the time. I may enjoy a lot of things, but I'm not easy. Since my last relationship, I accepted that there is no sense in planning or defining lines. I'm more concerned these days about work, ensuring I'm first in line for the fresh cinnamon rolls at Jolly Joe's, and trying to survive Hadley's barre Pilates classes. I'm not a model or anything like that." I feel like I'm in good shape, and I'm confident with my looks, yet still I don't spend hours on my appearance.

This time it's Vaughn who swipes a few strands of hair behind my ear.

"A girl who isn't afraid of breakfast pastry, you say?" Did he even hear me? "I dated models, and it's not for me," he adds.

I chortle and use my hands to indicate my outfit. "Great, your standard is models, and here I am before you in yoga pants and a sweatshirt."

His dimples appear again from his wide smile. I really do love dimples. "Oh, but your sweatshirt literally says 'A Simple Woman' with an icon of a donut, wine, and a hockey puck with sticks. That indicates that you're exactly the woman I need."

My face falls into my hand where my arm is propped on the bar, slightly embarrassed by my outfit choice, but I'm having a blast. "Least it's not my 'I like life in the penalty box' sweatshirt."

His eyes grow bold. "We can make that happen."

I search the room and see only a few people here, mostly watching the television or checking their phones. "Shouldn't we seek safety or something?"

"We're fine. Almost everyone is staying on the second floor, so not too high because of wind, and we're okay from flooding even if it rains a lot."

"You thought through all aspects, huh?"

"Even included snacks, flashlights, and bottled water," Vaughn deadpans.

I lean in to whisper, "What a thoughtful person. So…" My voice turns awkward, as I'm not sure what is next—well, I'm aware what is next, but I'm trying not to appear too eager.

He answers for me. "Take my hand and let's head upstairs." His tone is straightforward. He's past trying to persuade me; he knows that he has me. "But you might want to bring your suitcase so we can be kind citizens and let others have your room."

Good judgment is way beyond me. I think I was committed the moment I turned to find him next to me.

Which is why I easily take his offered hand.

————

QUICKLY, I grabbed my things and checked myself in the mirror before I went to Vaughn's room which was only a few doors down. I told the front desk they can have my room back very aware that I appeared in a rush and eager. Arriving, Vaughn lets me in with a sly smile. Behind him, I see he is watching the radar on the screen. It's raining outside, and I notice the trees blowing, but it's tame so far compared to the storm fronts that pass through Illinois.

Vaughn turns the TV off and throws the remote onto the bed before he strides my way with an overpowering heat in his eyes. My chest is on fire from my heart rate that's higher than normal because I love the pure purpose that seems to have possessed him.

We bypass small talk, and he grabs the hair at the back of my head to yank me forward, a power move that tells me he has a dominant side. When his lips slam down on mine, I'm already sinking into this moment.

He kisses hard yet tantalizing, his tongue swiping into my mouth, and it's the right amount of tickle against the tip of my tongue. A hum draws out from the back of my throat because I'm eager for his mouth to explore more. The feeling of his hands framing my face to ensure I can't escape is a sexy move that I enjoy.

We gently part to lock our eyes and check in with one another, only for him to growl and meld our lips together. The man devours me through a kiss, and inside, my body screams more, more, more.

But I refuse to just stand here, which is why my hands begin to roam his body, searching for the bottom of his t-shirt so I can encourage us to keep moving. I tug then yank as we walk in a circle with our mouths never parting. That is, until we must, to pull his shirt up and off. I can't help myself and lean slightly back so I can give him the once-over, and my pussy clenches from the view of his chiseled chest and stomach, and the tattoos on his shoulder and chest; a small black Celtic pattern. My fingers trail the lines of definition on his skin, biting my lip in the process because he is magnificent.

"Isla, you clearly see something you like, and I refuse to be the only one undressing here. Let's get this off of you." Vaughn begins to guide the fabric of my sweatshirt and tank top up, and when that's off, his eyes laser in on my pink lace bra. I've always been lucky with my cleavage, a perfect C cup.

Taking the liberty, I crawl onto the bed on all fours and glance over my shoulder as Vaughn watches, then I crook a finger to invite him to join me.

"Damn, which one of us is luckier tonight?" he says right before he grabs hold of my hips to flip my body onto my back, causing me to squeal in delight. He hooks his fingers around the waistband of my yoga pants and tugs them down and off. Vaughn's gaze rakes over my body, and he nibbles his bottom lip as he gently shakes his head in approval, clearly satisfied with the view. When my fingers begin to draw circles on my cleavage and I drag one hand down below my navel, his eyes grow big and his patience breaks. He is over me in no time, with his hands pinning my wrists to the mattress.

"I bet you're ready to go." He's sure of himself.

My head dips back into a pillow as I offer my neck to Vaughn, which he gladly trails his mouth with the occasional nip before heading lower to my breasts. His lips skim my skin and send vibrations down my body, causing a tight knot to form between my legs.

"This round you might not need to work so hard." My breath is heavy. "But something tells me somewhere between round three and four, you're going to have to use that tongue of yours and go incredibly slow."

A deep chuckle leaves his lips. "Babe, that's already going to happen this round. So spread those thighs of yours."

Obeying, I soak in the feeling of his tongue circling a nipple through the lace, while his hand delves between us, and he slides his fingers into my panties, instantly hitting the aching spot that I desperately want relief from. His hard cock rests against my inner thigh, and I just want to wrap my legs around him.

"Fucking hell, you're drenched," he notes with a rasp.

"I guess that happens when you're around, and I know any moment you will demand I get on my knees to suck you off."

Something about this man breaks open the doors inside me, making me let go of all inhibitions. The attraction between us feels like luck, because this simmering need to go wild is unbearable to most.

Vaughn curses under his breath. "You're a mind reader, which is why you know a spanking is going to come to you next round when you're lying over my lap with my hand tangled in your hair." Then he's slithering down my body, ready to prove a point.

He roughly pulls the lace to the side right before his tongue flicks against my clit, and his finger finds my entrance. My entire body writhes under him as I moan in response.

Vaughn isn't going to treat me like a delicate flower, and I'm completely here for that. Heat sends a wave through my body, desperate for him to continue.

"You taste so fucking good. Now, let me make you come," he urges before his tongue returns to my bundle of nerves that will unravel me. I don't even question why we're moving so fast; I guess our attraction is the type that combusts.

He adds another finger inside of me, and I swear I'm getting dizzy with overpowering lust.

I hum in approval, enjoying every second until I vibrate against his mouth, and he grips my hips down to keep me stable. He even interlaces our fingers against the mattress to steady me, or rather, be possessive. Either way, I'm not complaining. Give the man a reward for allowing me a few seconds to recover.

But we are a blazing flame, and he flips me over to my stomach and tilts my hips up. The moment the tip of his cock explores my pussy to coat his length before he circles around my entrance, I'm desperate for a new orgasm. When he fills me up with his cock I must appear as a woman wantoned by neediness.

His first thrust feels far too good, pleasure that I'm not quite sure I could have ever fathomed. We're on a wild train due to our eagerness.

We're fast, primal, and raw with one another.

It's only when he curses to himself that I'm broken from my cloud of ecstasy.

His breath is already heavy. "Condom, Isla. We completely forgot. I'm safe but…"

I have a strong instinct of trust with him, and I'm not logical right now. "I'm on the pill. Safe. Now don't stop." I string words together in a sentence.

His crusade to thrust into me with abandon continues. "Isla, I'm going to fuck you so deep that you'll discover new spots that make you want to scream and come all over my cock."

Him inside of me with no condom. Bare and hard. It only ups the ante between us, and my moan is as loud as the wind outside.

———

LYING IN BED, I catch the protein bar that Vaughn just threw at me. "Really?" I'm entertained.

He smirks to himself. "Gotta keep us strong for the night ahead… but really, I forgot I had one in my bag."

It causes me to smile as the lights flicker because the storm is going to hit us in the next hour. The outer bands are already overhead.

Vaughn throws his phone onto the chair. "We will miss the eye but looks like we might get the right side of the storm." He joins me back on the bed.

"I'm not worried."

"See? That's what the safety of my cock does. Calms you down."

I breathe out a sound as the corners of my mouth hitch up. We're both lying on our sides, resting from round three. I feel this is the moment to highlight the obvious.

"What happens tonight is what it is, okay?"

"Absolutely," he agrees. "We're making up for our missed opportunity during the wedding reception."

"We can pretend nothing ever happened," I add confidently. Deep down, I think that's what I want too. Our lives barely overlap. "Even if you have a game against my brother." Okay, I ignore that our paths will cross then.

Vaughn bobs his head side to side. "I don't know. It would really throw your brother's game off." I give him a death stare, and his response is to touch my shoulder. "Relax. You're right. I'll even make it easier and be gone by the time you wake."

Oh.

"That's maybe for the best." There's disappointment somewhere within me, even though I initiated this conversation, but I choose to ignore it.

Vaughn grabs the protein bar from my fingers and throws it to the side before he pulls my body flush on top of him, causing me to lean onto him. It's warm, and ooh, I'm going to enjoy myself tonight.

"What are the chances I can get you to ride me reverse cowgirl right now?" he mumbles into the top of my head, nuzzling my hair.

The thought of what his fingers could do to me while I ride him is too overwhelming. "Very high," I tell him, and instantly the tip of his finger comes to play with my clit, creating that internal agony of needing a release again. He encourages me to get in position.

The rain pours outside, the wind picks up, and there is an unusual feeling in the air. I'm not sure if it's the change of air pressure or the fact that tonight is one that I will remember, because I am truly happy by this very planned coincidence.

Which is why I'm grateful he keeps his word. Because when I wake, Vaugh Madden is gone, just like the hurricane that passed.

ISLA

My nails strum against the wood of my dining room table as I stare at my laptop screen. This is all pointless. I know I'm not going to learn any new facts. I squeeze my knee closer to my chest and sigh as I rub the back of my neck before I glance to my side.

Sometimes in life, you just have an uncontrollable feeling that you're right.

The pregnancy test taunts me from where it's lying on the table. Unceremoniously, I flip the test over to see the answer.

Positive.

It's not even a big deal because in my head I already believed it. The test is confirmation that I was right.

I felt it in my bones that something was off. The dizzy spell after the staff meeting. The slight case of nausea when I was at the general store picking up groceries. By the time my period never came, my head had already done the calculation. It never once occurred to me that maybe it could be a flu or virus; it was straight-up intuition that I was pregnant. A different feeling.

I thought the pill was enough. Obviously not.

Here I am blankly searching up on the internet what to expect over the coming weeks, with a realization that I need to get an appointment on my calendar to see the doctor and check on everything. Sure, I'm aware that I have options, but for me, this is the decision I'm making.

My groan this time is longer, and I bite my bottom lip to stop it.

I should be focusing on buying gifts for the holidays. Yet my eyes dart between a positive pregnancy test and the screen that tells me I'm carrying a blueberry-sized human, the creation of Vaughn and me.

Moving to stand up, I walk to my kitchen to grab a devil's-food chocolate-mint cookie from the box. Taking a bite, the sugar relief does fuck all to relax me.

I pull out my phone to call my doctor and make an appointment in two weeks.

Once that is done, I text Hadley.

> Sorry. Can't make it to barre class tomorrow, a bit of a cold is coming on with chills.

It's a lie, but alas, the internet told me to stay away from certain exercises during the first trimester.

> HADLEY
>
> Oh. Need anything? The moms will miss you at coffeetime after class.

I laugh to myself, because it looks like I can join the moms club. But then an affectionate smile overcomes me. Hadley's mom April, plus her mother-in-law Brielle, and her husband's aunt Violet would only be supportive, probably constantly asking if I'm okay too.

I'm not ready for that.

Another time. Sleep is calling my name.

So is figuring out how to tell my baby daddy.

Sweet dreams.

I have Vaughn's number, but neither one of us have texted since that night in Florida. And tonight, I'm not ready to try and reach out. How does one break the news?

I better come up with a way and fast.

———

Sitting in the waiting room at the doctor's office, I fully recognize that scrolling on my phone to check out how Vaughn played during last night's game against Boston is not the way I should be heading into this appointment. Nor is getting side-tracked that he is so ridiculously handsome in his pre-game suit that it's all over social media.

The door to the doctor's office opens, and I freeze when I see Violet. Not only is she now related to Hadley through marriage, but she's also the wife of the owner of the Spinners, and a friend in a way, as she joins the Pilates classes. She's only a few years older than me.

Her face grows crooked as she takes off her wool hat to reveal her dark hair. "Hey, Isla… uhm… didn't expect to see you here."

Because she's about five months pregnant with her second child, so of course she's at the OB/GYN's office.

I give her an awkward look because I already see she's puzzle-pieced things together in her head, and saying I'm here for a yearly gyno check-up doesn't seem like it's going to cut it.

Throwing my arms up in a loss, I ask for a favor. "What are the chances we can keep this visit between us? Like, completely sealed so not even your husband is aware. I'm not ready for the world to know."

Violet comes to sit next to me in the waiting room, and she nudges my shoulder with her own. "Absolutely. I never saw you here… Is this why you missed barre?" She rejoined when she hit her second trimester and skips a few more strenuous exercises. Then again, she doesn't need to exercise at all —she's stunning.

I pull out my devil's-food cookie box and grab one before offering her the box. She takes one on offer. "Something like that. This *obviously* wasn't planned." I hold my hand up. "Please don't ask about the father."

She quirks her lips out. "Does he know?"

I shake my head. "I'm kind of wrapping my head around the fact that I need to stock up on diapers before telling him. Another point for me, we're *obviously* not in a relationship."

"I gathered." She touches my arm to comfort me. "He has a right to know at some point, don't you think?"

I nod in agreement. "I'm trying to focus on one thing at a time."

Violet smiles warmly. "Okay, are you excited? Babies are a lot of work but oh so fun. And pregnancy can be the best time of your life too."

The corners of my mouth curve up. "Actually…" A radiant smile hits me. "I am excited. Other than Briggs, I don't really have any biological family, and well, this baby will be helping my family grow. Plus, I might have already looked at some baby clothes online, and well... they're so cuuuute."

She laughs. "I know. We have a bunch of girl stuff if you end up having a girl. It's a boy this time around, so I get to shop all over again."

My eyes drift down to my still-flat stomach, curious if it's a boy or girl inside of me. "Time will tell."

The door opens to the corridor for the exam rooms and a nurse appears. "Isla Chase?"

"That's me." I stand up and look to Violet who gives me an assuring smile.

"My appointment isn't for a while if you don't want to go in alone."

It's really sweet of her to offer. "It's okay, I think I need to do this solo."

"You've got this," she offers in encouragement.

I take a deep breath and leave her to follow the nurse who takes me to an exam room, where a minute later, I'm sitting anxiously on an exam table with a paper gown, and the doctor arrives.

"Hi, Isla, I'm Dr. Forest." The woman in her forties smiles. "Yes, like the forest with trees and deer."

"It's a fun name," I say. "Not easy to forget. I'm sure you get a lot of jokes about Bambi."

She smirks at my humor and glances down at her tablet. "Okay, so what brings you in today?"

"Shouldn't you know, since you're looking at my file?" I sound kind of surprised.

Dr. Forest laughs. "I do know, but I would like you to confirm it."

"That's kind of your job. To corroborate that a pregnancy test at home claims that I'm pregnant."

She sets her tablet to the side to grab some gloves,

still smiling. "Sounds like I don't need to tell you that your blood work came back also positive, and HCG levels put you at about seven weeks, but we're going to have a look because your file said that you had an ovary looked at a few years ago for a cyst, but everything checked out."

An audible breath escapes me. "Pregnancy, yay," I flatly say and give myself a weak fist pump.

Dr. Forest pauses to look at me. "You're not sure about this pregnancy? We can, of course, discuss options."

I shake my head no. "I'm ready for this, the baby, I mean. It is what I want. It's just... this was really unplanned. Like, 'surprise November hurricane, a hotel room with a hot hockey player who just so happens to be your brother's enemy' kind of unplanned. So... yeah... not exactly sure how to celebrate this one."

She rolls a machine toward the exam table. "Wow, that's quite a..." She debates what to say. "I can understand why your thoughts may be everywhere."

"You're telling me," I snort.

"How about we focus on you. How are you feeling?"

My head bobbles side to side. "Tired, nauseous, but so far, doable."

"Good. If you lie down, I'm going to do an internal ultrasound to check on baby."

I begin to lie down, with my pulse quickening. Lying on my back, I attempt a few relaxing breaths.

"I'm going to start now," I hear her say.

But it feels like the thrum of my heart is taking over my ears because I'm a good kind of nervous. I can only imagine what's about to happen. And when the swooshing sound of a fast heartbeat overtakes my nerves, tears instantly sting my eyes.

I look up on the screen where the doctor is pointing to a blob. "Healthy baby right here."

A warm tear falls down my cheek. I'm instantly in love. Life-changing emotions hit me in a giant wave.

She zooms in and tilts her head in various ways. "Is there a point to me confirming how far along you are, as you mentioned the one-night hurricane kind of thing?" I appreciate that she has humor.

"Least we can easily calculate, right?" I shrug, with my eyes laser focused on the screen.

"Yes, but don't forget, pregnancy starts from the date of your last period."

I raise my long finger. "Yep, got that. I'm quite aware how pregnancy works, which is kind of funny, as you would think I'd have had sense to double up on the birth control, but hey, we're not always wise."

"Normally you should be okay on the pill, but sometimes, travel or not taking the pill on time can decrease efficiency."

"You're telling me that eastern standard time, that one hour ahead of us, really screwed me over?" I'm sarcastic. I'm 100% sure that I forgot a pill.

Dr. Forest takes a few screenshots. "I don't think analyzing what went wrong will help. You have a healthy baby inside of you, and you seem at peace with that."

"You're right." I finally tear my eyes away from the screen. "Do I get to take home the photos."

She smiles widely at me as she slowly brings the wand out. "I'll do even better and upload the video and photos to the medical app. You can share it with…"

I hold my hand up. "The father? Yeah, that's taking a little time to process in my head, how to tell him."

"That's up to you."

"Yep." I pop the P, well aware that I can't rely on the excuse that I was waiting to confirm with the doctor anymore.

———

I PACE MY LIVING ROOM, while I struggle to hit send with my thumb. Instead, I type a text then delete and do this on repeat.

Hey, long time. Is it okay if I call you?

Obvious, Isla, obvious.

Hey, Vaugh, it's been a while. Nice goal last night.

Perhaps a good opening.

We need to talk.

Again, horrible.

Hope you're doing well. I know we said we would leave the hurricane night as a one-night thing. But we kind of have a situation...

That will just make him freak out.

Photo of ultrasound. *SURPRISE.*

That will just give him a heart attack.

"Just call him," I scold myself. In person is better, but there is no way that can logistically happen in the next few days.

My phone rings, and I see it's my brother calling. Briggs is in St. Louis for a game tomorrow. Guilt hits me because I feel like I might disappoint him. He's my older brother, but at times we're inseparable, and he supports me in so many ways. I don't want to let him down, and I know a surprise pregnancy isn't on his list of wants for his sister. And he will for sure kill Vaughn. Still, I answer.

"Hey, Sis, how is your cold going?" It sounds like he's walking.

"Fine. Ready for your game?"

I'm not telling anyone until I inform Vaughn. It's the right thing to do.

"For sure. The Spinners are playing somewhat better than last year." He's not afraid to be cocky.

"I know. It's a marketing gold mine. Thanks for that." Maybe he can hear my smile.

"Someone mentioned that you weren't at work today. Everything good?"

"Spying on me? Damn it, why does my brother have to practice at my place of work."

He growls in frustration. "How about you just answer me."

"How about you tell me how your 'operation win over your masseuse' is going?" I counter.

He's ridiculously hung up on his masseuse who doesn't want to give him the time of day. But now he is going full swing trying to win her over. I had to take extra photos of him in his hockey uniform holding a puppy with a Santa hat.

"I'm going to get that date. Just you watch. Now, work?"

I'm aware that I can't squirm my way out of this.

"Relax. I went to the doctor to check on this sinus infection. Just a virus that will pass," I lie.

In about seven or eight months.

"Okay, take it easy. I'm going to grab some dinner with the guys. Send me your Xmas wish list, by the way. Two weeks to go, I need to figure all that stuff out."

I already bought him his gift. I saw it in October. A remote-control car that delivers beer bottles from the kitchen. It's simple yet him. Briggs will go all out; he always buys me expensive stuff I don't need.

"Sure. I'll think of something. Good luck tomorrow."

"Love ya, Sis."

"Love you, too."

You're going to be a great uncle, I think to myself. I pull up the ultrasound photos on my phone, with a smile tugging on my mouth again.

"It's time to do this," I say to myself. Vaughn has a right to know. This baby deserves to have a chance to get to know their father. I also want to be ready if Vaughn wants no part in this. I can do it without him. I'm going to give him an out. I just hope he doesn't take it. I *pray* he doesn't take it. I want to believe that there are good fathers in this world. Nothing like my own.

I purse my lips and blow out a breath, ready to rip the band-aid off.

My thumb hits his name and the call button. My entire body is about to burst with nerves. He didn't have a game tonight, so hopefully he answers.

It takes three rings before his phone picks up. I could scream that this is going to happen.

"Hello?" A woman's voice answers, she sounds my age.

Every feeling inside of me collapses to my stomach.

"Hello?" she repeats. "Hey, babe, don't forget we're meeting Sam for drinks in an hour," she seems to call out to someone in the background.

Babe?

No, no, no. Tell me he isn't seeing someone. Maybe, I guess, he could have met someone, it's been a while since our night.

"Oh, uh, I'm looking for Vaughn," I nearly croak out.

"He's a bit busy, if you know what I mean." Her voice is like a purr of a taunt. I don't like it. No clue her name, but I already want to wipe that smug leer off her face that probably has lip gloss and overdone foundation.

"Do you… do you know when he might be available?" I

nearly stutter, but I'm desperate now because he is within reach, so close to his phone, he's there… just not alone.

"Listen, Irene, Isabel, whatever name that came up on Vaughn's phone. A request from Vaughn, unless you're his publicist or from the team, then he isn't available. In fact, he will be quite occupied later, so don't bother calling back… ever." She hangs up on me.

I stand there speechless with my phone to my ear, unable to move. This is the worst-case scenario. Vaughn has moved on and really wants us to forget about that night.

My hand gently touches my navel. It will be hard to do that; we have a reminder.

A tightness forms in my throat and a cry is working its way toward an escape.

"It's just you and me, kid. It'll be okay."

For now, I need to focus on my pregnancy. Telling Vaughn is no longer a priority, at least not any time soon. Feels like I need to recover and come up with a new plan.

4

VAUGHN

Sliding the door of the balcony closed behind me, I wish I wasn't leaving the Gulf water views of this penthouse downtown. Especially since my eyes land on the woman who causes pure aggravation, tapping her finger against the screen of my phone.

"What the hell?" I snipe as I approach her with speed. I had my phone on the charger while I went outside to say hi to a few guys since this is my neighbor's place, and a soft drink before sunset sounded somewhat relaxing.

The bleach-blonde woman instantly pouts her plump lips that are in no way natural. Amber has been the headache that never goes away. Borderline crazy if I'm being honest, maybe even stalkerish. She is also friends with my neighbor's girl-friend, which makes her sometimes inescapable. I wouldn't have come had I known she would be here.

"Baby, I was just checking that your battery was full so I could bring you your cell, of course." She purses her lips then perks out her tits that I have zero interest in.

I snap my phone out of her hand with fake white-tipped nails. "What did you do?"

"Nothing." She plays innocent, but I can sense a lie.

One mistake from six months ago, a drunken mistake, not even a full-on performance. More like in a haze of tequila, apparently, I kissed her, and here I am with her claws never letting go.

I examine my phone. "How did you unlock my phone? Do you know my password? Did someone call me?" I ask, because the call log is open, although I don't see anything new. She seems like someone who would erase the evidence.

"Of course not, silly." She touches my arm and flutters her lashes with an overdone giggle that I'm not buying. I'm pretty sure she is a replica of the doll that my teammate's daughter plays with.

"Then why is my screen open?" I grit out.

She squeezes my arm right before I rip away from her touch. "Oh, that. Wrong number, a cold call of someone trying to sell you hurricane shutters for next season." She's avoiding the total breach of privacy.

Shaking my head, I'm not going with this. "Really?" I cast my doubt. "My number is unlisted." My eyes narrow in on her for an answer. "Besides, my phone doesn't show any new calls. Did you delete it?"

"Did I?" She begins to twirl hair around her finger, playing innocent.

I pinch the bridge of my nose, beyond frustrated. "I don't know what clue to give you that I'm not interested, nor ever will I ever be interested."

She steps closer to reach for my hands, but I step back. "Come on, baby, we can go for drinks, relax. I'll give you a massage, maybe a little bit more." She bounces her shoulders in pride, as if she just gave me the best offer.

In another world it would be enticing… if it was from another woman. Isla, to be exact.

"I swear to God, I'm losing a brain cell right now." I was speaking to myself, but her puffed-out cheeks indicates she heard me and is no longer happy.

Luckily, a hand lands on my shoulder; it's my buddy Scott. "Didn't realize my girlfriend invited crazy, sorry about that," he mutters to me. Then he throws on an overdone smile. "Hey, Amber, how about you go find my girlfriend in the kitchen and stay there. This guy is probably on a plane tomorrow for his next game and just needs… well, not you."

Amber seems pissed off and sharply pivots to storm off to the kitchen, flicking her hair in the process. I turn to Scott and sigh an exhausted breath.

He winces at me. "Sorry, I didn't realize she was stopping by. I wish Nicole would warn me about these things, or even better, ditch Amber altogether. But you know Nicole, has to be kind to everyone, and Amber was in her sorority."

I laugh without humor. "She's batshit crazy."

Scott grins to himself. "That and I think you still have your mind on someone… anonymous hurricane girl."

My mouth stretches slightly at the memory of Isla. I haven't told anyone about who she is exactly, just briefly mentioned my fling during a hurricane.

"You know I'm focusing on the season." Partly a lie, since I think of Isla every single time I need a release with my hand.

"Doesn't mean she can't occupy your thoughts. Have you texted her?"

I slide my phone, now fully charged, albeit touched by Satan, into my jeans pocket.

"Nah, we had a blast but agreed to keep it at that," I reiterate what I've mentioned before.

Scott drinks from his beer before he tips it at me. "Should

I head into the kitchen to get you a drink so you can stand clear of psycho?"

I wave a hand. "Not feeling it, and besides, I think Amber killed the mood for any casual hangouts. I'm going to head back home. Could use the extra sleep," I explain.

He gives me a comforting nod. "Okay, have a good game up in Memphis."

"Thanks." I scratch my cheek. "Kind of full-on during December, on the road most of the time."

"Good. It just means you can focus, right?"

"Yeah, I'll see ya."

After heading out and back to my place, I ensure my security system is on to prevent any unwelcome guests. I would move states just to live in peace.

Heading straight to my sofa, I flop onto the cushions and turn on the television which instantly has hockey highlights on the sports channel.

Scott is right, I should be able to focus.

But I can't, I really can't.

I need to play harder to prove that I still have skill. Everyone is predicting this will be my last season—hell, even in my head I'm predicting it too. I just don't say it out loud, as that makes it too real.

I've thought about what's ahead. Back at Connor's wedding, his uncle mentioned a possibility for a spot somewhere within the Spinners organization. I'm sure a lot of teams will be vying for my attention to be involved next season in a non-athletic sense. However, Declan runs a tight ship, a team that has a large group of fans and that gives back to the community. Their social media presence draws a lot of eyes to the Spinners…

Social media is marketing, marketing is… Isla.

My eyes dart up to the screen that shows the hockey league's schedule for the coming two weeks.

I scoff a half-smile to myself when I read what I am already well aware of. We have a game against the Spinners coming up on the schedule, the last game before Christmas. It's at their home arena.

Which means that the probability of seeing Isla is disproportionately high.

Grabbing my phone from my pocket, I debate unlocking it to type a message. It isn't a good idea to check in with Isla, it will probably make my focus on the game diminish. She could be a distraction. I'm confident that we agreed on the right plan of action; nothing.

But I'm bound to see her, even a glimpse of her. Surely, she'll either be working or sitting behind the boards to watch her brother. I'll try to give her a nod or something when I'm skating by—wait, no, if her brother saw that, he would go mental. I promised Isla I wouldn't rile him for the sake of goals.

Maybe I should send a text. I mean, we will be in the same zip code again. It's just stating the obvious. Connor and I text, and even though we have to play against one another, off the ice we're friends. Which is why he sent me a "looking forward to seeing you in Lake Spark" text.

Isla and I can be friends. That we can do.

Growling, I toss my phone to the side. My life is one of confusion right now, no point in dragging another factor into that.

———

Skating onto the ice at the Spinners arena after a last-minute team huddle, I find myself facing off with Briggs.

"Vaughn," he says my name rather curtly.

"Briggs. Hope you woke up on the right side of the bed to keep your head in the game." I bend down to get in position.

He mirrors the move. "Oh, I did, with a beautiful woman right beside me. So, I'm fully ready to swipe that Florida vitamin D right off your pretty-boy face."

It's on the tip of my tongue to retort with something about Isla. But I can't, I have too much respect for her. It would be so easy, though.

"Only makes us stronger," I dryly reply.

The referee drops the puck, and it's on.

For the next few minutes, it's a constant back and forth on the ice with Briggs.

Then it happens.

I push Briggs into the boards, and a few seconds later, Connor is behind me. I have to keep friendship aside for the moment, and I aim low to pin Connor against the boards, gripping his shirt in the process. Helmets fall off as one arm elbows into Briggs, and Connor begins to scuffle with me. It's always a moment of high adrenaline when these incidents happen. Your body just reacts the way it needs to, even if it's a bit more aggressive than you would ever be. Which is why I give it my all.

Briggs ends up on the ice and his stick out of reach. Connor, now pissed, aims a little too high with his stick, landing on me. The ref blows the whistle, and Connor is sent to the penalty box for two minutes, which gives us a power play.

"Asshole," Briggs seethes as he skates off from me.

"Yet here I am, still on the ice to ensure you're in misery," I call out.

Finally getting a chance to breathe and shake off that

outburst, I notice movement in the corner of my eye, then fully examine the scene before me.

Isla's walking down the stairs to go sit with Hadley who is right behind the boards. The rink cam showed Hadley a few times on the screen. It's marketing gold. Isla has no idea I'm staring at her. But she's here, which means she's watching the game, wearing her brother's jersey number… can't fault her for that.

As much as I want to attract her attention, I have a game to win.

Maybe after the game, I'll be able to subtly say hi.

"What did I miss? I heard booing," I ask as I slide back onto the seat next to Hadley.

"You picked the worst moment to go to the bathroom, which by the way, are you okay? You do that a lot lately." She sounds frustrated with the game.

"Feisty. Sorry if nature calls," I defend.

It's been a few weeks since I found out about my pregnancy, and I still haven't told my friend. Part of me isn't ready, because it leads to questions, and I know that the baby will become a central topic for every coffee date. It makes it all even more real.

Hadley's dad, who was sitting next to her, excuses himself with the cover of finding snacks. I get the feeling he is giving us a moment alone so we can talk, even though he has no clue that my news will require a full-on play-by-play.

My nerves are rocketing because Vaughn is here. I'm thankful for the helmet which blocks me from staring at his smoldering eyes. It will also hurt less, because seeing him is like a knife to my body. It's clear he is in a relationship with someone and wants to keep to our word and forget our night.

The thought of this situation causes me to feel a little tight.

"What's up with you?" Hadley wonders. She must be picking up on my somber mood.

"Nothing," I lie but also sigh.

Hadley seems to be studying me as I stare aimlessly at a patch of ice.

"Nothing to do with who is on the ice?" Her eyes go bold.

It's a struggle, however I manage to shake my head.

She touches my arm. "Spill it."

An overwhelming feeling takes over me, and it just rolls off my tongue. "You know how I had that conference in Tampa a while ago?"

"Yeah, the one where you got stuck there because of a hurricane."

I nod. "I wasn't exactly alone when I safely rode out the storm in a hotel."

She seems invested in this gossip. "You were riding someone during the storm, weren't you?"

I bite my bottom lip. "It's not ideal," I admit.

"Why not? It's great. You are allowed to have fun. Who was it?" She's far too curious.

I nervously scoff a laugh, very well aware that I shouldn't give her clues to who this baby's father is, the baby that nobody knows I'm having. "The guy who just put your husband in the penalty box."

Hadley's jaw drops. "Vaughn Madden?"

I scrub a hand across my cheek. "Nobody can know. Especially since my brother isn't a fan. It was a one-time kind of thing."

"Really? I mean, he's not bad on the eyes. Long-distance isn't ideal, but it's no different than if he played here in Lake Spark and has to travel for the season." This is probably why

I didn't tell her; she's excited for a probability that will never happen.

I place my hand on her arm, needing to calm her. "Take a chill pill. It really was a one-time spur-of-the-moment kind of thing. He wasn't even there when I woke up."

"What an jerk." Hadley isn't impressed.

"Can we forget about it?" I attempt to plead. We both notice Connor leave the box to hop back onto the ice.

She rolls her eyes. "Fine. But give him a piece of your mind after the game. You're entitled to that."

"No, Hadley. We're all entitled to a no-strings night, and we agreed on the morning protocol. Now, will you focus on your man who just intercepted the pass?" I try to refocus her attention.

I'm very well aware that I might run into Vaughn after this game.

I SHOULDN'T DO THIS. Not after that call. But I need to make one more attempt.

It's the least I can do for him or her who is currently in my belly and causing my stomach to swirl. It's as though the baby can pick up that I'm anxious and decided to make my stomach flop with nerves a few extra times.

I'm standing in the hall near the locker rooms for the opposition, thankful that I'm able to be back here. Still, I do my best to blend in and stay out of the way. The Spinners won, which means Vaughn probably isn't in the best of moods. However, quite frankly, his dickish move of having someone else deliver the message that I'm never to contact him again causes me to not particularly care about his precious post-game feelings.

I nervously fidget with my fingers as I wait, reminding myself that I need to do this. My head perks up when I hear the door to the locker room open and a few players leave, but not Vaughn.

Oh great, let's draw this process out.

I'm not sure how many times I glance at the door when it opens with a brief excitement that I can cut the tether on this situation off. Finally, the door opens, and my chest tightens at the sight of a freshly showered Vaughn in a navy-blue suit. I want to scold myself for melting a little at the image before me.

His head hangs low until it doesn't. His eyes zap up because he caught sight of me in the corner of his eye. It surprises me that his mouth tugs, as if he's happy to see me. He quickly scans the area to see if anyone would notice, but everyone seems busy with their own tasks. Vaughn takes a few steps in my direction.

"Hey, Isla." His voice sounds soft. "Thought I might see you here."

"Hi." I give a ridiculous little wave like I'm a schoolgirl with a crush, but I clear my throat when sense hits me. "Uhm, listen, I know you don't really want to see me—"

"What?" Lines form on his forehead.

I glance away because his blue eyes on me feel too much, almost as if I should let him off easy. "Come on, Vaughn, I'm a big girl and got the memo that we are very much forgetting… late-season hurricanes." I can't muster the words to describe our explosive night.

He reaches out his fingers to gently touch my shoulder, and again, he studies the hall to make sure we're under the radar. "Again, what?"

"Your… a woman delivered the message that you are very much occupied and—"

Vaughn looks at me as if I'm an alien. "I'm sorry, I'm *very* lost. I know I didn't text, which is kind of a shitty move considering we were bound to run into one another tonight. But I don't understand about a woman delivering a message."

I roll my eyes. "It's okay, you don't owe me an explanation."

He seems to be thinking and then something dawns on him before he pinches the bridge of his nose. "Oh no. Ugh," he grumbles. "Did this woman sound like Barbie?"

I lift a shoulder to my ear. "I guess."

"Isla, she's no one."

I hold my hand up. "You don't need to justify it."

"Really." He's adamant, and his eyes bug out. "My neighbor has a crazy woman who visits their house, and she won't get the hint that I'm not interested. She had my phone. You must be the call that she erased from my call log."

I could cry. Hope fills me to the brim; this is a promising turn of events.

"She called you babe and said you two had to go some-where for drinks." I need to double-check that this beacon of light isn't a lie.

He scoffs a sound. "Trust me, that never happened."

"You only talk to women who are your publicist or from the team she told me," I list.

Vaughn shakes his head. "Wishful thinking on her part."

"I was never to call you again."

"Jesus, that sounds like her... wait, you called me? Why?" The corner of his mouth snags up, and he seems pleased with that news.

Tucking a few strands of hair behind my ear, I bite my lip. I can do this. "I can imagine you have to get on a plane with your team soon." I'm stalling.

He tips his head down, then back up to capture my gaze.

"Actually no, we're about to go on a three-day break for the holidays, and I'm going to see my brother in the city tomorrow morning."

"Oh?" My voice rises on octave.

Vaughn licks his lips and his dimples shine, creating the illusion of a sweltering look of trouble. "We were kind of adamant about leaving things the way they were, so I'm not going to tell you my room at the Dizzy Duck is number 107." The mischief in his voice while his gaze pierces straight through me is almost too much, I'm forgetting my mission.

I need to stay on track, not lose my panties.

Tightly, I smile, soaking in the fact that we had a classic miscommunication mix-up, and he just gave the sign that he would bend our promise a little. Honored as I am, sex is really the last thing that should be occupying my brain... yet it's crossing my mind.

Flicking my eyes up, attempting to ground my feet and stay strong, I shoot out an alternative. "Maybe a coffee or something... I don't mean that kind of something, not that I have complaints, it's just we could chat." Holy hell, I'm rambling.

I must look like a confused squirrel who really could nibble on him right about now.

Yet, Vaughn's eyes burn me with a type of affection that could be my misfortune. "Sure. Send me a text of where to meet you."

Our eyes are trapped in a holdout for a few seconds, but then I offer him a half-smile and walk away.

———

WAITING IN JOLLY JOE'S, the soda-shop-styled diner, with my tea mug in one hand, I scroll through my phone to admire the ultrasound photos. It never gets old, that feeling of aston-ishment.

That's what I will do, tell Vaughn, then show him my phone as proof.

It's not a cute announcement, but we're not a couple. We're two people who accidentally made a child.

The door opens, and Vaughn gives me a nod. He's now in jeans and a winter coat that he takes off to hang on the coatrack while he stomps his boots on the mat.

I laugh to myself as he approaches me with a stride that everyone calls swagger, complete with a suave smirk that oozes coolness, and my biggest fear comes alive when I notice that determination burns in his eyes. For what? I can only imagine, as I'm smart.

Vaughn slides into the booth seat across from me. "Welcome to Midwest winter. I would say I hope you can handle it, but your job is literally on ice," I joke.

He rubs his hands together for warmth. "True. Were you waiting long?"

"Not at all." My eyes dip down to my tea that I've barely touched, as I'm doing my best to cut caffeine for the pregnancy. Drawing a line back up to Vaughn who is now studying the menu, I take a deep breath. "Sorry about your loss, the game. I didn't get a chance to tell you since we got occupied trying to figure out the mystery of why I wanted to kill you."

He raises his brows entertained. "You wanted to kill me?"

"I thought you were not being a gentleman."

"I'm always a gentleman. Your body should know that."

Crap, did Jolly Joe's crank up the radiator? Because I'm refusing to believe that my body warms due to Vaughn's ability to make me weak and the fact that our banter just flows.

Snap out of it, Isla.

"Uhm, maybe we can keep this coffee… I don't know, as friends?"

A shade of disappointment is hinted on his face, and he eases his attempt to flirt. "Sure. What do you recommend?"

"Anything. Are you hungry?"

"We ate a few things after the game to restore calories. That's kind of boring stuff, wild rice and salmon."

I push down the menu he holds to the table. "Then try the grilled cheese with curly fries." I can steal a few fries.

"I shall follow your expertise."

That awkward air floats around us again in silence. It's crisp and could easily break if we just give into our attraction. A few images flicker in my mind of that night, and my mouth nearly waters.

Vaughn waves a hand in front of my face. "You okay? You seem to be deep in thought."

"Yeah, just, uh, forgot that the gossip train runs strong in Lake Spark, and my brother could discover I'm enjoying an evening snack with you."

"Enjoying? That puts me at ease."

I quirk my lips out then wave him off. "It doesn't matter. He's busy with his new girlfriend, and he doesn't get angry at Connor for talking to you, so why should I be any different, since you and I are just two people who are chatting over grilled cheese."

Vaughn folds his arms over his chest. "That we are. So why did you call the other week?"

Shit, I *nearly* forgot why I'm here.

"I saw your game with Memphis and thought I would check in. Tampa isn't having the best of seasons this year."

He rakes a hand through his hair. "We've had better. Why do I sense that isn't really the reason why you called?"

The waitress arrives, interrupting my opening to answer. Vaughn orders, and I ask for warm cherry cobbler with vanilla ice cream, although I can't stomach so much.

A screeching sound of a child hits our ears, which draws our attention to a young family leaving their table and a baby that looks near one getting pulled out of their highchair.

"Yikes. I'm so happy that I get to enjoy dinners in peace," Vaughn notes.

His comment instantly causes my eyes to whip back in his direction. "You don't like kids?" Doom hits me, then I remind myself that I always said I could do this all alone if I had to.

"Only if I can return them to their owners. Don't get me wrong, I think it's great when kids are at a game or I help out at a camp, but babies are a whole different ballgame. I see my teammates with kids, and I'm not ready to give up the life I have for that."

I cough once to rid the fear that is taking over my body like an exorcism. "So, one day you do want kids?"

Vaughn shrugs. "I can't think that far ahead. I'm not really sure that I would be a great dad anyhow, I don't think I even have it in me. Right now, my focus needs to be on my last season and gulping down this grilled cheese that my table companion has raved about."

I attempt to offer him a closed-mouth smile, but it wilts far too quickly. Vaughn has just in plain terms stated that he doesn't enjoy or want kids. He needs to focus on his career. I'm circling back to earlier in the day of imagining the worst-case scenario.

"Oh… we forgot to ask them to include onions. It makes it so much better." Give me the award for avoidance.

However, this is perhaps the biggest news that I could share in someone's life. What I'm about to say will alter his life completely, whether he is involved or not.

"I'll ask them to add some." He moves to slide out of the booth, but I reach out to grip his wrist to keep him from leaving. Vaughn looks at my adamant hand on his wrist then to me.

"You know, I think I have a better idea. We can ask for it to-go."

"To-go?" A smirk begins to stretch on his mouth, and he looks impressed. "Sounds like a plan."

Great, throw me in the horrible-human category.

———

WE WALK to the parking lot because I'm not sure what I'm doing except filibustering. I need more time to figure out where his head is at.

"Are you excited to see your brother for Christmas?" I ask as we walk side by side, with the snow crunching at our feet and twinkly white holiday lights hanging all over Main Street. He's holding the takeout bag as we walk.

"Absolutely, we're going to kick back with a few beers, and Stone is cooking a turkey. Way too much food for us, but we have college football to watch. It's sort of a tradition. Growing up, we had simple Christmases, all of our mom's savings went into hockey. Then when my brother went pro, followed by me, we still chose to keep it simple. Between hockey, endorsements, PR commitments, and fancy events, it just feels so good to sit back and relax."

God, I can relate. "I hear ya. It was kind of the same for Briggs and me, or at least until our grandmother got a job typing up hospital records. It paid well, and life kind of changed a little. I had a scholarship at college, and I'm relieved about that. It meant I wasn't relying on her."

Our shoulders occasionally touch on our leisurely stroll,

and we slow down as we approach my car, not wanting this conversation to end.

"You have a strong head on your shoulders, Isla." His praise causes my cheeks to lift, because I think I needed to hear that; it's the only way I can be now.

"I can imagine you must be able to relate. It must get lonely focusing on hockey. You don't ever want to have people waiting for you when you come home?" I'm testing him again.

He stalls in his step, and it causes me to side-eye him to investigate the look on his face, highlighted by the streetlight.

"Why do you ask? You're not holding out that maybe I want more, are you?" I hear the concern in his voice, and it only confirms my theory. Yet he isn't harsh either. Maybe he feels it too, that beyond our attraction we're able to connect on a different level that feels like a relief since he can relate to so many things.

My head goes side to side. "Not at all. Just asking." I don't dare ask him if he would have been happy or confused if he had answered the phone. "I needed to call," I mumble to myself, only realizing the thought in my head escaped my lips.

"Right, how come you called?" A deep low sound escapes his mouth in contemplation. "I guess I would have been a little confused if I had answered, as we kind of had a plan to leave it at one night, but I was also debating sending you a message."

I think of a fib. "Because we knew we would run into one another."

"Yeah. There isn't much more that I can offer." He sounds serious, but his smile remains gentle.

"Except screwing me. You've implied it once or twice tonight," I tease him.

He laughs. "Well, that is on offer. We're laidback around each other and are well aware that we're not going to be anything more than a hookup… maybe two."

Except we made a baby.

The words to make the announcement seem to be vanishing. I'm too scared, as his views are clear. A baby is the last thing he wants. I knew this was a possibility, but I hate the thought that another father figure has failed me.

"So, this is me." I indicate my car.

Vaughn nods as he steps forward, guiding me until my back rests against the door of my small SUV. There is heat blazing between us, despite our breath visible in the cold air. "It is. Going to offer me a ride?" He came by taxi.

"I think that would get us in trouble." I grin to myself.

His fingers adjust the wool hat on my head. "I'm starving."

My head lolls gently to the side to swipe my cheek along his hand. "A good thing you have the food then."

Vaughn sets the bag on the top of my car. "Except that's not what I'm hungry for."

I snort a laugh. "That's a ridiculous line, and you know it."

He nods in agreement, his eyes pleading like a man entranced. In this moment, I hold the cards more than he will ever know.

My brain is crossing wires, and I do the stupidest thing I can think of.

I take hold of his coat and yank him forward so that we can share a kiss. However, I know better. Instead, our lips are within breathing distance, tracing one another, both eager for more. A brush of our lips gives us a hint of what could be our night. A feathered-feeling reminder that our attraction is dangerous… but I won't give in.

Which is why I nuzzle his nose and inhale his scent, as if it will give me strength for the months ahead.

"I think," I whisper, "we're in a risky situation. I had every intention to drive you to the Dizzy Duck and get out of my car with you. But it's better if we say goodbye here, trust me."

"I disagree," he chides softly.

His lips nip at the corner of my mouth, and I retreat slightly.

Taking a breath, I do what's best because I'm far too petrified right now due to our conversation tonight. "Bye, Vaughn," I simply say.

Because I can't tell him about the baby.

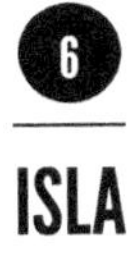

ISLA

I'm the first to arrive at Hadley and Connor's house for Christmas dinner. Funnily enough, I was on wine duty. Not that I can have any, but I think I picked up a few excellent bottles. Quickly excusing myself after trying some cheese from the charcuterie board, I went upstairs to change, as I was still in my yoga pants and sweatshirt to conquer this winter day. Now, I just want to change into something cute.

Instead, I'm sitting on the edge of the bed in the guest room and a waterfall of tears hits me.

I didn't tell Vaughn. I'm pregnant, and nobody knows. It will be a while until I show, although the array of emotions and nausea just seems to hit me in full force.

Sniffling away a tear, it's hopeless, as a fresh one hits my cheek.

"Isla?" I hear Hadley's voice. Just great, ruin the host's gathering.

The door that was slightly ajar opens with a little bit of hesitation, and Hadley finds me a hot mess on the bed.

"What's wrong?" She sounds concerned.

What the hell, I need someone right now. I thought I

could do this all, alone or with Vaughn as co-parents. I'm unraveling, and in ten minutes I need to be downstairs to smile at everyone while we stare in awe at April, Hadley's mom's cooking that she's bringing over.

"Hadley, I need to tell you something," I cry. "I can't keep it in anymore."

"You're scaring me," she tells me as she comes to sit next to me. Hadley touches my arm in comfort. "It's okay. If you don't like my attempt at a charcuterie board, you can tell me. Is that what it is?"

I have to smile through my tears at her statement. "It's delicious, just my stomach didn't agree."

Hadley frowns. "Oh gosh, I can't afford to poison people, not when a hockey team is relying on two of the guys at dinner tonight."

"They'll be fine. It's me. All me… I'm pregnant." Whoosh, there, I said it.

Her eyes survey my body as if she's checking that I'm not joking, then it turns to shock. "What?"

"Well, ten weeks to be exact."

"Huh?" She can't formulate words. "How?"

"A hurricane," I hiccup as I swipe another tear away.

Her eyes swim side to side as she registers my timeline. "As in…"

I blow out a long breath. "Nobody knows. Not even…" It's difficult to say Vaughn's name now, and I'm not sure if that's because I feel guilt for not telling him or sadness that he so clearly has no interest in having a family of his own anytime soon.

"Vaughn Madden," she croaks out.

I nod and grab a throw pillow to hug. "Isn't this a fun Christmas," I say sarcastically.

Hadley's hand travels up to my shoulder. "Why doesn't he know?"

"I haven't told him. First because I thought he was with someone, and then last night he said a few things that make it clear he would have no interest in this development." I glance down at my belly, still the same as ten weeks ago.

"He has a right to know, even if he doesn't want to be involved. Don't you think?"

I swallow and feel ashamed, even though that's not her intention. "You can't tell anyone, not even Connor. You promise?"

She nods. "It's not my information to share. I promise… but I think you should tell Vaughn."

"It wasn't the right moment. He said it himself that he only wants to focus on his last season without distraction."

"This is a little more than a distraction, it's a baby."

"I'm aware. I just got scared. Trust me, I wanted to tell him, but what's the point of making his life a mess?"

She massages my shoulder. "Is that what you think this is? A mess?"

Glancing to my side, a beaming smile hits me. "No, actually it's great. I think that I can really do this." I grab my phone lying by my side and swipe to show her the ultrasound photos. "Isn't he or she cute?"

"For sure." She examines the photo, and when her face goes slightly crooked, I have to laugh.

"You don't see it, do you?" I ask.

"Sorry, I'm trying."

I point with my index finger to the circle on the scan and outline the shape of a bean.

Her face brightens. "Wow, this is awesome. If you're happy, then so am I. Everyone will help you, anything you need. I know my mom will want to plan a baby shower. I would, but I rely on my mom for actual decent food."

"It's way too early for all of that. I have bigger fish to fry." I grab my dress from the bag at my feet. God, I wish I could stay like this and not dress up. I'm fairly confident that I'll need a nap in about an hour.

"Bigger fish, as in…?"

"My brother," I answer.

She offers me a sympathetic look.

———

SITTING at the counter in my brother's house, I fear the next five minutes. I decided that I wanted to wait until after New Year's to break the news. He's still in the early days with Ivy, the woman that he has spent months trying to win over. I wanted him to enjoy his victory, and they're good together. Plus, the last week, the only thing that I wanted to do was focus on work and sleep. They say it gets better once you head out of the first trimester, but that's just not happening.

Briggs offers me a glass of water and joins me at the kitchen island. He seems content and relaxed, even though he had a game on New Year's Eve.

"How is your *new girlfriend*?" I smile at him and nudge his arm with my own.

He couldn't hide his grin if he tried. "It's going well. I think she could be the one. She's good for me."

I like Ivy a lot. His interpretation of her being good for him is spot-on. I'm also fairly confident she figured out that I'm pregnant already at the team holiday party yet hasn't told him, so she automatically gets another point from me.

"Enough about me. How are you? You seemed kind of off at Christmas, well, the last few weeks really. Quieter than normal. I wanted to press, but you seemed like you need a little space." He examines me the way he always has when he feels that brother bear needs to come out of hibernation.

It's why telling him seems easier than informing Vaughn. Briggs won't leave me no matter what, I'll always be his sister. Whereas Vaughn is free to walk away.

"Yeah, that's kind of why I'm here," I reply and look down at my fingers twiddling together. When I look up, his nose is slightly flared, and he seems angry, as though he should be worried.

"What's going on? What haven't you told me?" Pure concern is apparent in his voice.

I touch the top of his hand that rests on the counter and pause for a second to gather my courage. "The thing is… I'm pregnant."

His face falls, and shock hits him at record speed. He croaks out a sound but can't gather words. Until he does. "W-what?"

I roll my eyes as I wait for him to digest the news. "A baby. You know, those little humans that cry and giggle, plus wear cute little socks. There is a baby growing inside of me."

"How?" He's in disbelief.

"Really? We need to go over a biology lesson right now?" I'm cynical.

A hardened look hits him. "Who? Who the fuck do I need to talk to? You don't have a boyfriend, so who is it?"

I rub my face in aggravation. In truth, I was kind of prepared for this. "Should we rewind and you ask how your only sister is doing?"

Briggs's face shades to a sweeter smile. "I'm sorry. How are you?"

"Healthy. Although nauseous and tired."

"Shit, that's not great… Now, who is it?" His hunt to kill returns.

I gently shake my head, annoyed. "It doesn't matter. I'm doing this on my own, so accept that. Do this one thing for me and don't push for more info. I'm happy with my choice and this surprise." I'm adamant and stern with my voice.

He takes a moment to reflect then rolls his lips in. "Okay… I don't like it, but okay. If that's what you need."

"It is. I don't want you to be disappointed in me. I really am excited for this."

Briggs gives me his signature warm smile that lights up the room. "I know you can do this. I'll be there for you. I'm just a little taken aback, but I won't leave you hanging. Anything you need, okay?"

"That's what I wanted to hear. It's still a ways to go, and I need to find a new place with a bit more room, not to mention stock up on supplies. But it just feels right."

He pulls me into a hug, exactly what I need right now. It gives me strength. It means the world to me that Briggs is on my team.

I'm not naïve, I'm aware at some point he will circle back to who the father is. But I'll hold off as long as I can, because I know there will be repercussions when he discovers the truth.

And I'm still undecided if I'll change my mind and tell Vaughn.

VAUGHN

Looking out at the sun over the Gulf, I hold a scotch in hand.

That's it. The end of my career.

A AC joint injury and it's over. One injury too many and I'm out early in the season. I refuse to leave as a man sitting on the bench, unable to play. Instead, I'm going to come to an agreement on the buyout that both sides want so we can end my contract early. I would much rather retire as a man who had a good last game until the injury in the second period than a guy watching from the offside.

It's already over the sports news, the speculations of my next move.

Still, my career is setting like the sun out ahead.

My phone vibrates in my pocket, and I choose to ignore it. For the past week, I've been getting an abundance of texts, but I'm simply not in the mood to answer.

Not the one from my brother. Nor the one from Connor.

I'm allowed to wallow in this moment, right?

This time my cell rings, and I pull it out purely to hit decline and set my phone on silent. But then I see a name that I wasn't expecting in the slightest.

Isla.

And for some reason, I answer.

She's the last one I should talk to right now, considering she made it clear that we really were a one-night thing. I even got the impression that she really didn't want to speak to me anymore. Since we originally did agree on one night, then I haven't put in any effort to contact her since Christmas.

I bring the phone to my ear. "Isla." My tone is simple.

"Hey… Vaughn…" She seems to be struggling to put together a sentence.

"That's it? You called to say 'hey, Vaughn?'" It causes her to half-laugh which kind of annoys me.

I walk inside, closing the double doors behind me, listening to Isla hum a sound.

"I heard the news and watched the replay. You all right?" Huh, she sounds concerned.

"Yeah, I'm fine. Bound to happen. Is that why you're calling? To be the hundredth person to check up on me?" I sound exhausted, but I don't want to keep repeating myself.

"Yes and no."

"What's the no part?" I set my glass onto the counter and head to my sofa to kick up my feet on the coffee table.

It sounds like she is walking around. "For some reason, I felt the need to check in, like genuinely check in. See how you've been. Did you find a new cheese to like? That kind of thing."

My lips twist in an attempt to smile because it sounds like she sincerely means it. "I've discovered a Dutch cheese that's sharp and hard. I would say it's like my thrusts, but it is actually a very slow cheese that takes 10 to 14 months to ripen and must contain a fat content of 48%. But damn, it's good."

She snorts a laugh, perhaps remembering Connor's wedding weekend where we mentioned cheese during our flirty yet odd topic conversation. "You can go slow, maybe not 10-to-14-months slow, though."

"You phoned to talk cheese?"

"No, actually, I phoned to ask you to open the door."

My eyes dart to my front door down at the end of the hall. "Why would I do that?" I shoot up and begin to step down the hall.

"Uhm, the Spinners played your old team, as you know. I guess you didn't want to watch, which is understandable. I decided to come down to watch Briggs and also shadowed someone I met at that conference who works in marketing. Then I thought, hey, why not check on Vaughn."

My pace picks up as I head straight for the door. I think she is insinuating what I think she is. Opening the door, I'm faced with Isla who has her golden locks down, a bit darker than last time, framing her face. She's wearing a sort of long baggy dress that has buttons and stops short of her knees, and I wish this whole getup would show more.

I slowly bring my phone down until my arm hangs at my side.

Isla's lips lift gently. "Hi," she softly greets me.

"Hi," I rasp.

"The front gate wasn't keen on letting me in, but an old lady who lives a few floors down took pity on me and let me in."

I don't move an inch. "Why are you here? Our last encounter you kind of pushed me away slightly."

She nods in agreement. "I did. But I figured you could use a friend."

I can't think of any reason why she would show up right now. It would take too much energy, and I don't have that right now. "Are we friends? Because I'm really not in the mood to attempt to be anyone's friend right now."

"Fair enough. So, am I just going to stand here or are you going to let me in?" She gives me a humorous look.

I hesitate for a second before I step to the side so she can come inside. I watch her saunter as she slowly enters my home and examines the setting while I lazily close the door behind her.

She notices the scotch glass that I forgot on the side table; I've been nursing the glass for the last hour. "Are you somewhat sober?"

"Sober enough to wonder how you got my address." I follow her until she's by the window looking out at the near-dark sky.

"Hadley had your address from when she sent out wedding invitations last summer." Isla seems nervous, and God, I hope it's because we are alone with my bedroom not far away.

"Look, Isla, I have to be honest right now. I'm not in the best of moods. I can't be a friend, and I sure as hell can't be anything but a great fuck. So that's the boundaries for tonight."

She scoffs a sound and crosses her arms over her chest. I could swear her tits seem firmer or larger, which causes my dick to press against the zipper of my pants.

"That's clear then. You do seem like you've seen better days."

"It's fine. This time was always going to come, but it's a subdued feeling."

She takes one step in my direction then pauses. "You don't want to talk about it?"

"Nope."

"Hmm, sounds like you might see the light at the end of the tunnel after allowing a few days of misery first." She's analyzing me, and it's irritating but spot-on.

Glancing to my open kitchen, I'm tempted to pour a fresh round. "Want a drink?"

"Oh, uhm, maybe water?" Not what I had in mind, but sure, I need her hydrated if she's planning on staying any longer, because I do need her support right now. In a way that only she can offer.

Into the kitchen I go and straight to the fridge to grab a water bottle, and when I turn, she's there. We bump into one another when she reaches for the bottle, and the touch of her hand blasts a carnal need to bend her over the counter behind her.

"Thanks." She takes the bottle from my hand, causing our fingers to skim with a friction of energy crossing. I'm tempted to capture them and pull her to me tightly.

Isla twists the cap then takes a long drink. "I think you're not in the mood for conversation." She sounds near deflated.

"That's obvious? Great." My tone is mundane, and it causes her to raise her brows, not exactly pleased with my attitude. I don't care and trap my sight on her lips then slip my gaze down to examine her breasts again which only makes me harder.

"I have to be honest. I came here hoping we could talk, have a few snacks and… never mind. This was a mistake for me to come here." She begins to turn to leave, and as she walks away, I'm trailing hot on her heels until her hand is on the handle of the front door. Isla's barely been here and now she's escaping, that's just not fair. I'm quick to grab her arm, causing her to glance at me sidelong before her eyes draw down to examine my hand on her arm.

"You came here for something. In fact, I'm confident you knew the risk of what would happen when you did." My tone is serious, I'm not going to play games.

Her breath hitches slightly. "Trust me, all scenarios have crossed my mind." Why does it feel like she has her own version of tonight that I'm not familiar with? How could she not expect that it was dangerous showing up at my door?

Our gazes connect, and a wistful glaze shades across her eyes. "You're really not in the best of ways, are you?" She states it more than she asks.

"Again, I'm allowed to have a bittersweet goodbye to my career and sulk a little." I don't let go of her arm.

"Vaughn, I'm not sure what to say to make you feel better. I can only bring you complications if I open my mouth." Her sentence causes me to ponder for a mere second. "Anyway, I need to get out of here. This was a horrible idea. I'll go downstairs and order a cab."

Everything inside of me sinks to the ground with disapproval. I have whiplash over what the last few minutes were. I could pin her to the door and make her admit that she wants what I desire in this moment, but her eyes seem to plead for me to give no such attempt.

I do the next best thing.

"I barely drank… let me drive you back to your hotel." Being a gentleman, that is a turn of events I wasn't expecting.

She sighs but then nods that it's okay. I grab my key fob from the side table, and we head out in a silence, the entire elevator ride down with tension sharp between us and our gazes fixed. We're both probably thinking a dirty thought and simmering in an attraction that isn't good for me.

Heading out of the elevator, my Ferrari beeps when I unlock it, and we get in the car, where she tells me the hotel, and I type the address into the navigation. But before I start the engine, she speaks again.

"I wish I could help you right now." Her authenticity is strong, and she's looking forward, lost in a thought.

"You're a confusing woman, Isla. The queen of mixed messages. Yet still you manage to keep me on this thin tether which is fucking annoying." I'm getting aggravated.

Her eyes dart to mine. "A tether is a connection, you know." Her tone is simple.

"We have a sort of fucked-up one, don't ya think? Somehow, I have no regrets either."

Her mouth opens and a sound croaks out of her lips. "I'm not sure… maybe I might be a regret for you soon."

My eyes squint as I try to figure out what in the world is going on with her. "You're speaking in tongues. You have me at a loss."

She nibbles her bottom lip and appears to be debating with herself. "I'm sorry. I just… Forget it. You're right, I'm all over the place, but so are you currently."

"Thanks for highlighting that."

A deep breath escapes her. "I shouldn't say anything anymore, it may just send us down a hell of a night."

We stare at one another for a few beats. It's intense but somehow profound. Two people glued to an inability to end the gravity that keeps us close.

Which is why I snap.

I yank her arm. She yelps in surprise and immediately turns to me with knowing eyes. "I meant what I said Isla. I'm only good for one thing right now, and if you can't help me with that, then I now realize this drive is going to be far too excruciating."

Her breath seems to have picked up before she observes

the garage where there isn't a person in sight. "Should we really be doing what I think is about to happen?" She tilts her head to the side, asking as if it's a dealbreaker, as it probably should be.

"Yes."

"Is this what you need right now to feel better?" she rasps.

I don't even answer. Instead, I crash my mouth onto hers. At first, she's taken aback, but then she melts into my kiss with a murmur. I'm not gentle. I kiss her hard as I wrap my arms around to guide her as I drag her across the middle console to have her straddling me. Instantly, she loops her arms around my neck while her legs link tighter around my hips.

Our kiss grows fervent as I bring my hand to roam the soft skin of her thighs and sneak under her dress that is now bunched at her waist. "If you want to help, then let me fuck you right now." That's my way of asking permission, and she nods once.

I jerk her panties to one side, and my fingers land on her sensitive nub. Her moan is instant, and I'm satisfied that it doesn't take long for her to experience a buildup that I'm not going to let her have yet. My fingers get soaked by her arousal pooling between her legs.

We stay connected by the mouth while she unbuckles my jeans, and I lift her enough that she can lower my boxer briefs. "Pull up your dress," I demand as I slip my finger inside of her, and she struggles to breathe normally, but a few buttons from the top of her dress snap open, and her breasts push together.

"Fuck, I shouldn't be doing this." She's scolding herself but tilts her body to use my fingers when I add another to her opening.

"Maybe you need this as much as me," I husk right before my mouth dives down to kiss her cleavage. "Bra down. Now."

Isla lowers the cups of her lace bra, and I examine her full breasts, so enticing and beautiful, with peaked tips. They definitely feel different than last time I got to bury my face and cock into them. I drag my tongue down to latch onto a nipple and wrap my lips around to gently suck and bite, only urged on by her crooning noise.

"Don't stop," she breathes heavily, with her fingers raking through my hair.

I groan from the feeling of my length rubbing against her body. "I'm not going to sugarcoat this. I'm going to jam my fingers into your mouth so you can taste exactly how much you want me. You're fucking sweet, Isla. Then I'm going to make sure my cock is buried deep inside of you. We're not going to go slow, and you'll let me go hard as I thrust up while you ride me. Tell me you understand."

"I understand." Her throaty voice is too sexy, and it only makes the heat inside of me ignite more.

I keep true to my promise, and my fingers find a new home on her eagerly awaiting tongue, right before she sucks them off as good as when she's on her knees for me.

Aligning with her center, I nearly lose it when I feel her hand grip around my cock to guide me in, instantly feeling her tightness coat around my cock. She feels far too warm, near hot, but I don't mind in the slightest. One slow pump is all I give her before I pick up speed and ensure I fill her to the brim. We keep our bodies close due to the logistics of fucking in the front of my car and her bouncing body.

I didn't realize how much I needed this to relax until a few minutes later when I'm coming inside of her as she bites my neck because she's shaking.

We end up tangled in a mess and in silence, recovering from spontaneous sex in my driver's seat.

But then she does something peculiar and begins to straighten her clothes, now eager to slide off me and back onto the passenger seat. It's maybe a fair move since I've given no indication that this would be an all-night thing now. If she was offering then I would use her to release tension, over and over back upstairs. I don't mind sharing a bed with her one single bit, because I like her hair splayed across a pillow. However, she is creating distance between us again.

Isla gives me a look that is near remorseful. "I hope this is what you needed, but I really need you to take me to my hotel."

I blow out a breath and do as she says, the short ten-minute drive far too quiet. Before she opens the door at her destination, she pauses.

"This…" She motions between us. "It can't get complicated, and we are only maybe friends who seem to do other activities." Her tone is near flippant.

"Wow, thought I would at least get a bye. Wasn't expecting you to be so eager to run away, but fine. I'm not in a state to argue."

"Just trust me, this is for the best." She is so damn resolute.

A sound of doubt escapes me. "Right, you take care then."

"Remember, you're the guy who doesn't want anything, and we agreed on only one night then. You're most definitely not going to tell me that something has changed. Are you?" It doesn't feel like she's trying to be wise, it's almost as if she is checking.

"No. I need to focus on my next career move."

I honest to God swear I see a shade of distress fall on her face.

"Obviously." Her voice is uneven. "Take care."

Then she's out my car door, forgetting the last half-hour happened.

ISLA

carfing down the ice cream sandwich that I'm holding, Hadley comes to join me on my couch.

"Still addicted to ice cream sandwiches?"

"Yes. I moved on from those chocolate ones that have vanilla ice cream in the middle that you buy at the store. I'm now on to two chocolate chip cookies with vanilla ice cream in the middle. I think this is a craving," I explain as I capture some melting ice cream in my mouth.

Hadley gets comfortable by tucking her knees under her. "So? Did you do it?"

I swallow my last bite and then pause for a second to prepare myself. "I messed up… a lot."

Over the last few weeks, a stirring feeling chased me. I calmed down a bit and reentered the circle of wanting to tell Vaughn.

She studies me for a second. "You didn't tell him, did you?"

It all comes out of me. "It's worse, way worse."

"How? You still haven't told him you're pregnant and you're nearly halfway." She isn't impressed, as she keeps reiterating that he has a right to know, yet she doesn't judge me either.

"We had sex."

"What?" she shrieks, and her face turns confused.

I cringe. "I know, it's not what I should have let happen."

"Isla, you went to Tampa to tell him. You literally used your brother's game as an excuse to fly there to tell Vaughn in person because you feel like it isn't a conversation to have via phone or text. Yet you didn't tell him and instead had sex with him?"

I rest my head against my propped arm on the back of the sofa. "He is in no place right now to hear that he is going to be a father. I swear that I went to his home to tell him. It's just, when I got there, I could see that he wasn't in a great space in terms of moods. He also made it clear that he didn't want to talk nor be a friend, and he only wanted one thing in that moment."

"Yeah, he just wanted to fuck," she bluntly states.

I hold up my other palm to ease her. "It felt like it was what he needed to not be so down, and if I'm honest, I wanted it too. Really, you should have seen him. If I had told him then, he would have combusted. He also mentioned that he has no interest in further complications in his life. This…" I point to my belly, "is a complication."

Hadley slides her jaw side to side, clearly digesting this development. "You made this far more complex. Once he finds out, he will look back at this." I don't answer or say anything. She reaches out to hold my hand between her palms. "Can we *really* talk for a second?"

"Always."

"Not telling him after three attempts is your easy way out. It's by far harder to inform him than not. You keep having excuses why you can't tell him. They are not the real reasons, though." She stops and waits for me to pour my heart out, but again, I stay mute.

"Isla, you're scared he will be exactly like your dad and want no involvement. This is more about you than it is Vaughn," she delicately explains.

An ache hits my face as my tears come tumbling down in droplets from my eyes. Her theory didn't take much for my body to react. Simply because she's right.

"It really sucked at times not having a dad who wanted to be involved in my life. He was barely around during Briggs's first two years of life, and our dad completely took off when my mom was pregnant with me. What if this baby gets the same treatment?"

She squeezes my hand. "The only way to find out is to ask the man who is the father."

"He is in a dwelling cloud, that I'm not overreacting on."

"So, what are you going to do then?"

I sigh. "I thought about it on my flight back. I'm going to do nothing, not until he figures it out—my pregnancy, I mean. He can discover it in his own way. I can't keep attempting to tell him and then feel horrible when I don't, and I know that's selfish. I fully agree that he has every right to know, but I just don't have the strength to break the news for the reasons you mentioned. And I need my strength to ensure this baby is healthy, it should be my focus. I'm choosing my battles."

She licks her lips and sits there in contemplation. "If that's what you feel you need to do then… fine. I'll support you." I can tell she doesn't agree, but she will be on my team anyways.

"Thank you."

"Anything for you. Crap, is it me who made the pregnant lady cry?" Hadley is trying to make me smile.

"Nah, I think I managed this all on my own."

"Should I grab you another ice cream sandwich from the freezer?" She hitches her thumb over her shoulder. "I know that you stocked up."

I chortle and wipe my tears away at the same time. "Nah, I'll be big enough soon, and I want to watch my sugar intake, as it's important for the baby."

She throws a fond look my way. "You're really going to rock this mom thing."

"I hope so."

Hadley claps her hands together. "Okay, so plan of action is to give up on trying to tell Vaughn, and he will need to figure it out either by word of mouth or seeing that you're carrying prized goods?"

"Could you maybe ask Connor not to mention that I'm pregnant?" I warn. "Not sure that's the way for this all to unfold."

She points a finger in the air. "Right, check that option off the list. We are sticking to Vaughn maybe running into you and figuring it out himself."

"Exactly. I'm lucky, I guess, that I haven't really started to have a belly, especially if I wear baggy shirts. But I'll start showing soon, no way around that. My jeans barely fit. I've moved onto using an elastic band to keep them up. Which means everyone will figure out that I'm pregnant soon. At least, the people who I haven't told." I sigh and feel that pain build in my throat again. "It's really not that I'm trying to keep him out of this baby's life, I swear… it's just… he's only given me signs that I will be hurt, and I just can't bear it now," I remind her. "After I have the baby I won't feel so fragile, as if I'm about to break, and my determination to tell him will return."

She gives me a sympathetic look. "I know… it's your own fear that you need to overcome." A long silence hits us before she changes her demeanor and attempts a smile. "We should go shopping for maternity clothes. Ooh, and are we finding out the sex of the baby at your twenty-week ultrasound? A gender reveal cake is completely in order." Her excitement is overtaking her.

"Yes, to clothes, and no, I don't want to find out, so no cake, sadly."

She throws me a pretend pout. "Hmm, we'll just have to go all out at your baby shower before the baby arrives."

I look around my living room and my eyes gently gawk at the scene. "Well, at this rate I won't have much space to store anything. I need to add moving to my list. I use the second bedroom in this place as a closet."

"A closet housing dresses and your shoe collection *is* important."

I appreciate that she has detoured from our serious discussion. That's the kind of friend I need, someone who follows my cues of what to say or do.

"Ready to implement the plan of action?" I ask.

It takes only a beat before she squeezes my arm. "No telling Vaughn and Big Isla, here we come."

I laugh. "I'm hoping for a cute bump. But yes, plan confirmed."

One day, I just hope Vaughn will understand.

Iᴛ's a few weeks later when I'm sitting at my desk going over project timelines in our Kanban boards on our project tool when my phone buzzes with an incoming message.

I finish typing my sentence when I quickly skim the screen of my phone, then my eyes shoot wide open in attention when I see Vaughn's name on top of the bubble box.

VAUGHN

Hey, I just wanted to touch base. A few
weeks ago was kind of unexpected, and I'm
well aware that it wasn't my finest move.
Just wanted to ensure that you don't feel
used or think that I'm an even bigger ass
than you probably already did.

I tap my finger against my desk, taking in the fact that he's been thinking about me or that night, which is why he texted now. I'm surprised for sure, but also remind myself of my plan of action that feels more like a strong conviction.

Still, the magnetic pull of his words causes me to type back.

You didn't use me. I also offered.

Okay.

I should flip my phone over and move on, but I don't. A speck inside of me is wondering if this is a tiny door to try again or at least figure out if he is in a better place.

Hope you are feeling better?

The dots on the phone indicate that he is typing back, then he stops, then types again.

I am actually. Maybe even partly excited for
what's next. Sure as hell not in the state that
I was in when you last saw me. Although I
guess I'm always a little demanding in
certain ways...

The corner of my mouth hitches at his attempt to lighten the conversation. I'm also happy that he seems to be in a different mood. For a second, I think about breaking the news. But then I remind myself that text isn't the way for me, but I could ask that we speak. Maybe a video call is better than nothing.

> I'm happy to hear. You mentioned what's up next, so what is that?

Maybe I'm testing the water.

> Yeah, general management for a team, and I already have a few teams interested. It's a hell of a lot more demanding schedule, but I'm at a stage in my life where I can devote my time and go all in.

My stomach sinks again, as any light that I thought might help me unlock my secret just vanished. The idea to ask that we talk is a sentiment that I now ignore. Yet again, Vaughn has no clue that he planted more doubt in my head. All indications are that our baby news is the last thing he would ever want to hear right now. And in a selfish move, I need to focus on this pregnancy and being healthy both physically and mentally. It's easier if I just leave this be.

Which is why I simply write back and brush past his innuendo.

> I need to get back to a project. Take care, Vaughn.

It's what is best right now.

9

VAUGHN

Staring up from the paper lying on the conference table, I watch the three men before me in their suits.

One is a lawyer, the other my own, and they both sit mute in their years of experience. They only interrupt when legal clarity is needed. Then there is Declan Dash, my friend's uncle and the owner of the Spinners who has been quietly pushing his case for the past year. He wears a subtle wry grin with triumph as he says all the right things.

My eyes dart down to the contract that I've already read over with my lawyer during the past few days, then back up to Declan who is patiently waiting.

He picks up a pen and wiggles it between his fingers. "What do you say? Is the offer appealing?"

I lean back in my chair, surprised that he made the effort to fly down to Florida to speak to me. Since my last season ended, I've received offers for various roles. Yet here I am with the only one that caught my interest. The wheels have been in motion since last month, but now we need to cement it all down in ink if I choose.

"Should I be thanking the GM you just fired?" I joke to lighten the mood.

Declan wobbles his head slightly. "Well, probably. I mean, I've been wanting to shake up the team for a while now. Just so happens he made that easier when the Spinners were out mid-playoffs because of a bad trade this year, so we chose not to renew his contract. And after next season, the head coach has got to go, as I don't like his methods to train the team. You made it clear that you are not eyeing any coaching position. I heard the rumors, I know Phoenix asked."

"You're right. I want a bit more of a mix, working with the scouts and coaches, getting a chance to add a little of the business side into things."

Declan splays his hands out. "And me." I chuckle softly. "You and I will have daily contact. You'll be up in my box at every game and talk to the press. I believe you are exactly who we need to shake things up. I want a man who knows hockey from the other side, and I've seen other teams hire young fresh blood, often with no hockey knowledge, and it's a success. We will need to throw you in the deep end to talk with our scouts about draft picks, and you'll play a key role in forming our new team strategy. It will take more than one season to completely reshape things, which is why a four-year contract is on the table, with every intention to extend."

A deep inhale hits me. This would be a great move. And working with Declan would be a good match. He is the type of owner who wants to be involved, as he himself used to play, and I'm the guy who wants to be the spider in the web to see through all lenses of the sport.

It's a no-brainer.

"Any way you could add Florida weather to the agreement?" My mouth tilts up, and my joke earns a chuckle from the gentlemen in the room.

"No, but you would be heading to Lake Spark during the off-season, so the next few months will feel like you never left a tropical paradise," Declan counters.

I huff a laugh. "Don't fill me up with lies. We all know summer in Illinois is not exactly predictable. Besides, the off-season is arguably just as busy for a GM, as a draft is fast approaching. Not to mention that players are at development camps. I'll need to hit the ground running."

"I can't deny that, but lucky for you, we'll get moving fast and have you in Lake Spark within two weeks. Besides, we have a great realtor that works with the team, I'm sure they can find you a not-so-humble abode that will be ideal for winter and summer."

I pause for a second as the paper is taunting me.

Lake Spark.

It does have charm. It also has Isla. The woman who made it clear back at Christmas that we absolutely will be keeping to our agreement of having only one night, only for her to let me take her again weeks later. She's hot and cold. In fact, for a split second, I could have sworn that she didn't quite want to see me again. That situation might be tricky.

However, the seven-figure salary before me is persuasive. This is a no-brainer, even if it means I'll need to forfeit my Caribbean holiday that I thought of taking next month to unwind.

Truthfully, I don't need Declan pulling out the stops. We wouldn't be here if we were still in negotiations.

Quickly I glance to my lawyer who gives me an assuring nod. There is no more stalling.

"I get to keep the pen, right?" I smile.

Ease hits Declan's face, and our lawyers even crack a smile.

Declan reaches over the table to hand me the pen. "I'll even buy you a set."

I quickly sign my initials on each page then add my signature on the last page next to where Declan already signed.

As I slam the pen down, our lawyers are already shaking hands, and Declan stands to button his suit jacket and circles around the table to shake my hand.

His other hand lands on my shoulder. "I'm excited for this. I'll be sure that someone from the team contacts you right away to sort out the logistics of the move. We need you up there as soon as possible. Of course, my wife will be expecting you over for dinner. My nephew will be thrilled, that is, if he doesn't sign with another team for next season."

"If we give him a good offer then maybe he will stay," I say. I already need to think like a manager.

Declan chuckles. "I'll stay out of that one." He leans down to look at the signed contract and then slides it to his lawyer. "We should get a bottle of champagne in here before I need to fly back. My daughter has a ballet class where the parents can watch. She's only three but watching her wobble around is the cutest."

I only nod because I can't exactly picture it.

"There is one matter that we might need to discuss. As much as I'm sure grown men can be professional, uh, Briggs Chase does absolutely hate me," I point out.

It only causes Declan to grin. "He does. But he is going to have to suck it up. Besides, I'm not sure he will be sticking around. I know contract talks might be difficult with him, as he is an unrestricted agent now, plus maybe he has gotten softer lately since his personal life has had so many changes."

That piques my interest. "Oh? Everything okay?"

"For sure, just his personal life is occupied with his girl-friend and sister. Plus, he lives in Lake Spark, and you can't not be happy when you live in Lake Spark."

I laugh because his small-town pride is a far cry from his days as bonafide bachelor, with his city penthouse.

"Be sure to send me a welcome basket," I joke.

Someone opens the door to the meeting room and brings in champagne on ice with flutes.

"That can be arranged."

It hits me that I'm going to move to Lake Spark.

———

SITTING on the private plane a few days later, I trace the button on my phone near Isla's name.

Maybe I should text or give a warning. They are announcing my new role tomorrow to the press. If she really doesn't want to see me, then she's going to have a hard time avoiding me. Plus, maybe I want to see her. She occasionally lingers in my thoughts. More than she should since that night of comfort sex in my car.

I shake off the idea of texting her and glance out the window to see corn fields, which has mostly been what I've seen for the last hour. Luckily, as we approach the private airport near Lake Spark, the view begins to change. More greenery, tall pines, winding roads amongst small hills, and an emerald lake in the far-off distance.

Tucking my phone away, I get ready for landing.

This is my new adventure.

The landing is smooth, and when I disembark from the plane, I'm instantly greeted by Declan standing on the tarmac next to Connor.

"Welcome!" he calls out while Connor grins broadly.

"Where's my fruit basket?" I tease as I step down the stairs.

When I get to the bottom, I greet him with a handshake and give Connor a side hug.

"I'm not supposed to know why you're here, but I have connections," Connor jokes.

"I would love to say I planned to stand here and wait for you, but I'm going to Detroit for a meeting and need my plane once they refuel," Declan clarifies but still grins.

"And since I'm here to drop him off, then I'll drive you into town. The Spinners are trying to go as green as possible." Connor smiles tightly while his eyes bug out and indicate the plane behind me. "So, no need to drag another car here." His sarcasm is underlying at how ridiculous this policy seems.

"Sounds like a plan." I'll get my rental car later, as they will deliver it to the Dizzy Duck Inn in town until I have a new house.

"Alright, a winning team here we come." Declan claps his hands together before he picks up his laptop bag. "Don't forget to hit up Jolly Joe's, everyone needs their coffee with an overly-food-colored jellybean." He does a little fist pump in the air.

Connor gently nudges my arm. "Ignore him. He's hyped up on coffee from Jolly Joe's, and it has mystical powers on people." He scans the area. "Ah, I see that someone is bringing your luggage to my car. Let's get out of here. You must be hungry. We can grab some food at Catch 22 if you want."

"I guess I could eat."

We begin to walk toward his SUV, the latest model. "I would have picked you up in my Jag but figured you had luggage."

"It's cool," I promise.

Sliding into the front seat, I quickly see a message from my brother.

STONE

Enjoy small-town life with a big career. The
perfect balance. What are we missing in that
equation? ;) Good luck, Brother!

I'll text him back later. It will be nice having a shorter flight time and more flight options to see him. It was one of the reasons this move was more tempting. As we drive away from the airport, I feel content that it's the right choice.

"Whether I stay with the Spinners or not, I think you made a good decision." Connor must have read my mind as he focuses on the road.

"Thanks, buddy. How is married life treating ya?"

"Fucking fantastic. No complaints. Hadley is the best. Then again, we've known one another almost our whole lives. It's just now we dirtied it up a bit."

I sputter a laugh because that is something he would say. "And your good friend Briggs?"

Connor grimaces. "We told him the news earlier today to warn him. He'll get over it. Besides, he has enough happening in his private life to keep occupied from killing you."

Huh, he is the second person to say that Briggs has stuff going on.

"I guess my uncle has you jumping right in, but if the weather holds up, then we should do a ride out on the lake. My dad always has his boat out for the season."

"Nothing like Florida water, but I'll give it a go," I respond.

Looking out the window, I'm trying now to count the ridiculous signs on the road. I've now counted a sign warning for deer, another sign for ducks crossing, and a sign cautioning for, I think, raccoons. Do they even make a sign for that?

"We don't have great seafood up here. But I think we beat out Florida when it comes to hot dogs and pie season. We have some skills in that department," Connor justifies. "How is the house search going?"

"The real estate agent that the team uses is like a shark. Already had a few options sent to me last night," I explain.

"You need to give me the name of the agent. Isla has been trying to find a new place to no avail, trying to buy instead of rent. Even had a successful offer on the table for a new house the other week, but the seller pulled out. There is absolutely nothing on the market. Then again, she isn't the guy who just pocketed a solid seven figures."

Interest inflames in me. "Isla wants to move?"

"Yeah, for so many reasons. She's been looking since February," he mentions.

"In Lake Spark?" I shouldn't really care, but maybe the idea of running into her is more enticing than it should be.

"Uh-huh." Just then a call comes in on his Bluetooth, with Hadley's name appearing on the dashboard screen. "Sorry, I should take this."

"Of course, happy wife, happy life."

He sidelines his eyes to me with a smug smirk before answering. "Hey, Sprinkles." Damn, that's a little sappy.

"Connor." I hear Hadley's voice. "I need you to come right away to the hospital."

Fear hits Connor as he grips the steering wheel. "Wait, what? What's going on? Are you okay?"

"I'm fine, I just need you to come right away. Can you do that for me?" She sounds upset.

I mouth yes to Connor, assuring him that we can take a detour.

"I can be there in ten minutes, okay?"

"Hurry."

———

TEN MINUTES later we are running into the hospital and up two floors to find Hadley standing by a room, pacing the hall. She immediately runs into Connor's arms.

"Hey, it's okay. What's going on?" he asks as he holds her tight and rubs her back.

She gently pulls back. "It's Isla."

Instantly, my body tenses, and my eyes shoot to the door to Isla's room. Hadley notices me, and her face is indescribable, as if she is surprised that I'm here and equally worried.

"Oh, hey, Vaughn… didn't realize you would be here."

Connor interjects. "I mentioned this morning he will be our new GM, I picked him up from the airport."

"Right." Her T is tight.

I can't figure out why she is acting odd, but I can't focus on that. Not when I know Isla is on the other side of the door.

ISLA

I practice my yoga breathing while I sit up on the bed. Closing my eyes, I do my best to calm down while my hand is firmly set on my belly that has a belt of cords around it to monitor the baby, and I also have a pulse oximeter attached to my finger.

The door opens a crack, and Hadley slips through the tiny opening, careful to ensure nobody else can enter. Her face seems panicked.

"We have a problem," she states.

"What? The doctor said I'm fine and it was just a false alarm. They will just double-check everything when my doctor arrives after they notify her upstairs."

Her mouth is in a strained line as she shakes her head before her face squinches. "It's not that. I was so worried when we first arrived that I phoned Connor. I didn't say anything, so he thought it was me hurt, but that doesn't matter because…"

I stare at her blankly. "And? He's your husband. I sent a message to Briggs too because I was freaking out."

"So…" She quickly walks to my bed and perches on the

end. "When I asked you to meet at my studio to go for lunch, it was actually because I wanted to talk to you about something that Connor told me about this morning at breakfast."

"Get to whatever it is faster."

"He told me that later in the week they are going to announce the new GM for the Spinners… Vaughn."

My eyes instantly widen and my nose tips up. "Come again?"

"*Yeah…* and what I didn't realize is that Connor was picking up Vaughn at the airport, and when I phoned him to come to the hospital… Vaughn was in the car."

"What!" I shriek, and the monitor that I'm attached to makes a spike on the graph. "He's here?"

She nods once. "Outside that door."

"Oh fuck." I touch my forehead, as I'm about to have a meltdown. I knew this day would come, but does it have to be right now?

Hadley touches my leg. "He doesn't know why you are here. I gave Connor a pleading look, and I think it registered in his head a connection with Vaughn, and he got the hint not to tell him about your current state. But that will only hold out for so long."

I feel as though I'm levitating away from earth. There is no way around this. Vaughn is going to find out today. I've had a thousand scenarios in my head of how this could go, but him showing up to my hospital room is not one of them.

"This is not… how today was supposed to go."

"Maybe it's for the best. You've been lucky that you only started to show after you saw him last, but with Vaughn now in Lake Spark, I'm confident that he *would* notice that your stomach is harboring a baby, and saying you ate too many cookies isn't going to fly. You're glowing during this pregnancy too, plus, well, about to push out a baby," she explains.

I rub my belly and quickly glance at the screen that's now zigzagging in lines. "Hadley, I appreciate your stellar positivity, but my baby daddy is about to find out that I haven't told him about the baby… and I'm wearing a sweatshirt with a bar of chocolate printed on it that literally says, 'I have issues.'"

She shrugs. "Helps explain your reasoning?"

I bring my hands to my face to rub as tears begin to build behind my eyes. "How do I do this? I'm attached to a machine, I can't run away."

Her lips roll in, and a sympathetic look is fixed on her face. "Maybe that's a good thing. I don't think you should escape right now… You weren't really never going to tell him, were you? You had a plan."

A long heaving sigh leaves me. "No, I don't know, yes, I mean no." I shake my head. "I'm just scared. He made his views on kids so clear and…"

"You didn't give him a chance to walk away," she highlights.

That just unlocks the quiver on my mouth to upgrade to a tear that's been begging to fall.

As much as I'm scared, she's right. He hasn't been given the chance, and I want the information on his medical history to ensure that we can get ahead of anything we might need to worry about for the baby's health.

Fuck, I'm saying "we" in my head. Maybe it is we. Since the entire town found out my current status a little while back, it's been an outpouring of support. At work, we're preparing for my maternity leave that starts in a week. Ford is even giving me extra paid leave. Hadley has attended appointments with me. Her mom, along with Brielle and Violet, is planning a baby shower coming up. And Briggs? He has slowly been stockpiling toys that are far too noisy. It takes a village to raise a baby, they say.

But Vaughn has a right to choose if he wants to be part of that village.

What the hell do I do if he doesn't want to be involved? This town is only so big, and my emotional wound already runs deep.

Blowing out another breath, I decide that maybe…

The sound of the door opening breaks my thought.

"Are you okay? What's happening?" Briggs stalks into the room and quickly lands next to me to squeeze my arm.

I wave him off. "It's nothing. An active, kicking baby scaring the hell out of me. I totally overreacted."

"Of course not. If my nephew or niece needs medical attention, then we go all out." He glances at the monitor.

"Hey, Briggs, where is Connor?" Hadley inquires.

"He's here? Didn't see him in the hall. Must have gone to the vending machine or something," Briggs answers, and my eyes shoot to Hadley.

Oh crap, Briggs is here and Vaughn.

No, no, no.

The door opens again. "Heard we can start a party here, so we're letting ourselves in," Connor announces, with Vaughn in tow.

Then it happens.

Vaughn's eyes strike mine with a hint of a smile on his lips that twitch when his sight sidelines to the machine next to me that unfairly informs everyone that my pulse is picking up. Finally, his eyes drop to my belly that I'm cradling in my hands, with his smile now dispersing into history.

He blinks a few times. Is his brain registering?

"What the fuck is he doing here?" Briggs nearly hisses.

Right, because my brother is present. Nearly forgot that, as I think there are bigger problems right now.

"You're pregnant?" The words faintly escape Vaughn's lips.

"Uhm… in my third trimester, actually." My tone is neutral as I can't tear my eyes away from him.

Is it possible that I can see inside of his mind as he counts back the months?

An unusual silence takes over the room.

"There is some odd tension happening or something," Connor comments, and Hadley instantly elbows into his ribs to shut him up, and he yelps yet gets the clue.

"Tell me now if what I'm thinking is correct?" Vaughn grits out.

Fresh tears pool in my eyes, and all I can do is nod.

Vaughn nearly falls back as though I just knocked all the air out of his lungs and scrubs a hand across his jaw.

In the corner of my eye, Briggs is whipping his vision between me and Vaughn with everything registering. "Oh no… fuck no… tell me it's not him."

"Briggs, now isn't the time." My voice is shaking during my plea.

"Whoa, him?" Connor points his thumb at Vaughn and grins like this is great news. "Wait, when did this happen?"

I give him an unimpressed look. "A hurricane. Now can we skip the specifics?"

Connor's face turns blank. "Huh… Vaughn," he reflects. "Well, now this just got really fucking awkward."

Hadley swats him and glares at him, unamused. "Now is the time to stay quiet."

Briggs stomps forward to the middle of the room and directs his attention to Vaughn. "You're the guy who knocked up my sister?" He glances over his shoulder back to me. "It's him? How the hell?"

"Jesus, calm down. She doesn't need to explain the birds and the bees to you," Hadley chides.

Vaughn remains in shock.

"I'm going to rip your head off." Briggs begins to charge at Vaughn.

Vaughn is snapped out of his daze when my brother grips his shirt.

"Briggs," I screech. He only stops for a second. "Can we stop? The baby has ears now and can hear everything."

"Fuck off, Briggs." Vaughn yanks my brother's arms away.

But my brother only pushes him, not ready to give up. "Watch the language, the baby has ears now." He isn't even mocking; he's taking his uncle duty far too seriously. "So you just get my sister pregnant and leave her to do this alone? I knew I had a reason to hate you." He pushes Vaughn again who is visibly annoyed at him.

"Connor, do something *right now*," Hadley gravels out to her husband. He is quick to tend to the scuffle happening in my hospital room.

"Just great, I have a hockey fight in my hospital room minus the skates." My shoulders slump down when I mutter to myself.

"You know I can take you down in no time, so back the fuck off," Vaughn growls.

Connor steps between them again to keep them apart by holding his arms out. "Will you two knock it off?"

Briggs looks back to me while he points at Vaughn. "I'm not going to let this go. His intentions are not honorable, and I won't forget that."

Throwing my arms up in the air, I gawk my eyes. "Briggs, we're not in Victorian times. I don't need your approval. I'm not a damsel in distress," I say, raising my voice.

"You're my sister," he defends.

"Yeah, and I'm the sister who hasn't actually told the father of my child that I'm pregnant, so leave it alone," I justify.

My brother's face falls, and it clicks in his head that Vaughn is finding out for the first time. He even flashes Vaughn a look that for the most part is neutral.

Just then the door opens again, with Dr. Forest arriving and rolling in a cart. She warily studies the room. "What a collection of hockey players here that the medical staff seemed to notice gather in the hall earlier, but the nurses' station is picking up that your heart rate is all over the place, along with the baby being more active, so you seem to be stressed."

"Understatement," I highlight.

"I think it's time that we kick out the visitors." She smiles at me.

The room goes silent as we all look at one another.

"Let's go, guys, I think Isla needs a moment." Hadley does her best to usher Connor and Briggs out. She stops short at Vaughn, maybe even gives him a cautionary look.

"I'm staying," he states firmly, with his fists clenched at his sides and his gaze still drilling into me.

The doctor notices the tension. "You can only stay if my patient agrees."

Vaughn raises his brows at me, waiting for me to answer, and it's clear there is only one answer that I can give.

Blowing out a breath, I say, "He can. He's… the father. Would it be okay if we have a minute?"

"One minute," she says sharply. Give the doctor an award for professionalism as she clearly grasps this unusual situation.

With everyone abandoning us, Vaughn steps forward.

In the background, I can hear my brother. "I swear to God, I might just commit murder."

"No, you won't. Come on, let's go for a walk. You're acting like a wild animal who needs to be tamed," Connor suggests, and they must be walking away, as the background grows silent.

Except for the sound of the machine.

"Oh, Isla, Isla, Isla," Vaughn tuts, and it's sweltering, and it would even be sexy if it weren't for the fact that I know what's about to come. "You owe me a lot of answers."

VAUGHN

Isla's chest visibly moves up and down, but my sight keeps drawing back to her swollen belly. It's visible without a doubt.

A baby.

Our baby.

I'm completely blindsided by this news. I can't even process how I feel about the fact that I created a child. Instead, fury takes over me.

"You're already in your third trimester?" I repeat what she said earlier.

"Yes, due in a few weeks."

Fucking late-season hurricanes.

I step closer to the bed, undecided what I'm doing. "So, that means you're like, what, about to birth a child?"

She takes a long breath through her pursed lips. "Seems you're great with numbers." Is she seriously attempting to make a joke right now?

"You had nine months to tell me, yet here I am after *accidentally* discovering that you're pregnant." I'm livid I think, which is why my eyes narrow in on her, and she looks kind of uncomfortable, but I believe that I have a little right to feel this way.

"First off, it's not nine months, we still have nearly a month to go."

"Cute." I flash her a contrite smile.

"I-I tried to tell you… a few times."

"So, what? You were going to wait until I saw you carrying a baby? Invite me to their high school graduation and be like, by the way, you're a dad? Were you ever going to tell me?" My voice raises slightly.

Her eyes hood closed then open, with fresh tears, and the vision of her right now has me torn, because I'm angry, but she's the woman sitting on a hospital bed.

"No, I was going to tell you… eventually."

I scoff a sound and bring my hand to my forehead to check that I'm still alive. "When? When did you try to tell me?" I want answers.

"First when I phoned you and the crazy girl answered." Shit. "Again, at Christmas when you were here for the game."

"You wanted to let me fuck you and not even tell me that you were pregnant?" I'm astonished.

"I didn't let you screw me, thank you very much," she defends.

My hands slowly clap together. "Let's give you an award for having a conscience." I'm being cynical. "That only lasted so long," I snipe.

"I freaked out because you said you didn't like kids and you didn't see yourself wanting kids anytime soon," she adds.

I shake my head. "I did say that, but it doesn't mean you had a right to withhold this critical information."

"You have a choice to walk away if you want, I know that. I tried again to tell you when I came to your place, but you were so visibly not ready to hear the news. It felt like it was the last thing that I should say."

Again, looking back, I had an inkling there was something more at the time, but I was too frustrated in my life to press her for what it may have been.

"Instead, you didn't. You let us have sex while you harbored a secret." Unbelievable. I didn't want to think less of Isla, but right now, she has crossed a major line by keeping this big of a secret. "Seriously? This is a shitty thing to do. The last thing that I would expect from you." Then another fact dawns on me, and I rub my temples. "Wait, how the hell did I not see you were pregnant when we had sex?"

She lifts a shoulder up to her ear. "I didn't really start to show until more than halfway. I mean, I had a little bump, but I wasn't wearing the right outfit to make it obvious." She lifts a finger indicating for me to wait. "And to be fair, our position of choice didn't exactly get me naked, nor could you notice my belly."

"No, instead you let your bigger boobs entice me into ramming my dick up inside of you." It scrapes out of my mouth.

Her own mouth gapes open from my harsh words.

"Incredible, you're focusing on our ability to fuck between a seat and steering wheel when you should be focusing on other aspects. I mean, really? We had sex, a few good conversations, that doesn't mean you know me inside out," she refutes.

We've had a connection from moment one when we met, which raises the scale of my disappointment.

My face falls to my hands because we may go in circles right now.

"I need to process this," I admit. Then it dawns on me that she is in a freaking hospital. "Wait, why are you here?"

She chortles to herself. "I thought something was wrong. Turns out I was a little dramatic, and it was just eating the wrong thing and had Braxton Hicks contractions, which is like my body practicing for the big day. The baby was kicking more than normal too."

"Baby? You don't know…"

"If it's a boy or girl?"

Why am I asking as though I'm already invested? I haven't figured out my feelings.

The line of her mouth slants to the side. "No. I didn't want to find out."

I nod slowly, attempting to soak this all in.

The knock on the door kind of sends a surge of dread through me, in case it's her gladiator-hyped-up brother. Luckily, the doctor peeks her head around the door.

"Ready? I need to see you now so we can get you home soon," she explains.

"Sure," Isla agrees.

The doctor walks in with a genuine smile. "I would like to do an ultrasound just to be safe, but your blood work seems good, and the baby's heart rate is strong, just spiked earlier because he or she seems to be an active one. You probably need a little rest considering your body seems under stress, and it's also preparing for him or her to come out." She begins to roll a machine to Isla's bed. "Will he be staying?"

"Yes," I blurt out. I have had enough undisclosed information for one day.

The doctor smiles at me. "That's great, but again, the patient gets to decide."

My gaze snaps to Isla to inform her that I won't be accepting no for an answer.

She grasps my demand and quickly answers. "He can stay," she assures the doctor.

"Okay, lean back and lift your shirt. You're a pro at this now. A bit of gel and then here we go." The doctor removes the contraption belt around Isla then squirts something that oozes from a bottle and places the wand-shaped thing in her hand against Isla's belly. "You should probably get closer to Isla if you want to enjoy the show."

Reluctantly, I take a few steps next to Isla's bed near her upper body. She gives me a nervous look before her head zips back to the screen attached to the portable machine.

When I can see the outline of a baby, I'm taken aback.

"Wow, the baby has grown since the last ultrasound," Isla notes with a fond smile.

"It goes really quick now. The baby is almost so big that an ultrasound won't show many new things because the baby doesn't have much room to move around." The doctor stays glued to the screen as she zooms in to different sections.

The sound of the heartbeat fills the room, similar to the sound of being underwater, but there is a rhythm. Steady and fast, a sound that I wasn't expecting to cause a twitch some-where inside of me. For a second, I'm in awe that I played a role in creating that. It's really a baby. We're also way past the stage of debating what to do, in terms of options. I've missed the majority of her pregnancy, and this is a full-fledged baby that has a heartbeat and legs and arms… and is about to enter the world.

Isla doesn't seem fazed like I am by the image on the screen. I guess she has had ample opportunity to listen to this.

"Your file states that you didn't want to find out the sex. Still the case?" the doctor asks.

Isla shoots me a look as though I have a say. I'm not sure if I'm glaring or my face is frozen because Isla seems to try to break the air between us. "I didn't want to, but maybe…"

Is she waiting for me to answer?

"I do. I've been graced with enough shockers today." My voice is a little bitter.

Isla nods to the doctor that it's okay.

"Ooh, fun." The doctor zooms in then brings her finger to the screen. "Baby is giving us a great view today, as I can see very clearly that you're having a daughter."

"A girl?" Isla cries, but her smile indicates that they are happy tears.

I tilt my head to examine the screen, and I feel my mouth tug. *Yeah*, it's pretty visible, otherwise there would be a large line if it were a boy.

"Yep. Get ready for tea parties." The doctor keeps the wand in place so we can stare for a few seconds at the screen while she seems to be taking measurements of limbs. "Dad looks like he's already planning this girl's ice-skating career," the doctor attempts to joke.

Dad is planning nothing. I'm still in disbelief.

A daughter. Wow.

Isla seems to be searching my face for a clue to understanding where my brain is at.

"Okay, everything looks great. You're doing excellent, Isla. But really, try to be stress-free. At this point, the baby is at a good point in the pregnancy and has a better chance to live a long and happy life if born a few weeks early. The longer she stays in, closer to the due date is ideal, but any moment it can happen."

"About to go into labor." My tone is flat. "I find out when she's about to go into labor." I feel a hint of anger boiling inside of me.

The doctor stares at me with perhaps exasperation or a warning to calm the hell down. She removes the wand and turns off the machine before she begins to detach the cords connected to Isla's finger.

Isla ignores me and speaks to the doctor. "Don't worry. I'm taking my vitamins, ensuring I eat vegetables, no caffeine, not even any desserts with alcohol in the recipe, lots of sleep, and daily walks." Isla seems to be proud of her habits.

"You're doing great." She hands Isla some paper towel to wipe her stomach.

"Of course, and sorry I overreacted. I didn't expect the contractions or for her to suddenly hate Jolly Joe's cinnamon rolls," Isla apologizes.

The doctor stands. "That is a travesty. How can she ever be a true Lake Spark citizen?" she jokes. "You did the right thing. If there is anything else going forward, then call right away."

"Yep."

The doctor begins to walk out. "You're free to go. See you."

With the doctor now gone, Isla and I return to a stalemate with our eyes in a stare down.

"A girl," she whispers to herself.

An overwhelming feeling hits me, a need to assure her, but that anger keeps poking at me. I want time to process still, I'm not that type of guy who forgives so easily. She didn't tell me for months, with no plan in sight that she would have.

"How?" I state more than I ask. I'm near numb from confusion.

A sound escapes her mouth. "The low pressure in the air from a hurricane increases your chances of getting pregnant."

My head perks up in astonishment. "Really?"

"No," she deadpans. I shake my head that, of course, I'm being an idiot. "We didn't cover it up, and I forgot a pill, so this is all on me."

I debate how to answer her. "I think a man is still

involved in that equation, and that just so happens to be me. I'm moving to Lake Spark. That was already happening before I discovered your little secret. We have a big discussion ahead of us, but it can't happen right now. I'm sure as hell not going to jump in as if you didn't keep this from me," I snipe.

"Are you saying that you don't want to be involved?" Disappointment floods her face. "It's fine. I can do this alone; you have an out."

I scratch the back of my head. "Isla, I'm pissed. No, furious. I need time to process. So I'm leaving and finding a strong scotch. We'll talk when I'm ready."

Then I walk away.

VAUGHN

I seem to be engrossed with the deep blue water next to the deck and dock of Catch 22, the restaurant in Lake Spark that has a great steak. Although, I'm not hungry.

I'm waiting for my brother, Stone. I'm thankful he lives in Chicago and just had a meeting with his publisher first thing. Go figure, a former pro athlete is writing books. I called him last night saying I really needed to see him if possible, and with no hesitation, he said he would drive out to Lake Spark this morning. He should be here any minute, which gives me time to read an email from the real estate agent. I may not have gotten much sleep last night, but I'm comfortable enough to answer back and hit send.

I toss my phone onto the menu lying on the table just as my brother arrives.

"What's up with you? That phone is getting the treatment of an empty beer can at a kegger," he observes as he takes a seat across from me, leaning across to touch my shoulder as a hello.

"Sorry, I just bought a house."

His face turns puzzled. "You only got here yesterday, and you already saw a house to buy?"

"Nope. Didn't see the house, just purchased it, all cash. I'm sure it's a great house, at least the pictures look like it." I grab my glass of water to drink.

Stone gawks at me. "You what? That doesn't sound like you."

I tip my head slightly to the side and flash my eyes. "Well, a house is a small problem right now, and I need one ASAP. And quite frankly, I don't particularly care if the walls are green or blue." Or pink if that's what Isla is going for.

Stone stares at me blankly. "Okay, what am I missing? You look like you've seen the eye of a storm."

A humorless laugh escapes me. "That's a wonderful reference considering my predicament."

"I thought you were completely excited for this move, plus your new job."

I scratch my nose before I lean into the table with my arms. "I sure as hell hope I'll be able to focus, considering I just discovered that someone I slept with is pregnant."

My brother's eyes instantly grow into saucers. "As in… you're the dad?"

"Yeah, as in I'm the dad. It's not just that… she's already about to pop, which means she never told me, with no plans to tell me."

"Shit."

The waitress arrives with a bright smile then locks between my brother and me, sensing the tension. "I'll come back in a jiffy."

"It's okay." My brother looks at his watch. "It's twelve o'clock, I'll have a beer. This guy here looks like he needs a clear mind, so bring him an iced tea."

She offers a polite smile and scurries away.

My brother snaps his gaze back to me. "What do you mean she was never going to tell you?"

I hold up three fingers. "I've seen her three times since the night we conceived a child. All of those times, she didn't mention a word, not even a clue. If it weren't for the fact that by *accident* I showed up to the hospital, then I don't think I ever would have known until I saw her on Main Street carrying a kid." I sound livid because I am.

He blows out a breath. "Holy hell, this is… big news."

I scrub a hand across my face. "I'm so furious."

My brother studies me for a few good seconds. "Do you know why she didn't tell you?"

I scoff a displeased sound. "She said she tried but every occasion there was a reason not to, not the right time."

He nods in understanding. "Now that you do know, what does she want? Wait, who is she?"

"Isla Chase."

"As in… Briggs Chase's…"

"Little sister, yep. Give me another point for making this more complicated."

He swipes his hands across his face. "Damn." It drags out.

"Again, minor detail, as we now need to figure out what's happening going forward. Stone, I don't care what she wants. She doesn't get to decide if I'm involved or not."

"She doesn't want you involved?"

I flex my jaw. "She didn't… exactly say that."

A knowing smirk appears on his face. "Jumping to conclusions then?"

Maybe he has a point. "At this rate, I don't have a lot of time to guess. You know the doctor said that the baby could actually come at any time now and still be okay. What if I wake tomorrow, and *poof*, there's a baby here?"

His eyes narrow. "You sound like you are kind of already

on board. If a baby did just poof…" He makes a gesture with his hand. "Then it seems like you want to see him or her."

"It's a girl." That overpowering pull of my mouth to smile hits me again. It happened a few times during the night while I tossed and turned.

My brother smiles widely. "You're having a daughter. That's kind of cool."

"Her heartbeat is strong." A soft spot within me causes my voice to grow almost tender.

Staring at my brother, the realization hits me yet again. I'm going to be a dad.

It's a moment before Stone states the obvious. "I think… you know you're invested. Just scared."

The waitress deposits our drinks, and Stone gives her an indication to come back later.

I stew in his observation. "Yeah… I am. First it was digesting the news, I felt like someone swung a bat into my stomach. I wasn't sure that I wanted this. Then it was trying to figure out what role I would play. But the real kicker for why I didn't sleep more than an hour last night is because…" I hate saying it.

Luckily, Stone does it for me. "You're not our dad. You can be so much better than he ever was. Just believe it."

"What if I get it all wrong?" I'm throwing it all on the line because we can talk about anything.

"What if you get it all right?" he counters.

I lick my lips and glance at the lake, trying to capture some peace in my head. Then I return my gaze to my brother who's observing me without judgment.

"I don't know how to handle a girl. At least with a boy, I have hockey. A girl? I don't know what to do."

He raises his brows at me. "Now you're scared of a daughter? Nah, you're equally excited. Either way, a child of your own is a whole different territory. You'll just be seeing a lot of pink and purple."

A half-smile hits me like a wave. "I guess so."

"And just like that, we've confirmed that you're doing this. You're going to be a dad."

I nod once in agreement. "Is it bad if I thought for a millisecond last night that I should just give Isla money in a trust fund and sign away my rights?" Shame floods me that the thought even crossed my mind.

"Uh…" He scratches his chin, debating the right words to use. "I think… if it was only a millisecond then you can let it go. Because a millisecond is a speck on the spectrum of your life, not even noticeable. Hell, you can't be the first guy to think it if he discovers he is unexpectedly becoming a dad. Besides, you're here telling me all of this because you *want* to be a great dad. That's by far more important."

I think about it. "I'm not backing away from being a dad… I just don't know how to deal with Isla."

"Maybe… I don't know. She can also be scared or have some reason deep within that prevented her from telling you. You're not the only person in the world to have fears, Vaughn."

My lips quirk out, as my brain feels fried from trying to solve the mystery. "I told her I needed space and walked away."

He chuckles. "Sounds like you really don't want to make this easy."

"She never clued me in that she's about to have a baby," I reiterate.

"And? She didn't exactly say you can't be involved either. You need to talk to Isla. Sometimes we have to take the high road when we shouldn't have to. She's the one who is pregnant, so in this case, she wins."

I shake my head, aggravated, as two people approach our table. I recognize Connor and Hadley right away.

"Hey… well, this is timely," Hadley greets me, while Connor greets my brother since they know one another.

"Excuse my wife. We came for lunch and she noticed you here. Now she has a strong feeling to insert herself into situations that she should probably stay out of," Connor attempts to explain what is about to happen.

Hadley throws him a playful glare before sharply turning her head back to me. "Isla is in misery." She gets right to the point.

"And? She kept a big secret about my baby."

She stands taller. "You said your baby. Isn't it *our* baby, as in Isla and you?" She's keen to correct me.

Connor smiles tightly at me. "Hadley is concerned."

"You know, she has her reasons for why she couldn't tell you. She tried, a lot. So while you sit here debating how to punish her for that, just remember that all she's done is focus on the baby, while internally she is scared out of her mind because she *didn't* get the life that this little girl is going to have."

Fuck, it only dawns on me now that Isla and I share a similar upbringing, with absent parents playing key roles in our probably broken behaviors.

"I don't think I should be having this conversation with you," I inform her.

"You're right. You should be with Isla, planning a future whether together or not. It's eighteen years to life the way you're now bound together." Hadley is feisty but raises valid points.

Connor affectionately touches his wife's elbow to usher her away. "Come on, I think you need to give the guy some space."

She glares at me as her body turns away. "Fine. But she has a craving for ice cream sandwiches, just so you know."

Connor rolls his eyes while his wife nearly stomps away. "Sorry. She's protective of Isla who is like family to all of us. We'll get out your way and do takeout, it's safer for all of us." He begins to turn but pauses. "For what it's worth, I doubt Isla did this to be cruel or spiteful. That's just not her."

As he walks away, I do my best to take in their words, but that livid feeling of betrayal still lingers.

"See? Maybe you should put your feelings aside and hear her out, focus on the one thing that is important. Is it being angry at Isla or preparing for this little girl?" My brother is challenging me, getting my brain to rewire, that's what he is trying to do.

I sigh. "You're right. I should cool off a little more then go to see Isla."

The corners of his mouth twitch with a comforting look. "That right there is what real dads do."

A feeling of hope begins to creep inside of me near my chest. I can do this, the father thing. It's not what I have to do, it's what I *choose* to do.

"I'm doing this. I'm going to become a dad," I confirm before I blow out a breath in an attempt to chill the fuck out.

"I'm proud of you." He avoids getting too sentimental and holds up a menu. "Now, let's fuel you up."

It's a half-hour later when our food arrives, yet I only manage a few bites, instead opting for a coffee.

"Eat," my brother demands as he throws a fry into his mouth.

I take a bite of my egg salad sandwich to keep him at bay. "Sorry, my mind is still a little distracted."

"That's cool, I get it. As much as I don't want to get the

wheels turning in your head again, but... could you see a future with Isla, not just as co-parents?"

Harsh. He's going for the deep questions to make my mind stir.

"I really can't say. We've only seen one another a handful of times, not talked much more than that, but somehow, I feel more linked than most." I'm being honest. As much as I felt a spark and connection with Isla, it's hard to determine what the future will bring when I've always been adamant that a future with someone wasn't for me at this moment in time.

"Do you want to find out?"

"Stone, right now, we just need to figure out the logistics of having a kid."

He takes a sip from his beer. "Right, babies need things and a roof over their head. Silly me for thinking a bowl of water and a ball would suffice."

I snort a laugh at his attempt to lighten the mood. But his mention of a roof gets me thinking about living arrangements. I vaguely remember Connor mentioning in the car that Isla has been searching for a new place; I can only imagine that she needs more space for the baby.

"Got it," I say confidently. "Isla is going to move in with me."

Yep, that's the answer for now. I may be slightly pissed still, but I'm not going to miss more moments of this pregnancy, and I'm sure as hell not missing the first weeks of a newborn.

My brother looks at me in doubt. "Surely, you need to ask her first."

"Nope. She doesn't have a choice in the matter," I say, adamant.

ISLA

I've barely slept, I lack coffee, and I'm doing my best to check the graphics for work, as I wanted to send a few more notes even though I'm on leave. The banana peel and crumbs on my dining room table from my toasted waffle are just a bonus in my life that is now in chaos.

The sound of the doorbell already has me dreading my wobble to the door. It's an array of options who could be on the other end, and I've done my best not to be hopeful that Vaughn would be so quick to talk.

When I reach the door and look out the side glass, I'm confused. The woman appears to be holding a sign, but she looks normal enough to avoid stranger danger.

I open the door. "Can I help you?"

The woman in her forties smiles brightly at me and seems awfully cheery. "Yes, I'm Katherine from the agency and just wanted to let you know that I'm setting up the sign now, so we should be getting some action quite soon."

"Sign?" My face must seem perplexed.

"Of course, you can't rent a house without the for-rent sign. It's an essential to get traffic to view this place."

Blinking my eyes a few times, I try to make sense of this. "Sorry, but did my landlord send you? She said she wasn't thinking of selling until next year. Did she change her timeline? Normally she's really good about talking to me directly. This is the worst possible time, right now." Now I'm internally freaking out because this is too much to add to my current state of life.

Her smile drops and she begins to look confused. "The landlord? Well, I'm here because the landlord called and said she wants to rent out this address since it will be vacated soon. The paperwork initiating the process was signed yesterday evening."

A skeptical laugh escapes me. "I assure you that I didn't hand in any notice to leave last night. Hell, I'm not even sure I left my bed last night. You must have the wrong address."

She grabs her phone from her big purse and immediately brings up a message that she quickly reads. "This most certainty is the correct place. Vaughn Madden wrote it down specifically in the email after speaking with the landlord on the phone who is down in New Mexico. He even got her to send over the paperwork via email."

"What?" My curt response has me nearly spinning.

Before she can answer, I notice a car pull up to the curb. A fancy rental, with a guy in the driver's seat that has a sharp jawline that I've enjoyed a time or two. We both watch Vaughn get out. I'm sure Katherine here is drooling and getting her panties in a twist. Vaughn is sporting a pair of jeans and a white t-shirt that is tight enough to see the outline of his muscles. His hair seems to have a little gel, as his wave is swept back, and I'm not quite sure what the small box is in his hands.

He instantly smiles a welcome to our real estate trespasser. "Hey, Katherine, you beat me here. You go on, do your thing, and keep me posted. Isla and I need to talk."

"Of course, I'll be quick, as I need to go take down a sign over on Duck Road," she greets him in passing.

I warily assess Vaughn, as I'm unsure what is happening or if I am still on planet earth. "Please explain." My sharp tone hopefully informs him that I'm not impressed.

Vaughn is unfazed by my direct tone and strides straight to me before touching my arm to guide me inside. I quickly look back to see a sign getting hammered into my lawn.

That isn't the kind of hammering I enjoy.

Vaughn kicks the door closed behind us, and I break free from his touch. "You're leaving your house and moving in with me." His tone is dismissive as we face one another.

I ogle my eyes at him as an electric shock seems to hit me. No words can express this bombshell demand, because he isn't asking, he's ordering me.

He hands me the box with a fake sweet smile. "Here."

Examining the box, I'm torn between backtracking on what he just said or being happy. "I assure you, ice cream sandwiches are not going to solve this conversation." That's the road I choose; serious discussion.

His smug appearance has me worried. "Oh, you're right on that, sweetheart." The way he says sweetheart isn't an endearing term, it's a warning. "You kept the single most important news of my life from me, and I have every intention of rectifying that little judgement error, and you may or may not like what I have in store for you."

My body straightens and again that swirl of confusion is on full flight through my body. A concern for what his decision may be, but damn, his word choice makes me hot and very bothered. I may be pregnant, but I'm ready to pounce on a little anger sex.

My glare is hopefully burning a hole through him; however, we have to put this aside. I indicate the sofa, and he nods once before going to sit down. I follow, holding the box of ice cream tightly, because despite what I said, I may need one to calm me down.

We get comfortable, and I'm waiting for him to begin. Not going to lie, I feel as though I deserve a lecture.

His head rolls to the side to look at me. "Here's the deal, Isla. I've already missed enough thanks to your doing. I'm not going to miss any more, especially if the baby will be here before we know it. I heard you were looking for a new place to live, and I just so happen to have a house that I bought on a whim. Solution found." His firm voice is far too cocky for me right now.

My face must be turning red due to irritation. "I'm sorry, okay? I should have told you no matter what. I've thought about it every day, trying to push my fears to the side. But you can't just contact my landlord without asking. How do you even do that?" My voice cracks, because really? How *do you* do that?

"Connections, and a promise of a financial bonus on her part. I'm fairly confident you will sign what needs to be signed to make sure you vacate like the good little tenant I'm sure you are." His piercing gaze is chipping away inside of me.

"Vaughn, okay, I *have* been looking at houses because I will need more space. It's not that I can't afford a slightly bigger house to buy or with higher rent, it's simply there isn't much on the market here. People tend to rent out their three-bedroom homes for weekend and summer rentals," I explain, as I don't want him to get any ideas that I need to be saved. "Besides, I can make it work here for a bit, as the baby will sleep in my room the first few months."

He holds a finger up as if he is going to correct me. "No, the baby can sleep in her own room in *my* house where space isn't an issue."

I grumble a sound before opening the box of ice cream, not caring that it's all going to melt. Ripping open a wrapper, I stuff a bite into my mouth. "I get the memo. You want to make me move as punishment, but just throwing a sign in my yard is a step too far and far too permanent," I say with a full mouth as I chew, then I point at him with my free hand. "You know, before the baby news, I was a fun and spontaneous woman who would spend a night with hot hockey players," I begin my tangent.

"Players, plural?" he cuts in.

"Fine. You. Actually, you're the only hockey player. I've never done that before, but I am a spontaneous and fun woman. It's just when I found out I was pregnant that full-on mother bear mode kicked in. Roar." I pretend to claw him with my hand not even in fun, I've gone psychotic.

His brows arch, and his face is dead serious. "Did you just roar and try to claw me like a bear?"

I blink my eyes a few times, realizing how crazy I am acting.

His head cocks gently to the side. "Now, let's stay focused. I wouldn't say demanding you and my daughter live in my house is punishment, as you say, but it means you don't have a choice but to rely on me and my place to stay, no fucking escape. Our daughter deserves to have both her parents around her. Isn't bonding crucial the first few months? Then we can figure it out."

My head perks, and I slow down chewing my mouthful. He said *our* daughter. He isn't running away. I need to retrace my thoughts a second and break down the information that he's throwing at me through dominant demands. "Wait, you made your decision… about being involved."

Vaughn takes the ice cream sandwich out of my hand and flops it on top of the box that's now on the coffee table. Apparently, he needs me focused. "Didn't you get that clue with the whole 'you will move in with me' thing? Yeah… I'm involved." His voice is pure reverence, delicate, but in the best possible way.

I lift a shoulder. "That probably… was an obvious clue."

His nostrils flare slightly as he inhales deeply. "Isla, I'm not going to lie. Timing? Uhm, not great." His face is near cartoonish. "Although it's off-season for hockey players, it isn't really for me, and I have a lot to do to prepare for next season, especially with the draft approaching. Which is why I need you at my home, ready whenever I need."

"Ready?" I gulp.

Holy fuck, something inside of me is clinging to logic for survival while I feel a pool of wetness between my legs. I subtly shift my gaze down to double-check that he won't notice that my nipples are now tight and hard, nor hidden thanks to flimsy fabric.

His tongue darts to the corner of his mouth while his eyes stay glued to me. "I mean it's easier on my schedule. I will be traveling with the team, so I don't want to be puzzling with our calendars. When I get back from a late flight, then I better be able to simply walk in to see my daughter."

"Our daughter," I correct him, but I stay mesmerized by first the image that was in my head, followed by the emotions soaring up through my body, because as prevailing as his request is, it's because… he's invested in the baby.

The fear I had is fading away bit by bit.

"Our daughter," he repeats. "I get the keys for my place

tomorrow since it was an all-cash offer and the former owners were already out. I have movers ready to pack up what you need, I have all the furniture… wait, except the baby furniture." He's making a mental note that he forgot something.

This is another side of Vaughn. I'm still in a trance.

"I really don't have a choice in this matter and guilt is taking over. Plus, I really need to nest for the baby. I was waiting for my baby shower next week to get everything in order. We were supposed to have it a few weeks ago but had to postpone due to a lot of us out with the flu," I point out blankly.

Vaughn pinches the bridge of his nose. "I'm not entirely sure what a baby shower entails, but fine. Look, we focus on the baby, but damn, Isla…" His look is now stern. "I didn't sleep, I'm still numb, and you really fucking hurt me by keeping this all a secret."

"Crap, oh no, we keep using bad word choices, and the baby can hear us."

"Really? We're still on that?" His tone is mundane.

He's right, it's silly. I comb my fingers through my hair. "I can say sorry a thousand times. I was scared, and every time it just didn't seem the right moment."

His look isn't changing, he's not impressed. "My cock inside of you while you were bouncing on my dick in my car didn't seem like the right moment? We could be as intimate as can be, yet you couldn't share the news?" he dryly highlights the replay of events.

Taking relaxing breaths, I remind myself to keep my debate from boiling up. My hands begin to rub my belly as I think of the best way to move on from this topic.

"Look, as much as I am ready to do this all on my own if needed, I still feared you wouldn't want to be involved. I'm sorry. It is what it is." I swim my eyes away from him because I can't handle seeing the disappointment on his face.

It takes a few seconds before he responds. "Like I said, that issue still needs to simmer down inside of me. We should just focus on the baby."

"I agree."

A butterfly feeling flutters underneath my ribs before a hard nudge hits me from within. It causes me to smile, as it has done every single time.

"What's wrong?" Vaughn moves to touch me, with panic appearing in his posture.

"Relax, she must be awake now and is just letting me know. Or it was the sugar kick from the ice cream." I keep my hand steady on my belly to feel her shuffling her little feet inside of me.

Vaughn seems unsure what to do.

Without thought, I grab his hand and bring it to the spot where he will feel her. "That little jab against your hand is her kicking. They say it will slow down once she is ready to rumble in her life outside of the womb. Her space is getting limited, so it restricts her from moving the way she did a few weeks ago."

The warmest of smiles begins to stretch on his mouth. "Wow, she has strength."

"Tell me about it. When she decides to kick me in the ribs at two in the morning, I'm wondering if she's trying to escape already."

I close my eyes for a moment and take in the fact that Vaughn's hand is firmly planted against my body to feel the baby we created. Something about this feels promising... and special.

"Does it hurt?" he asks while he stares at my stomach to see the little pops of a foot from inside of me.

"Nah, it's more of an ow that's quick and just makes you laugh."

"I guess we have to think of a name other than baby or she," he mentions.

Is this happening? Is Vaughn Madden really sitting next to me, touching my body and promising he will be involved?

I hate how buried emotions that aren't even his doing prevent me from fully believing him, but everything from the last few minutes gives me a little hope.

"A name, packing her hospital bag, installing the car seat, and ensuring the baby stroller is ready are all on my list. I have some stuff stored in my spare room."

Vaughn can't tear his eyes away from the spot where she kicked, even though she has stopped moving for a solid minute.

"Wow… so this is really happening." He blows out another breath.

"You said the hurricane was nothing to worry about; turns out that it was way more than that." I point to my stomach while his hand moves away to rake through his hair.

The corners of his mouth twist. "Guess so."

We stare at one another in an intense way that's filled with a lingering attraction, maybe even heightened because anger and fear tend to fuel it even more.

Vaughn clears his throat before he stands. "I need to head to the training arena."

"Sure. I'm just doing a few things on my laptop today."

"Good, you should take it easy. I guess I'll need to keep an eye on you."

My eyes bug out as I stand. "Vaughn, I'm an independent woman who won't tolerate a possessive man." It comes out a little too bouncy, and in truth, I kind of like it.

He chortles a sound before his smirk returns. "I beg to

differ. You will absolutely tolerate it. You don't have a choice. I mean it, Isla. I'm not going to play a game. My mind is clear that I'm a little wounded from the secret you kept, but I'm choosing to focus on what matters. You're carrying our baby, and that's what matters right now."

I nod gently and roll my lips in response.

His eyes draw a line up and down my body for a once-over before he begins to walk away. "It's also fucking annoying that even in this situation, this attraction around us doesn't seem to fade."

A sly smile hits me. "Tell me about it," I respond softly in the same casual tone he used.

"Within three days you better be in my house." he calls out without throwing me a glance.

When he leaves, he is like the breeze that blows through a house on a summer day; chilly at first but then a welcome relief.

Let's just hope it stays that way.

ISLA

What in the world am I doing?

I keep thinking it to myself as I carefully rummage through the box for lighter items to take out and set in the room that most likely will be the nursery in Vaughn's beautiful modern home. It's on the side of the lake that gets great morning sun.

Fortunately, he is in his home office for a video call with a scout who is currently in Sweden. I'm kind of grateful that the last few days he has been very busy. Meeting after meeting and strategy planning, which is why we haven't spoken much. Instead, he sent me the time of when the movers would arrive. In truth, from what I have seen from afar, he seems content with his new role and maybe dare I say more relaxed than he was during his last season of playing hockey… Then he looks at me and a shade of indescribable mixed feelings hits him.

Since the movers placed my stuff upstairs, I've been wondering how this situation will all play out. I can't think clearly as my brain goes in multiple directions.

When my phone rings on the side table by the bed, I

wobble over to answer because the screen flashes Briggs's name.

"I'm outside. Let me in." His curt tone has me huff a sound because I know what is about to come.

I've been lucky that Hadley and Connor have kept my brother at bay, telling him that he should give me some space and time. That was only going to last so long. "Okay," I answer and pull up the app that Vaughn sent to me for the front gate and the house door.

I manage to walk down the stairs, recognizing that I'm a tad slower than I was even a week ago.

Opening the door, I'm greeted by my brother who charges in and instantly searches the area, probably for Vaughn.

"He isn't within earshot," I inform him.

"Fine," he grits out. "I came to talk to you anyhow."

I lead him to the living room, and we each find a spot on opposite ends of the sofa.

"Get on with it." I must sound unenthused.

"What the hell, Isla? He waltzes back into town, and you just go along with moving in with him?"

I hold my hand up as if it could be an attempt to calm him. "Trust me, this wasn't part of the plan, but he makes a point. He is the dad, and when the baby comes, then he has a right to be involved, and logistically, this probably makes sense as I can't just hand over this little girl on a schedule the first few weeks, especially if I breastfeed. It was never my intention to keep him from the baby, it was only I struggled to *tell* him."

Briggs rubs his eyes as he takes in my explanation. "Not going to lie. This feels like a bit of a betrayal that of all the people you choose to hook up with… it had to be him. But this is the situation we're in."

"No, this is the situation that *I'm* in. I kind of put myself here too," I clarify.

"Admittedly, I'm relieved to hear that he didn't know and hadn't abandoned you. That is the only little speck of compassion that I'm going to give him. What happens now?"

My shoulders slacken a bit. "Truthfully, I don't know. It's kind of hard to focus when all I can think about is the fact that she can come any day now, and I have nothing ready because I wanted to wait until I knew this would be a healthy pregnancy just in case."

"That makes sense. I'm trying to wrap my head around how to handle being in the same room when that asshole is around," he nearly snarls and looks around the room to take in the décor which is quite basic yet chic, with a few boxes of baby furniture in the corner that just arrived.

It causes me to smile because I'm entertained. "Briggs." He doesn't look at me. "Briggsy Chase," I try again. "Look at me." He obeys like a child who needs to be explained why they're in timeout. "You have to find a way. He will be around. Maybe, just, I dunno, focus on your niece when you're stuck in the same room for personal gatherings. For hockey, I don't know what you'll do."

Guilt seems to hit him, and his silence plus my sibling intuition causes me to realize that there is more.

"I need to tell you something," he starts, and it doesn't feel great. "There is a rather large chance that I won't be signing with the Spinners for next season. I'll sign with another team, perhaps out in Seattle. The paperwork hasn't been completed yet, but I've been thinking about this since before Vaughn entered the picture."

"What?" I screech.

"I didn't tell you yet because I didn't want to upset you."

My throat tightens as a cry builds. "You're going to leave? You're my only family here."

He slides down the sofa to be closer to me and touches my shoulder in an attempt to comfort me. "First off, I'm keeping my house here, so every off-season, I'm here. And I'm not your only family here. Just look at everyone who is throwing you a baby shower this weekend. They love you as their own."

Tears fall. "B-but you're my brother," I stutter.

He offers me a warm smile. "You always knew this was a chance, and I'm ready for a change. I wouldn't be much use helping you with my niece in a few months since I'll be on the road. But next summer? I'm all here. Isla, you're growing your own family, whether that's alone or with…" He groans. "I can't even say his name."

"Vaughn." A firm voice causes our heads to shift to the opening between the step that leads to the living room and the open hall.

I roll my eyes, wondering what is about to transpire between my brother and the father of my baby.

"If you're going to be in my house then you can say my name," Vaughn adds.

Briggs stands. "Great, you're here. Was hoping I could avoid you, but since you're gracing us with your presence, then let's have it out."

"Geez, this isn't some battle of honor, Briggs. Please, for the sake of the heavily pregnant lady here." I hold up my hand. "Can we just calm it down a notch?"

"She's right." Vaughn steps down to be on our level. "So, what is it you want to say to me?"

"F-you." He's direct.

"Try harder," I mutter to my brother.

Briggs's jaw tenses. "Fine. My sister deserves the world,

so don't be an idiot. Whether I stay in Lake Spark or not, you best believe I will be getting the full report on how you treat her and my niece. To be honest, congratulations, because having you now be the GM just makes me more eager to sign elsewhere."

"I'm not talking hockey right now with you, so let's keep the topic on Isla."

"Then answer me," Briggs volleys back.

Vaughn's piercing gaze remains on Briggs. "You have my word. Now, if we can save the lecture for another day when I actually have patience for you, then I'm sure you can find your way out without the door hitting you in the ass. I need to chat with your sister."

I stretch both of my arms out to my sides. "Both of you chill and accept that you eventually need to find neutral ground. I can't deal with this every single time."

They both glance at me then adjust their shoulders, as if they're both struggling to accept my request but will go with it.

"Fine." Briggs goes first, and I'm having a hard time believing him, but I'm choosing my battles today.

"Also fine," Vaughn adds.

I sigh in relief and stand up. "Great, let's move on."

"Sure, I'm out of here anyway. I'll text you later, Isla," my brother informs me before I nod in understanding.

He throws Vaughn one more steely glare in parting.

The moment that Briggs is out of the house, the tension in the air deflates and turns to a new kind of tension, the unknown abyss that I'm heading down with Vaughn.

Vaughn has one hand tucked into his jeans pocket and he scrubs the other across his jaw as his eyes draw a line up my body to my nervous smile.

"Settling in?" he asks.

I salute him and give a coy smile. "Yes, master."

His lips form a contrite smile. "Charming."

I turn serious. "Yeah, I am."

He indicates the boxes with a nod. "I'll have someone come to construct this stuff, just tell them where to put it."

"Oh, you don't want to have a say where it goes in the room?"

He seems kind of exhausted. "I don't care nor have the time."

"Okay, then can you have someone come to paint the walls gray?"

Lines knit together on his forehead. "Gray? That's your choice for the baby's room?"

I walk a few steps to him. "Yeah, I don't want to do pink, and gray is neutral." I continue my walk to my purse on the stool of the open kitchen and pull out samples to show him. "I think North Rain Gray is a better choice to Cloud Gray, so North Rain Gray it is."

"Cloud Gray," he counters, and it feels like he is doing it on purpose.

"You don't care," I say, calling him out on his attempt.

"Cloud Gray," he repeats.

I drop the paint samples, now aggravated. "Is this your way of saying you're still pissed at me? Because I'm positive that debating shades of gray isn't going to solve it."

Vaughn's lips roll in. "You're right… North Rain Gray it is."

"So accommodating," I say, my tone frivolous.

I begin to walk past him, but he reaches out to touch my elbow and my feet become stuck to the ground, unwilling to leave, because he has me invested in what comes next.

"I'll calm down eventually." He means it, I can tell.

"Enough to stop by the baby shower?" Maybe I sound

hopeful, and I'm not sure why, considering he wasn't even in the picture a few days ago.

Now a half-smile appears, lighting the air between us. "Guys go to those?"

My shoulder rolls back. "Not particularly. I mean, some baby showers have the guys there, and they do ridiculous little games. Not this one, it's more a ladies' high tea. But the dad… normally stops by."

"I, uh, I'll see."

"Right, of course." I swallow my disappointment. Suddenly, it feels like we're not taking any steps. Besides, I was going to go to this party before he ever found out anyhow.

I begin to move again, but his hand is glued to me. "Isla…" It seems he has something profound to say. "Do you have any names in mind?" It feels like a cop out, but fine, I'll run with it.

"No, I'm struggling with that part," I admit.

"I can imagine. She'll take my last name?" His voice sounds elusive.

"Oh, I didn't really think about that yet." I'm truthful, as I just assumed she would have mine, but now that he's in the picture, I'm not sure.

"She should have it." He nods once then lets my arm go.

Feeling as though this is my opportunity for an exit, I walk away until I stop and spin on my heel. I notice that his eyes are still on me, filled with a blaze that isn't anger as his finger traces his jawline.

"Vaughn, I really am sorry," I repeat for what feels like the hundredth time.

His head tips lower before striking back up. "I think if we have any chance to make it the next few months and to raise this baby together, then you need to stop saying sorry. Eventually, I'll understand."

I appreciate that so much that a wry smile creates a line on my mouth.

"I'll send you the baby shower details."

"I'm not sure if I'll come, but maybe."

Inside something hurts a little. I recognize that it's that fear again, that he won't be fully invested in our daughter's life.

"Fine." I charge off, needing to go lock myself in my bedroom, wishing that it was his, because all is well, not only for our baby… but us.

● 15

VAUGHN

Staring down at the tablet in the training arena's boardroom, I'm looking over stats for the list of players that we'll hopefully manage to get in the upcoming draft next week. I'm changing windows on the screen as I compare one sheet to the other, which are contract negotiations. As much as I enjoy seeing Briggs with the other names that will probably leave, I also feel slight remorse for having that feeling. He is a great player and Isla's brother, so I better get on that bandwagon. However, I know if he goes to another team that Isla will probably be devastated.

I don't particularly want her upset, which is why I feel like a bit of a jerk lately that I've been distant and sometimes cold then warm. As much as the secret she kept is a hole somewhere within, I was right when I told her that she needs to stop apologizing if we have any hope of focusing on the future.

The future.

The one I have no clue what it will hold for us.

I've ignored every time it flashes in my mind that eventually we will need to confront the issue of us, but then it blows out of mind just as fast.

I glance to one of the guys from the management team to see that everyone is busy at work with various tasks. At least one thing is clear and it's that this career move was right, near exhilarating.

"I'll be back, just going to check in with the admin staff about travel next week," I say.

Someone in the group gives me an okay.

Sliding out of my chair, I head into the hall where I stroll until I turn a corner and instantly nearly run into Isla.

"Oh, hey, forgot you were here," she says, looking up from her phone. "Didn't see you this morning."

I've been avoiding her slightly at home, it's better that way. She was always beautiful, but right now? She's glowing, and she has my baby in her belly which just shoots the appeal to the sky.

Then it hits me. She works here, not for the team but for the facility and their training programs. And she's working today.

"Why are you here?" It comes out a little short.

"Oh, hello to you too." She's already exhausted of me.

Reaching out, I touch her arm then rub up and down. I can't not touch her. We may not be together, but I have the best claim possible.

"I mean, you should be at home resting, not here," I clarify.

Isla scoffs and her eyes widen slightly. "I'm pregnant, not incompetent. Plus, even though I'm on maternity leave, technically by law I can work until this baby arrives."

I smile tightly, a wave of protectiveness hitting me in full force. "I think not. Money isn't an issue, and you really *should* be resting. Not here."

"I enjoy my projects and want to ensure a smooth handover." She's clearly offended.

I roll my lips in to tame my temper. "That's great." Sarcasm sinks those words down. "However, as long as I can keep an eye on you while you're under my roof, then there is no escape. In a few days, I fly to Nashville for the draft picks, and then I can't ensure that you're taking it easy."

Her tongue hits her inner cheek, and it seems that she's in a similar mood and suppressing her anger. "Vaughn, as much as this alpha male behavior would be sexy in normal non-accidental-pregnancy circumstances, I can't handle this right now. You're stressing me out more than work, where I get to use fancy highlighters to write notes."

I clench my one hand, hoping it will keep me calm, reminding myself to get over my ego for a hot minute. "Okay… fair enough."

Her free hand comes to her hip, but she can barely tip her hip out because, well, she's heavily pregnant, and that area kind of merges together in a way that seems healthy and cute.

"You know, we can't keep avoiding one another considering we live together, but I get it. This is the worst time for this…" she points up and down her body, "to transpire. So, I'm letting you off the hook, as I know you want to start your job on the best possible foot. That doesn't mean that I'm enjoying this ride."

Fuck me, I was right. I'm being an ass.

She sighs one more exhausted breath. "I'll take it easy because I want to take it easy. It's not due to your demands." Isla walks past me, and I'm tempted to say something, yet I'm not sure what.

Isla beats me to the punch anyhow when she stops and turns slightly to glimpse over her shoulder at me. "Vaughn."

"Yeah?"

Her face softens and a half-smile appears on her mouth. "Thanks for leaving the new box of ice cream sandwiches in the freezer." Then she walks away.

Yup, I'm the king of unresolved feelings and actions.

My subtle act was because I have a sentimental spot for Isla. I can't deny that I've felt that way since the moment I saw her.

———

GETTING HOME LATE, I scrub my face, trying to wipe the tiredness from my eyes. It was a solid fourteen-hour day, and it will be that way again tomorrow. The house is dark, and I make my way up the stairs. Noticing the door to the nursery open, I decide to peek in, because somehow the reminder of a child entering my life feels calming in this moment, which is odd, as I was freaking out only a few days ago.

The moment that I open the slightly ajar door to the dark room, I notice Isla right away. She's leaning against the window wearing a long tight cotton nightgown, with her head resting against the glass as she cradles her stomach, completely unaware that I'm here, or maybe she is aware but chooses not to spare me a glance. The moonlight is bright tonight, which only makes this scene extra poignant. I'm tempted to take my phone out to capture a photo, but it would probably cause her to turn, and I want to soak in this scene a little longer.

I get those few seconds, and as much as I want to leave her in peace, I can't. And she seems to know that too.

"Thinking of running away?" she asks before her head turns in my direction, with her mouth sliding to the side.

I laugh under my breath and step farther into the room. "So you did notice that I'm here."

"Yeah, but I was waiting to see what you would do."

I saunter in her direction, my eyes circling the nearly complete nursery. I'm relieved that I'm in a position where I can hire people to handle this. If I had time I would do it myself, but time is sparce.

"You looked at peace, and I'm not sure how much I would ruin that." I join her at the window and lean against the edge. "Why are you not sleeping?"

"I'm restless. They say it happens as it gets more uncomfortable."

I nod in understanding. "I can imagine."

It happens yet again; our eyes get lost in one another as we take a few beats to stare.

"I'm sorry."

Her brows raise, as she seems confused. "For what?"

"I've been… well, a lot of things lately."

She hums a sound. "As much as it's whiplash, I… understand. I don't get points for doing what I did, and forgiveness isn't always fast."

Forgiveness, huh. I've just been on a train forward, focusing on this kid.

My thoughts float, and I glance to the side and stare at the crib for a hot second, then I return my gaze to Isla. "I've never been so scared in my life."

It causes her to smile. "Trust me, I can relate."

"What if, as much as I want to get it right, I just don't? The last thing I want is to be like my own father." I realize that speaking honestly with her is more of a relief than I expected.

"Sounds like we have the same fear. The last thing I ever want is for either of us to fail at this parenting thing. I want to do better than my parents, by far better. Be everything that they weren't."

Her hands stroke her belly, causing my sight to cascade down her body to land on the vision of the connection we will now forever share. "That's what I want too. Doesn't mean the anxiety vanishes."

Isla bites the corner of her lip. "Vaughn, let's just promise that we'll try our damnedest for this little girl. The parenting thing, I mean."

"I can do that."

"All I've ever wanted is to have more family, and this is my chance. Probably yours too."

I begin to smile from affection. "You seem to have become a mind reader."

"It's kind of obvious where our heads would go, considering our upbringing. Keeping it in just makes it hurt more. Saying it out loud is far too real." She doesn't blink.

Touching her arm first to comfort her, I quickly bring my hand to her navel, taking peace from this kid that somehow is the abundance of both hope and fear. Isla brings her palm over my hand. As much as this moment should be about our daughter, I can't help but enjoy Isla's touch. It makes my thoughts go haywire, because there are no warnings shooting through me, and there probably should be.

"I wish I didn't have to go away to Nashville for a few days next week, but if there is anything you need, then you'll call?"

She nods. "Of course."

I can't tear my eyes away from our binding life, yet I don't dare voice the question buzzing in my head. What about us? Partly since I don't have an answer for her. My view on relationships was thrown upside down the moment I found out I'm going to be a dad. But my attraction and wanting for her has been there from the moment we spoke about cheese all those months ago.

Easy seems to be the only solution right now. "Need anything?"

"No, it's okay. I'll just attempt to sleep again and think about what I'll wear this weekend for the baby shower." Her chin tips up, and it's obvious she's searching for an answer about whether I'll be there.

I should tell her that it's a no-brainer, but it's also a commitment. Those tend to make me indecisive.

"You mentioned."

That wasn't what she was hoping I would say. "Right, well, I should go to sleep. Night, Vaughn."

"Night," I say before she meanders out of the room.

I'm alone and look around, knowing I need to do so much better, while I admire the dreamcatcher hanging on the wall by the crib.

A moment later, I walk down the hall to my room, and Isla's door is partly open. Maybe she did that on purpose to tempt me. Either way, I watch from afar as she adjusts her body in her bed. Lying on her side, with one leg wrapping around her pregnancy pillow and her head getting comfortable on a normal pillow.

So fucking beautiful.

I realize something; she understands me on so many levels. That, mixed with a magnetism that is underlying, causes me to realize that for the first time, if I ever had a shot at something extraordinary, then maybe, just maybe, it's with her.

I just need to figure out what to do about it.

ISLA

Laughing, I can't help but inspect what I just unwrapped.

"This is a little… I don't know… What is it?" I look at Hadley's mom April, perplexed.

We're all sitting in a circle at Violet's house for my baby shower. She had her baby a few months ago, so it was the easiest solution of locations. The pink decorations are gorgeous, the games we played ridiculous, and of course, Hadley's mom went overboard with snacks. Also, presents…

"It's a unicorn outfit." She seems proud of her choice and starts pointing to various aspects of the clothing. "See? The little horn on the hood." I laugh again. "She'll be like a burrito wrapped up but with a special hat. Perfect for Halloween."

"That I can see, thank you." It's a cute gesture. I search for the next item from the pile of gifts. My head indicates the giant diaper cake in the corner. "Thank you, everyone, but it seems like a lot of diapers for the first few weeks, will I really need them?"

The moms in the group say *yes* in unison.

I'm not going to argue with their perspective that they calculated right. I hold my hands up. "Okay, okay. Forget I asked."

An abundance of unwrapped presents are around me, still with another pile to go. Not only do I have the usual ladies from my circle of friends who are the next best thing to family, but also a few colleagues, and of course, Ivy, my brother's girlfriend.

Hadley claps her hands. "Okay, everyone, let's take a little break before we continue to the big round."

"Great idea, I need to pee. This kiddo has been pressing against my bladder all day," I say as I stand.

By the time I'm done in the bathroom, I come out to find Hadley carrying a bag of ripped wrapping paper to the garage in one hand. "Surviving?" She grins.

"This is really a special day, thank you."

She waves me off. "It's the least I can do. You were my maid of honor, and I'm not having a kid anytime soon, so it keeps the ladies in there occupied." Hadley throws her thumb over her shoulder.

"They are *really* into this."

Hadley studies me, maybe trying to read me. I'm familiar enough to know that she is about to ask a question that I might not appreciate. "Um, should I bring up the topic?" Her face screws into a cautionary look.

I take a second. "You mean Vaughn?"

"Yeah." I hate her sympathy in trying to comfort me with her hand on my wrist.

"I invited him. If he doesn't want to come, then that's his choice."

Hadley takes a moment. "But you do want him here, right?"

I shrug my shoulders. "I do. Doesn't mean it will happen."

"What's going on between you two?"

"Nothing. Just focusing on this baby, and he's been busy with work. Not to mention, I think it's going to be a long time until he forgives me."

"So, no discussion of…" She's struggling to beat around the bush.

I shake my head. "Is there something to discuss? We are two people who gave into lust a few times."

A short laugh comes out of her mouth. "You had sex with him three times because you can't keep your hands off of one another."

"Two times. At Christmas, I was completely well-behaved, thank you very much… Besides, hurricane us were kind of at it more than once, so I'm not sure your numbers correlate." I sound far more serious than I should as I bring my arms to cross over my chest.

She tries to keep her loud laugh in but fails miserably. "I think you probably need to investigate *that*—" she circles her hand as if she is outlining a circle "—situation a little more. See if it is really just lust or a chance for something else."

I chortle a sound. "Not sure now is the time for it. Besides, I…" I lean in to ensure nobody can hear. "I'm not sure if I want to get my hopes up or if I'm already there and know I *shouldn't* get my hopes up." I stand taller. "Plus, he's been a little too posses-sive and broody lately. Not exactly getting points from me… Okay, it's kind of hot. But I mean, he doesn't even show up to my baby shower. Surely, a smart man would have figured out that my invite was because this means a lot to me. But no, Vaughn enjoys keeping everything in limbo, as if it's some game with my very hormonal emotions." I'm completely riled right now.

Hadley quirks her lips out, just listening, however, something feels like she won't respond to me as a sly smirk forms on her lips, her sightline over my shoulder.

The clearing of a throat instantly draws my attention behind me.

Oh shit.

Hadley doesn't say anything, because Vaughn will.

He throws me a tiny little wave. "The guy who is playing a game with your emotions is here."

My sight whips back to Hadley who smiles tightly. "Think that's my cue to leave you two alone." She walks on and spurts out a laugh.

Vaughn only steps closer. "Sorry I'm late."

I can imagine that my face must looked flushed. "Uhm… how much of that did you hear?" I ask awkwardly.

He smirks as he leans against the wall with his arm against it, and he crosses his ankles. My impression is that he enjoys making me squirm. "Enough."

I gulp and laugh nervously. "Sorry. I'm a little emotional today."

"I'll let it go. It seems like quite a spread in there." Great, he's changing the topic.

"They all went overboard, it's really sweet. Declan and Connor are in the mancave somewhere in this house… if you need an escape."

"I just got here," he states, matter of fact. "And I know. They warned me to avoid baby games like the plague, so here I am, hopefully saved from measuring your belly, although…" His head slants to the side. "Could be kind of interesting."

A smile curves on my lips. "Good choice of timing then. I still have another round of presents… the big ones. We will be needing two cars to get it all back to your house, for sure."

"You mean our house."

A sound of doubt hits my lips. "Is it, though? I'm pretty sure you dragged me there without my choice of humble abodes, and if it weren't for the fact that I'm going to be a kickass mom, then you would lock me in a tower."

He laughs. "Lock you in a tower? Nah, I'd lock you to my bed." It escapes him, and the moment he realizes, his jaw flexes.

We're flirting.

It seems we still have it in us.

Still, my eyes blaze slightly from the surprising choice of words. "I'm sure…" I try to stay calm while a painful feeling hits that nub between my legs, the kind of pain only he can relieve—or my hand, but Vaughn is so much better. "It would be an adventure." It's nearly a rasp.

His smirk pulls a tiny bit, drawing my attention to his lips.

But then he grumbles a sound, bringing us back to the present for our little offtrack distracting talk. "So, what am I supposed to do?" He straightens his posture, and his hand finds my arm. "Not that I'm not interested, it's just I really have no clue."

I giggle. "It's more that your appearance is a thank-you for all the gifts, and you sit with us for a little bit, preparing for a lot of *ahhs* and cooing. I actually have sympathy for you right now, because it's going to be a little much. Hopefully, they tame down their labor stories in your presence. They also all love to give unsolicited advice, but luckily, in a kind way. They just want to help. I'm so grateful for it."

A gleam appears to glaze his eyes. "I'm happy that you have everyone in there."

"I'm lucky. And it is great. It's just that it's… not biological, ya know?"

His head tips low. "I get it."

"Yeah… you do." An unsaid realization floats between us, an understanding. "Now come on, get ready to be sucked into an atmosphere of sickly-sweet goodness."

"Ready as ever."

Vaughn follows me, and I don't even realize until I feel a sizzle run along my spine that it causes me to glance down to see our hands holding. I'm not sure who initiated it or if it's just a natural magnetic need between us.

I like our hands interlaced, it's the type of support that needs no words. A signal that you've got one another's back. But it's also an act that only normally happens between someone holding a child's hand or between two people who are in a relationship or on their road to that.

I don't let the thought overtake me, and I can't even if I tried, because soon we are ushered by someone into the room which must feel like a pit of doom for Vaughn, but his smile seems the opposite. He must be acting polite.

The appearance of Connor and Declan in the back holding up a beer in support is also a solid vote of confidence for team Vaughn.

We sit down next to one another back in the circle and someone hands over a big box. Vaughn instantly holds it since my belly is in the way.

"Wow, this seems bigger than my body," I note as I begin to rip the paper.

A box with what seems like a highchair is soon revealed.

Violet pipes up. "It is Scandinavian design, has a few inserts so even the newborn can be table height when you're eating dinner, plus it grows with the child to the point that you can even use it as an adult as a normal stool." She claps her hands together. "We all got it for you."

I scan the circle, feeling emotions swell in me and a pool

of water forming at the bottom of my eyes. Vaughn seems to notice, and his arm snakes around me to pull me into a side hug, and he speaks up. "It's just what we need, thank you. Right, Isla?" Thank goodness he can read me like a book.

"Yeah, it's… perfect. Wouldn't have thought of it," I add.

The next few gifts are far too generous. A bouncy chair, a travel cot, a few cute little onesies.

"Okay, open this one. It's the last one." Hadley hands me a bag with tissue paper, and my eyes go round with curiosity at Vaughn, who just returns the gesture.

"Hmm, I wonder what this could be." I begin to pull out the paper. When my hand dips in, I feel only softness, yarn maybe. The moment that I pull out the blanket, I'm done. Tears fall from happiness. "Oh my."

"The moms and I attempted to knit a baby blanket together. It's the most colorful, mismatched, badly knitted blanket in the history of baby blankets. We even tried to have Piper, who owns the boutique, fix it, and she said it was a lost cause. But it's still a blanket, and it's warm." She's proud with a goofy grin.

I laugh. "I-it's the best blanket," I stammer out. "So incredibly sweet. The baby will love it."

"Really?" Her face goes lopsided. "It's a weird purple mixed with a mustard yellow then gray and pink. Not even sure what the other color is." She points to a square.

"Totally sure," I swear.

"We can stich on her name once you know. Do you have any ideas?"

Vaughn and I look at one another. "Not yet," he mentions. We can add names to the list of things that we really need to discuss, but now we are showered in complete kindness.

"Good plan, see the baby first," one of my colleagues says.

"I'm sure she'll have your eyes," Vaughn nearly whispers so only I can hear.

God, why am I melting around him today. Hell, it's not even just today. It was the moment he walked back into my life.

I'm saved by Brielle, Connor's mom, announcing that we have one more surprise, and she points to the kitchen where I think Connor and Declan got roped into helping.

We all migrate over to the kitchen island, with Vaughn being instructed to cover my eyes with his hands. This isn't helping my current predicament. He covered my eyes once, with a blindfold, somewhere between taking me doggy style and missionary during a storm.

Alas, I'm unable to relive my memory because he laughs right before his hands fall away from my eyes, and instantly a wide grin hits me.

"Best baby shower ever, right?" Hadley is getting a little cocky, but she's right.

Before me lie plates of all types of cookies. Followed by chocolate chips, pink sprinkles, mini marshmallows, and anything you might want to cover the ice cream that will stuff your make-your-own ice cream sandwich.

I grip Vaughn's arm tightly because I'm not sure I can stand any more, because this feeling of gratitude is too much.

"Thank you," is all I manage to say. "Yeah… best baby shower ever."

THE REST of the afternoon was just spent relaxing on the sofa and snacking while Vaughn spoke with the guys and drank a beer. Occasionally our eyes would catch, and a subtle smile would form between us.

Now, we're home. It feels weird saying that but also right.

Vaughn brought all the gifts up to the nursery, and I'm now sorting through it all to find newborn clothing that needs to be washed.

"They certainly covered everything," he comments while he stuffs diapers in a drawer, even studying a few because I can imagine that he has never changed one.

I focus on my task. "It's wonderful, isn't it?"

"It is. They even sent us home with a cheese plate, what are the odds?"

I chuckle. "Does it have the Dutch cheese that's hard and sharp?"

A bashful look falls onto his face. "You remember that?"

"One of the oddest references to sex, but I'll let it go."

We have had good times together, that we can't deny.

His look doesn't fade, which is promising.

I nervously swipe my hair to my shoulder. "Actually… uhm… I got you something."

"Really?" Stunned is an understatement.

"Bottom drawer. I didn't wrap it or anything." I do my best to downplay this, I don't want it to be a big deal.

He heads straight to the bottom drawer of the dresser. It's still empty except for the gift.

A closed-mouth smirk begins to form as he holds up the tiny onesie. "My dad can fire the coach," he reads out loud.

"General manager joke," I clarify.

"Oh, I got that. This may get me into trouble, but I love it." He examines the onesie and notices the Spinners logo and can't stop smiling.

"It's a little big because I thought she could wear it during hockey season. That is if you want her to visit you at work." I'm doing my best to keep this a simple moment.

Vaughn looks at me with intensity. "For sure, I want that.

Didn't really cross my mind, but since you said it, then absolutely… she'll need her mom with her." Now it feels like he is testing the waters to read me, or rather he doesn't want to say what he is really thinking. He does that a lot.

"Of course. Wouldn't miss it."

"Good, good…" He tries to focus on something else, our moment breaking, as we're both unsure of what to do with this feeling that keeps orbiting us closer.

"Vaughn… thank you for coming today."

"Truthfully, it wasn't something I thought I would enjoy, but it wasn't so bad. I got to see you completely happy, Isla."

I smile again. "I am. Well, as much as I can be." My eyes drop to my belly. "I have to push her out soon, and you… I mean we… no, I mean the situation between us is… I don't know what I'm trying to say. Can we forget this?" I ramble completely.

It only makes him more entertained. "Maybe."

I roll my eyes. Great, just great. Add this to my list of things I do to dig us deeper.

Vaughn begins to stroll out. "I need to call my brother, pack for Nashville, and take a *long* shower." Oh, now we're back to inuendo by highlighting "long."

Damn it, this isn't great for my stress levels.

"Take it easy, I'll lift the heavy stuff later."

I salute him. "Sure thing, sir."

That sexy smirk is back in full force. "Careful, Isla, I may just have to fuck our baby out of you."

My jaw drops, and he leaves me there.

17

VAUGHN

Pacing my bedroom with the phone to my ear, I wait for my brother to tell me something wise. Anything to untangle the thoughts happening in my head.

"So, you went to the baby shower? Preparing for my niece? What else are you two getting ready for? Doing one of the labor courses or something like that?" he lists his questions.

"Don't have time for any course, let alone reading a book. I'm literally winging it, all of this. Basically 95% of the presents we got from the baby shower, I have no clue what they are. Diapers?" I feign doubt in my voice. "No idea how that works."

"I bet you Isla does, and I haven't even met her," he assures me.

I pinch my nose before I sit on the edge of the bed, only to stand again due to my energy level. "I'm quite confident she's nesting or something like that, someone mentioned that's a thing. I keep catching her in the nursery doing something."

"But not doing you," he jokes.

I stop, frozen at his humor, because it brings me to my predicament. "We haven't even discussed how this lifetime as parents together is going to go."

"Ah…" I can tell he's kicking his feet up on a table while he gets comfortable for this discussion ahead. "You mean the you-and-her-together kind of thing."

My head bobs side to side in contemplation. "Again, thanks to her, I haven't had time to think about it."

"Still angry she never told you?"

My shoulders fall. "I think I've decided to bury that away so we have a chance to have some normalcy, as our focus should be on the baby."

Stone lazily claps his hands once. "Give the man an award."

"Funny. But yeah, we haven't really talked about it. I'm not sure it's even crossed her mind."

"Does it cross yours?"

Blowing out a breath, I finally flop onto the edge of the bed in defeat. "It might have appeared once or twice." Maybe I'm downplaying it. "I just can't be sure if it's the baby factor that makes me want to think it or something else."

"Hmm… well, what did you think of her before the baby equation?"

A smile jerks on my lips. "A lot of attraction, good conversation, she's funny, gorgeous, understands hockey, I think that we were both okay with our boundaries that we had set…" Damn, it's a long list.

"And do you really think those feelings just faded away? Maybe your anger and disappointment with her may have fogged those attributes, but now that you're not angry, then are they clear as day?" He's treading carefully.

"That's exactly the problem. I've never been a relation-ship kind of guy, but now my view might be altering, and I'm just not sure to what completely. And Isla? Well, she's as beautiful as ever, there's still good conversation, to the point I swear she can predict my thoughts, and well, she's funny yet a little feisty. All of it together is making it impossible for me to not want to kiss her. Which may surprise her, considering I've been a complete idiot lately."

The sound of something from the hall grabs my attention, but not enough for me to look.

"I don't know, Vaughn. You're nervous about becoming a dad, but that won't always be there, and eventually you can have a little more. You may be a dad, but you're not only a dad. You get it?"

"Yes, oh wise one," I mock him, but he has valid points. Strong points. Points that make me want to begin to unbrick any walls that I have inside of me.

My eyes sideline to the clock on the table next to the bed and see that I should probably go to bed if I have any chance for making tomorrow a clear-minded day, with strong focus on work.

"I'm going to dive off this call, I really need to head to bed," I say.

"Sure thing. Keep me posted and let me know if you need anything."

We both say goodbye and hang up. Quickly, I throw on a t-shirt and strip down to my boxers, eager for my head to hit the pillow… any pillow. Yep, a pillow, it's happening, and my mind is becoming a clusterfuck, and I hear another sound. Wait, a sound in the hallway. Now, I'm drawn to investigate the sound I thought I heard, which means going into the hall and passing Isla's door.

Still, safety first, right?

With my feet on a fast trail to check on whatever it may be, I don't see anything except Isla standing in the hallway, which causes me to nearly fall forward from surprise. Her eyes seem to have been watching my door, and I swallow because I have a strong feeling of what might happen. Especially as she's wearing a barely-there tank top and shorts, with her hair still partly wet from the shower that she must have just taken.

"Were you listening?" My tone isn't accusatory; the opposite really, I'm curious.

Her sight becomes fixed on me, her eyes unable to blink while the tip of her tongue finds the corner of her mouth. She pauses for a second before a wry smile appears on her lips, and her head lowers but her eyes then peer up at me.

"So…" She's dragging this out until her smile turns to a satisfied grin. "Tit for tat today. You heard me earlier, and now I heard you."

I have to grin to myself as my head gently lowers; I could swear that I'm near timid. I'm caught, and I don't mind one bit.

"Seems the case."

"I'm still beautiful, and I'm making it impossible for you not to kiss me?" A sultry look forms on her face.

I nod as we stare at each other, with a sweltering tension floating between us. No words needed. Which is perfect because I've never been a man to wait for what he wants.

I do what's my instinct.

I'm impulsive.

Lunging forward, I bring my hand to the back of her neck to pull her to me and kiss her. I'm not even gentle. It's deep, ensuring I leave a print on her lips. Her muffled sound into my mouth is only a sound of pleasure, which I know because her hands begin to roam up my arms to around my neck, and she tilts her mouth to give me more access so I can delve my tongue in.

My hand on her neck begins to twist her damp hair around my fingers, and I yank her gently, causing her to jolt back and catch her breath in surprise, meaning our lips part and her eyes fire with a need that's impossible to ignore.

"Should we really be…" It's a whisper from her mouth.

"Shh," I tut.

We're throwing caution to the wind, and words are not going to help our journey.

Our lips find each other again, and we begin to move. I'm walking backward, guiding her with me. She tastes sweet and eager, everything I need to drive me crazy. My thoughts leave my head because I just want to get lost in her. I can't seem to kiss her lips enough, and I'm torn to stay on her mouth or nip her neck. Her skin is extra soft, almost encouraging us to keep going, as the road is smooth. Her swollen belly currently housing our daughter between us doesn't seem to be a deterrent.

When we make it next to my bed, any hope for caution seems to be out of our heads as Isla tugs on my t-shirt, and we only slow down so I can peel her tank up and off her body, savoring every second of the slow tease.

Before the last few weeks, I've always wanted her every time I saw her. Now? I still want her but in a possessive fuck her kind of way.

"Hell, you're a vision."

Isla blushes, and I get the feeling that she might be shy as she brings up her hands to cover her breasts that appear full and heavy.

Her lips open to say something, but I instantly plant my finger against them to ensure she doesn't speak a word.

"You're more beautiful than ever," I rasp before ensuring our gaze doesn't break.

"I'm not shy, if that's what you are wondering. Not in front of you. You're the one who put a baby inside of me."

I'm about to lose it, she just unleashed a new kind of lust inside of me. A possessive and proud mood that leads my actions. "With that thought, I *need* to get on my knees for you."

That earns me a smirk from her swollen mouth.

She's standing before me like a goddess, and I'm at her mercy, but make no mistake, I'm leading us. I hook my fingers under the band of her shorts to lower them and get her naked.

I keep true to my promise and drop to my knees. I lean in to kiss a trail up her inner thighs, coasting my lips around her pussy then trailing up. I pause for a second to take in the view of her belly at my eye level.

This is very new for me. Not that I'm complaining.

I plant my hands on her sides before I kiss her gently by her navel.

"I never thought I would be taking you with my baby inside of you, but make no mistake, I want to now that I see you carrying my child. You're so fucking magnificent."

"Ours," she corrects me. The affectionate shimmer in her eyes is sentimental, and her fingers come down to rake my hair. My lips move back down, this time to her pussy where my tongue finds her soaking clit, and an instant moan releases from the back of her throat as she relaxes under me.

Why does she have to taste so subtly sweet? I want more and can't fathom stopping. I lap my tongue a few times up and down her pussy before focusing on her clit. I dip a finger inside of her then pause for a second to zip my sight back up to her.

"Does this hurt?" This is new to me, and she's heavily pregnant at that. My pregnant woman.

She half laughs. "It's fine. I'm extra sensitive in a good kind of way. It feels a little different, but I like it."

A grin begins to dance on my lips. "You've been touching yourself?"

Her mouth tightly slides side to side to hide her timidity. "How could I not with you only a few walls away."

Ditto. My shower has been my haven.

"Then let me make you feel really good."

I return to her pussy with my tongue and now two fingers. She feels extra warm, and her inner barriers are open yet welcoming. I want to bury myself in her, make her moan so loud that the only way I can quiet her is with a kiss.

"Don't stop," she whimpers, with her fingers continuing to grab my hair.

I pursue my quest until her cues imply she's close, and I stand, kissing her lips to let her tongue have a taste. My hands frame her face to ensure our stare indicates we're both on the same page before I guide her onto the bed, removing my boxer briefs before I join her.

Isla lies on her side, and I'm aware that taking her from behind will be most comfortable for her. Sliding right behind her, our bodies mold together, with my arm looping around her to cup her breasts while my cock firmly presses into her lower back. I twist her nipples, and she hums a sound that feels like sex to my ears.

Her breasts have always been my weakness, but right now, I may be an insane man. I need to take her right away and bring my hand to lead my cock inside of her, and this time we're moaning together. Breathing into her neck, I rest my hand on her belly as I take her gently yet deep. I'm constantly scared that I'm hurting her, yet I fall into a complete world of pleasure that's making me carnal.

Thrusting into her with her body in this state may become

my nirvana. I'm well aware that this can't be an everyday kind of thing, as soon our child enters the world. Then it hits me that I'm not fucking her. It's on a different level, one that I'm not sure of.

Her moans become pleading, and I finally come inside of her with our mouths fused.

I quickly identify that we just confused the situation between us by far.

But I'm not going to let her leave my bed, either.

18

ISLA

Vaughn is between my legs as I sit propped up against pillows in his bed, his tongue working me into a state. It didn't take long after our unexpected evening for him to go right back at it. The man has stamina and doesn't accept recovery for my dear body. But I don't mind because he's slithering up my body, taking a detour around my giant belly until his mouth covers a nipple and his fingers play with my other one.

That's when I nearly lose it.

Actually, I'm a few seconds away from losing it.

My breasts being sensitive in the best possible way doesn't even come close to this heavenly feeling of him worshipping my body.

Then I'm gone when his finger continues to stroke my pussy. I'm crumbling into tiny pieces as my orgasm takes over my body.

"Fuck," I moan out.

Then the devil studies my facial expression with a small laugh. "The baby has ears, remember?" he teases.

"Thank goodness we don't follow the cliché swear jar,

otherwise she already has a college fund based on the last few days." My breath is still heavy when he flops onto the bed beside me.

It's a minute or so before my cheek smooshes against the pillow when I turn to look at Vaughn in his glory.

"You've done the work of a superhero. I've been getting more uncomfortable by the day with this pregnancy, but you were the perfect relief to relax me."

He side-eyes me. "Except we are horrible at maintaining boundaries."

"Extremely horrible," I agree.

The back of his finger caresses my arm. "I'm completely on board with your body like this. Your tits are driving me crazy."

"I've noticed." My elusive smile can't seem to disappear.

Vaughn adjusts his body to lie on his side and look down on me. "You know, last time we did this, in my car, I swear I noticed your breasts were larger."

I breathe out a sigh. "Now you know why."

"I didn't realize I have this kink, but I'm going to struggle watching this kid suckle on your tits for weeks on end."

Now I just want to burst out laughing. "First off, I'll only breastfeed if it feels right. You don't know if you'll have enough milk, or the baby just doesn't want to do it. And secondly, many guys are into tasting milk or using it for other things." I flash him my eyes. Vaughn just looks at me, puzzled. "Like lubricant," I clarify, and his eyes bug out.

"Okay, I don't think that's actually for me. Not sure what rabbit hole of a conversation we're heading down."

I shake my head to myself, still smiling. "Think of something else. I don't dare to figure out what the hell we do now, with our spectacular ability to complicate things…" I'm not even trying to nudge him into a discussion; I really *don't* know what the hell we do now.

Thankfully he brushes past that comment and glances at the clock. "I really need to get some shuteye. My flight is tomorrow, late morning."

"Oh, I thought you said next week is the draft."

He bops the tip of my nose with his finger. "Tomorrow is Monday, that's next week," he points out.

That does make sense.

"Kind of a good thing to avoid the awkwardness that I'm sure will cloud us," I joke.

"The timing sucks, and I wish I didn't have to go, but the draft is probably one of the major points in the year for a general manager."

Vaughn brings his arms behind his head to rest on, and I can't help but follow the lines of his muscles and tattoos. I was never a tattoo kind of girl, but his are not that big and only etched in black.

Tiredness begins to take over me. Sex was great, but there's a tightness between my thighs I'm not familiar with, not in a bad way by far.

"I get it. I do. Anyhow, I should go sleep too if I can. I'm beginning to feel like an absolute whale," I note.

He touches my arm. "Stay, I'll go grab that giant pillow thing from your room." He's off before I can answer.

I guess we're sleeping together. Another point on the scoreboard for our really bad judgment to ensure we don't seem to clarify things between us. However, I want to feel a body next to me—his arms around me, to be exact. My wish wins by far right now.

Vaughn comes back and settles in behind me, and I do my best to get comfortable with multiple pillows.

"Here." Another head pillow is placed behind my lower back.

"Ugh, whale me is getting moody and frustrated. I'm not sure I will last many more days."

Vaughn rubs soothing circles on my back. "Try to relax. And did you not hear me earlier? Marine mammals did not enter my comments at any point."

I smile to myself. "Fine. I'll be cheery." I don't sound completely on the bandwagon, but then again, he's right. I've gotta go into birthing this little girl with full-on positivity and ready to party.

Vaughn's gravelly laugh feels good, and it causes me to close my eyes just before his palm finds my belly to rub circles.

It appears his hand has no plans on leaving either.

———

WAKING UP, it hits us as soon as we look at one another.

Yeah, Vaughn and I really did that last night. Had excellent sex, not worrying about repercussions.

Give us an award, because without any words and only a few good beats of searching one another's eyes, our bodies become flush and ready. He throws the pregnancy pillow to the ground right before he slides into me, and we smolder together.

This isn't fair. I'm always horny these days. He wakes up hard, and he's offering. What kind of woman would ignore all of that?

A smart one.

Nope, not me, with a college degree and motherhood on the horizon. It's me, I'm acting a fool.

But it's oh so good.

Vaughn's warm breath against my skin sends ripples through my body, and his mussed hair, with his accompanying gravelly noises in the back of his throat are just so freaking fantastic.

I would completely agree for him to tie me to the bed and take me like this whenever he wants.

He pumps into me, and it feels even more sensitive than last night. Vaughn's being tender, and our eyes connect while our hands entwine. I'm too far gone. And so is he when he's filling me up.

He collapses to his back, while I just breathe out a heavenly feeling and rest my head against the pillow.

Maybe we fall back asleep, or it's simply fatigue still circling me, but we rest for a few minutes before Vaughn vacates the bed and stands, and then I wonder if regret is now hitting him.

"Want to join me in the shower?" he asks as if this is a normal day.

I twist part of my body to look at him. "Hell no. Let's just pile up our lack of crossed lines even more."

The corners of his mouth twist. "Language, Isla," he teases.

"Oh shit… wait… no, ahh, I curse like a sailor sometimes." My eyes drop to my belly. "Sorry, little girl."

"You do that a lot? Talk to her?"

"Well, yeah, you're supposed to, so they get used to your voice," I explain.

His eyes roll. "That's just great. My daughter has heard me basically be an jackass and say really dirty things to her mom. That's how she knows my voice."

I snort a laugh. "Oops."

Then the air turns serious between us, especially when Vaughn sits on the bed next to me. "We'll talk when I'm back in a few days. Maybe my trip is a good thing, so we can both think without distraction."

"Yeah." My voice is soft. "You're right."

The back of his hooked finger glides along my cheek before Vaughn kisses my forehead then pats my belly. Then he's off to the bathroom for a shower that I choose not to join.

But I have no control of my mouth spitting out things I probably shouldn't say or ask. "Vaughn," I call out, and he stops when he is about to open the door.

He glances to me with a glint in his eyes. "Yeah?"

"Why did you insist on meeting me at the hotel?" I'm referencing Florida way back.

He tries to suppress his boyish grin, but his dimples appearing give him away. "It can be fun to follow the whirl-wind path of attraction. But I think… there can be a bolt of lightning between two people, and it simply can't be ignored… so I took the initiative."

I like his answer, but I'm just not sure what to do with it. "Well… a whirlwind path of surprise obstacles we have followed."

"Obstacles, hmm." His eyes drop down then fly up. "Last night… right." His T is sharp before he gives me a faint smile and leaves me for the shower.

Inside me, fear swirls again, in case we just ruined any chance to make the co-parenting thing work. Then realization hits me that it's not that; I'm scared it won't work between us as two people in a relationship.

A FEW DAYS LATER, I'm sitting with my brother in the living room on the couch.

"You're really doing it then, leaving for Seattle?" I am

sad about it, but Briggs is right that I'll still see him, especially during the summer.

"It's for the best. Besides, it means the dynamic between Vaughn and I can be strictly somewhat… I don't know… but you bind us." He struggles to form an explanation.

"You're not leaving because of him, right?"

Briggs waves me off. "Nah, I was already in discussions before he graced us with his presence, I told you that."

I touch his arm. "Good. If you're happy then I'm happy." It's a lie, I'll miss him.

Briggs ended up living in Lake Spark for the Spinners, and it just so happened that I found a job too. We've always been around one another, not only as siblings but also friends. Now part of my family will be away.

I begin to rub circles on my belly when a weird feeling hits me, one that I've been having all day, but it's not a cause for alarm.

He groans a sound. "Dare I ask if Vaughn is stepping up?"

I shake my head. "You have to accept all of this. Plus…" I splay my hands out to display the house. "Do you not see that he is providing?"

Briggs snickers. "It takes more than that to be a father. A good father, I mean."

"I need to give him a chance and so should you." I wince and a strained breath hits me.

My brother notices. "You okay?"

"Totally. How about a fresh round of drinks?"

He begins to stand. "I'll get it."

I grab his arm. "No, I need to keep moving, and this can be my exercise."

Briggs listens and lets me stand and walk in the direction of the kitchen. However, the moment I'm next to the kitchen island, I take hold of the counter when I feel an unusual sensation, and I swear I hear a pop.

My eyes draw a line down to my dress, and then I see water trickling down my bare leg.

"Oh no." Panic hits me.

Briggs is up on his feet and racing toward me in no time. "What is it?"

"I think my water just broke."

19

VAUGHN

Sitting on Declan's plane back to Lake Spark, the coaching and management staff study the schedule for our new players as Declan and I sit next together a good distance from everyone. The new players we drafted are very young, and we quickly need to get them settled in their new surroundings, while they also tackle development training and full-on marketing appearances.

"It feels great to have fresh blood on the team. I think our defensive players are strong," Declan mentions as he drinks from his water bottle.

I chuckle from his comment. "I've never seen an owner so involved. Normally a team is their hobby, and they only show up for games, when the board of governors need to vote, or when shit hits the fan with the general manager or coach."

He smiles proudly. "I'm not a normal owner. I played for far too many years to make me sit still. Likewise, for you. That's why we're a winning formula."

I lean into my elbow. "A good philosophy to have."

"I kind of need a break from team talk, it's been nonstop for the past few days. Ready for fatherhood?"

I chortle a sound. "Hardly, but not much I can do about that. Timing isn't on my side."

"Fate may be. You were moving to Lake Spark before you discovered the happy news. Now it just means that you get both without complication," Declan notes.

My brows raise up then down. "Uh, not exactly, but I guess it will figure itself out."

He chuckles in understanding. "That tends to happen to a lot of people. Violet and I eventually came to our senses and maybe one of you will too. There is always someone in a relationship who gets there first, yet it's not a race."

I scratch my chin, internally agreeing. An answer doesn't come to me, partly because our bedtime fun the other night may have taken us off track.

My thought is broken when a flight attendant arrives and whispers something in Declan's ear. His eyes nearly darken then he winces. When the attendant walks away, Declan looks straight at me.

He claps his hands once, as if we're about to enter a team huddle. "So, here is the thing. The pilot got a message, and it seems that Isla has gone into labor."

"What?" My voice raises an octave, and apprehension drops straight to my stomach. "She should have another week or two!"

Declan touches my arm. "The baby can also come early."

"Not while I'm on a plane she can't." I grip the armrests with full strength, trying to figure out if it's fear or worry that's the prominent emotion flooding me.

"We'll be back in an hour then get you straight to the hospital," he promises.

I shake my head. "This can't be happening... I haven't

even read the baby book yet." I'm stressing now. "Not to mention, I've only known that Isla is pregnant for barely a millisecond, and now she's delivering a baby?"

Declan looks at me with a strained expression. "To be fair, nothing goes to plan like those books." He slaps my shoulder. "Besides, the first baby is normally a long labor."

Blowing out a breath, I rub my face. "I'm not sure what to do right now. I'm going to go out of my mind. Isla's in labor, and I'm not there."

"In an hour you will be. Try to relax because it could be a long day ahead. What's important is that you show up for her."

"Christ, I knew I should have listened to the daddy preparation podcast. Fuck, first I miss an entire pregnancy, and now this? Someone upstairs hates me." I tip my head to the sky, only to grumble a sound because we're already in the damn sky, as in not on the ground, more so as in I can't drive like a maniac to the hospital.

"Just stay calm."

I give Declan an unamused look because his advice is absolutely impossible.

I'm not ready for this. I thought I had a little more time to adjust. Hell, I didn't even get a gift yet for this kid. And coaching Isla through this? Holy hell, all I know is to pat her back, except she isn't some animal who gets a treat.

She's Isla.

The mother of my child.

The woman who has flipped my world upside down.

And I have an hour to switch my mind and be there for her.

———

RUNNING down the hall of the hospital, I recognize Briggs pacing, and his head whips up at my arrival. He quickly stomps in my direction before grabbing my shirt and pinning me to the wall.

I can't even process until his mouth opens. "You listen here, Vaughn Madden. In there is the biggest game of your life. I couldn't handle it. She's in pain, and they talked about needles if she wants an epidural, and I nearly fainted. You suck it right up and take one for the team."

His pep talk sounds like we're going to war.

He doesn't stop there. "Do not falter on us. It's up to you to be in there no matter what."

"Where the hell is Hadley or her mom? Is she really in there alone?" I screech.

"They're in Chicago and driving back as fast as they can. Violet can't be here because their baby has a virus, and she doesn't want to risk giving it to Isla. I've failed her, because this—" he points to the door of Isla's room "—is not meant for brothers. Now get the fuck in there, and you do not leave." He lets me go, and I immediately go to the door, already hearing Isla weeping in pain. "For the team, Vaughn. You're captain of this ship," Briggs calls out.

For fuck's sake, his speech as a sailor going to war doesn't help this situation.

Opening the door, I find Isla sitting on a yoga ball and holding onto the railing of the bed with a nurse next to her. She's trying to control her groan, nearly screaming as she's in the middle of a contraction. As I run straight to her, the nurse backs away.

"I'm here. I'm here." I touch Isla's back, and she looks at me. She seems worn out, and her hair is damp from sweat, her eyes desperate.

When her contraction passes, she cries, "It's too early. I

mean, I had another week or so. This shouldn't be happening."

I cup her face. "She wants to come now. The doctor already warned us that you're pretty much ready." I do my best to ease her thoughts.

"This is our fault," she wails.

"How so?" I ask as the nurse brings a cup of ice chips and hands it to me.

Isla knocks it out of my hand with force, causing the ice to fall on the floor. "Screw the ice chips, they do fuck all. And yes, this is our fault." She breathes through pressed lips. "We had sex. They say it can induce labor." The hint of a barely-there smile graces her lips.

"Really? Why didn't you mention that to me?" I play along.

A humorous look of disapproval hits her. "Sorry if I didn't want to ruin the mood."

"Hey, you know I use these kinds of balls in my hockey training." I smile at her, but I'm met with a near sneer.

"Really?" She doesn't sound impressed. "This is the moment you want to compare labor to your training regime?"

I hold a hand up in agreement that she is right.

Another contraction hits her, and I rub her back as the pain appears to rip through her. Briggs was right, this isn't for the faint of heart. I'm hurting for Isla, but I can't show it because I need to be here for her.

"Give me the epidural," she pleads to the nurse.

The nurse looks over her shoulder, checking the monitor. "I'm sorry, Isla. You're too far dilated and so close. The best you can do is keep breathing through the pain. You're doing great."

Oh God, Briggs really was preparing me, because this is like a battle in the trenches.

Isla wails again as she abandons the ball. "Make this stop, it hurts too much." She leans her head against my shoulder.

I kiss the top of her head. "It's going to be okay. Before you know it, she'll be here."

Isla grips my shirt with both hands. "Promise me that no matter what you'll go straight to her to make sure she's okay. Focus on her, not me."

It conflicts me, because what if something happens to Isla? It didn't cross my mind until now. That thought unnerves me, but right now, she needs reassurance.

"Of course, Isla."

"Oh no, the car seat. We didn't even install it."

I offer her a simple smile. "I did. In my car before I left."

Her face brightens up with comfort.

She's delicate right now, which is why I can only be honest with her. "I think I believe that, even though I just found out about your pregnancy, it was because I am meant to be here in the moment to help you."

A lightness shades her eyes. "You're not still mad at me?"

"No, Isla, I'm not still mad," I tell her point blank.

It seems to bring relief to her, only for it to be interrupted by another wave taking over her body. I grip her arms so I can carry her weight as much as I can. I murmur encouragement until she sighs from the contraction ending.

"Okay, Isla, I think you're nearly there. I will call Dr. Forest."

Isla nods while our eyes lock. I'm not going to let her down, and I think she realizes it.

For a moment, while the nurse goes to the corner to make a call, Isla and I get a chance to have some privacy.

"I'm scared. I'm not ready," she breathes out.

Moving so she can waddle to the bed and lean against me, I hold her up, as she seems to be weak. "You can do this. I know you can. You've done everything so far because you want to give her a good life. So you'll make sure she enters this world on the right foot, and in order to make that happen, you have to get through this."

She laughs. "Easy for you to say. You don't have a baby goblin ripping through your body." Another contraction hits her, and she clasps onto me for dear life.

"You've got this. You're so close," I soothe her.

The contraction is short but seems to be stronger than what I imagined.

I smile at her and stroke her hair. "Goblin, really? That's what we're calling her now?"

It makes Isla laugh. "We don't have a name for her."

"You pick when she's here," I say to encourage her. "Well… the last name is not really up for negotiation, but you know what I mean." I try to make her smile again.

She nods again.

I kiss her forehead, reminding myself to stay calm.

By the time the doctor is here, Isla is ready to go. I believe that we're both petrified. Our lives are about to change, and we know it. The moment this girl enters the world, we'll see everything through a different lens, even I know that.

I sit on the side of the bed behind Isla to support her, with the doctor between Isla's propped knees and the nurse nearby, ready for action, and another nurse preparing things in the corner. It doesn't take long for an exhausted Isla to push, and she nearly breaks my hands when she squeezes them. Every push she amazes me with her strength that could take out any hockey player I've ever played.

Six pushes later… it happens.

A cry fills the room, and my heart grows bigger already.

"Your daughter is here," the doctor says as she holds up

the red baby covered in a white coating, with a squinched face and a full head of hair to my surprise.

Isla cries happy tears then tries to peek when they cut the cord, but then they take a little longer than we expected. They hold our daughter and check her body longer than I would expect, and in a moment that now feels chaotic, terror fills Isla's eyes as she looks at me. It's only a few seconds, but it's too many for Isla. "What's happening?"

I try to get a glimpse, but I honestly don't know.

"It's okay, Isla," the doctor explains.

I try to peek again to keep my promise and attempt to study the medical staff while our baby cries. I'm not sure what is happening, but it only takes a few seconds more for a nurse to smile at me as she hands Isla our naked baby to rest against her chest then quickly covers them with a blanket.

"She's a strong one. She looks good," the nurse says.

I watch as our baby finds a home against Isla's chest. My daughter's little eyes stare straight at me, and her cry seems to soften. I'm not a crier, but tears sting my eyes at this little bundle in Isla's arms.

I guess I am a dad now, and as cliché as it sounds, my world suddenly feels like it's turning differently.

I soak in the scene of a washed-out Isla, but she seems to find renewed energy when she soaks in our daughter. "She's here," I whisper.

Isla cries as she inspects every little inch of our girl and clasps onto her tiny finger. I'm quick to lean down to get a better view and kiss Isla's cheek.

"Nora Madden is here," she whispers.

I'm taken aback by the name. It's perfect. Our daughter gets my last name and a first name of the hurricane that brought Isla and I together.

Isla glances at me with a laugh and tears drying on her

face. "What? You think she will ever ask how she got that name?"

———

IT WAS a tranquil couple days in the hospital with visitors, help from the staff, and we didn't need to stay any longer. I'm positive Nora was the best baby there too. I also got to rest her little cheek against my bare chest because apparently that's good for oxytocin and bonding. Basically, it was nothing like I expected or could imagine.

Everything is better, a fog of bliss but unreal. It's only just sinking in that we had a little baby that we took home in my car. One day Nora wasn't here, then suddenly she is.

Returning home, the house now feels different. I notice that our friends must have been here. There is a balloon on the kitchen counter next to wrapped food. A few of the baby things that are for the living area are all set up, including that Scandinavian highchair with a newborn insert that everyone raved about.

I set the car seat down at the bottom of the stairs, and Isla lets out a sigh. "Finally, back home."

"You should probably rest, you warrior you," I recommend.

Isla doesn't tear her sight away from Nora. "What if I miss something?"

I chortle a laugh. "You can't not sleep for the rest of your life."

Isla bounces her head side to side in consideration. "Maybe you're right."

"I'll carry her upstairs. You'll be okay with the stairs?"

"I'm fine."

When we reach the top of the stairs, Isla directs me to her

room. "I want her to sleep with me in the co-sleeper. It will be easier to feed her at night when she wakes, and I don't like the idea of her all alone in the nursery yet. She's still so tiny and might get scared."

It feels like we are taking a step back since Isla seems to be returning to her room to sleep. It perhaps makes sense considering our circumstances.

But despite what's going on with us, I'm putting my foot down.

"She's not sleeping in your room."

"Oh yes she is, Vaughn," Isla challenges, with her hand on her hip with her sass clearly recovering well.

It causes me to smirk. "It's my decision, considering our timeline of events, or rather my lack of being on board for that timeline of events. You can both sleep in my room."

"You didn't think to bring up the sleeping arrangement topic in, let's say… the hospital, the car ride, or up these freaking stairs?" Isla seems taken aback. "Uhm…" She doesn't know what to say.

"I'm not taking no for an answer. I'll move the bassinet thing that attaches to the bed."

"A co-sleeper," she corrects me. "Or we can use the baby nest." Her palm flies up to stop me. "Wait… I don't think this is a great idea. I'm… my body is kind of, well…" Her hand outlines her breasts and heads lowers with awkwardness. "I… there are liquids coming out of my… body." She draws out the uncomfortable sentence.

I look at her, unfazed. "And? I just saw you push out a baby. I think we're good." Her eyes nearly turn into saucers from surprise or the fact that it's no big deal to me. "I don't want to miss anything, and soon I need to get back to work. Remember I said I want to come home and be able to check on her when I want. That means slipping into bed and she's nearby." *And you're nearby.*

Isla seems to be in contemplation. "It's… okay, uhm, limitations are clearly not us."

I lift the handle of the car seat, already prepared to direct this discussion straight to my room. "You're going to agree." I pretty much demand it.

Now a smirk plays on Isla's lips. "Fine. But she needs her dreamcatcher from the nursery for above the bed. I'm superstitious."

"Okay. Done."

She nods before slowly walking to my room to climb into bed to rest with our daughter nearby.

This is the only step that I know how to make right now.

Because everything between us changed the moment we became a family.

ISLA

Sleep is a glorious thing.

If only I could enjoy a nice deep slumber. Lately, I cannot, which is why I drowsily wake up at to the sound of someone quietly clicking their tongue.

My eyes dart to the baby nest in the middle of the bed to find it empty, which causes me to shoot up in a panic, but then I ease at the sight. One that I've become accustomed to the last week since we came home.

Vaughn is bouncing Nora in his arms while he stands near the window, greeting the day. He offers her his pinky as he makes little noises. His lack of shirt isn't helping the situation.

The view warms my heart.

Vaughn must sense that I'm up, as he doesn't take his eyes off our daughter but acknowledges that I'm here. "Your mommy should go back to sleep."

I laugh. "Very unlikely." The heavy fullness with a twinge of pain across my chest informs me that something has to give. "Mommy either needs to pump or go straight to the source. Someone may be hungry soon."

It causes Vaughn to glance in my direction. "Again? Didn't you feed her like a gazillion times during the night?"

Sliding out from under the covers, I grab my robe lying on the end of the bed. "That's kind of how babies work. At first, they need a lot of milk."

A humorous smirk hits his lips. "True. She is also a strong one, this one."

"You sound like she's going to be some future queen of a kingdom."

He chuckles. "Nah, she'll just be keeping us on our toes as soon as puberty hits."

I walk to them, admiring how this is a strange yet relaxed feeling. We share a bed, all three of us, as if it was the only way to be.

I'm happy Vaughn gets his moments with Nora, especially as he has a lot of work. Having a baby in the off-season should be a hockey player's dream, but a general manager? Hell no, it's full-on preparing for the season ahead.

My hand falls onto Vaughn's arm as we look down at our daughter. "She's already getting bigger." Still her baby clothes drown her a little, and we have to roll up her sleeves.

"Everything is a blur. Fast is an understatement," he notes.

We haven't discussed even once our events prior to Nora entering the world. How could we? We're occupied with a new baby.

"I'm going to head to the training arena soon, but I'll be home early because my brother is going to stop by to meet his niece," Vaughn informs me.

It grabs my attention, as I haven't met his brother yet. I guess it's not a big deal considering he is Nora's uncle. No different than Briggs, except meeting Vaughn's brother feels a bit more confronting and serious maybe. I want to make a good impression.

"Sounds good. I'm going to see Hadley this morning, and maybe I'll stop at the general store for some things later." Our local general store is anything but, it's a gourmet supermarket.

"Sure, just take it easy." He hands me Nora. I'm fairly confident that she has his eyes.

Nora is making little faces that tell me she's hungry. "I'm just going to head downstairs to feed her." As much as I don't mind Vaughn watching me, it still causes my lips to curl into an awkward smile. It's a sort of intimacy in a different strange way.

"Okay, I'll be down in a minute."

A few minutes later, I'm sitting on the couch with Nora at my chest and my eyes taking in the morning light streaming in through the big windows. I'm chewing on some fruit since I always wake up hungry.

Random sounds in the kitchen tell me that Vaughn is about to leave and probably grabbing his protein shake for the road.

We have a routine that we easily fell into. I'm grateful for that. If he was still angry at me for not telling him about my pregnancy or insistent that everything goes his way, then I would have been walking on eggshells.

"You'll send me photos throughout the day?" He smiles at me as he's on his way to the front door.

"Always," I promise.

He pauses for a second the way he or I do on a daily basis. I'm sure we both want to say something that has no relation to our daughter, but we always stop ourselves. We just let our eyes linger instead.

"Isla, uh…"

A closed-mouth smile hits me. "I know," I acknowledge, but I really don't. It's just a confirmation that we're both in the same state.

For now, that just has to work.

———

HADLEY HANDS me a decaf coffee and a croissant as we get comfortable on the bench by the gazebo in the park, with the lake nearby. Nora is sleeping in her stroller. Getting fresh air is important for me, especially with the great summer weather we've been having.

"Sleep tight. I'm your auntie who will be your godmother and be the one you can turn to when your mom goes strict during the teenage years. I'll fill you up with sugar when you're going through the terrible twos and be the best friend your mom deserves," Hadley coos and jokes.

I hold up my coffee. "Funny. Thanks for the croissant, I'm always hungry these days. Nobody warned me how feeding a pint-sized human makes you starving. I think it's worse than labor. I just want to eat and eat," I complain.

"At least you have an excuse. Don't you burn extra calories or something?"

My head tips slightly to the side. "Good point. But I'm jealous of your caffeine-infused drink."

She slides next to me to nudge my shoulder. "One day you'll taste it again. Speaking of tasting…" Her tone changes, and she gives me playful look. "Vaughn." Her eyes nearly pop out.

I just roll my own. "It's nothing. We're so occupied and running on adrenaline still."

"I can see that. Just… won't that wear off at some point?"

I snicker a sound. "I think we both realize that."

"How are you around one another?"

My face squinches, as I know one of her signature squeals is about to hit me. "So the thing is, we're sharing a bed. Don't get excited, we have Nora between us, and her parents are grasping for straws when it comes to sleep. Except… before I went into labor, we kind of did something stupid."

"No way!" Now Hadley is fueled by the latest gossip of my life.

"Simmer down, child. It happens. I'm fairly convinced it set off my labor too." I'm only half-joking, but it's a better story.

"Are you kidding me? Don't you two ever lock it up? Every time you see one another you just go at it."

I glance blankly to my side to face her. "Attraction is attraction, but we haven't once mentioned that night since."

Hadley brings a finger to her chin. "One day it will come up, and then what?"

"I don't know. Our priority is this little princess right here. I'm also in this cloud of happiness where everything is lullabies and cute little outfits. A clear mind doesn't exist for me right now. Maybe I'm also waiting to see what the impact will be once Vaughn starts traveling with the team." I slouch because the thought isn't exactly uplifting.

She affectionately touches my shoulder. "Do you still worry that he might bail on you?"

I shrug and don't dare say the word yes.

"I really don't think he will," she encourages. "He's totally in love with Nora."

My lips quirk out. "See? With Nora. When it comes to me, then it's still confusing for both of us."

"Maybe time is what you need. But maybe you should also plant some seeds in his head of what you're thinking. Men do great when we give hints."

I yawn from tiredness while I take in her advice. "You're probably right, but that's not going to happen today. His brother is stopping by, and I want to give Nora a bath tonight, plus catch up on laundry."

"Excuses." She gives me a knowing look.

I lick my lips. "I can guarantee you that Vaughn is probably doing the same as me."

"Then it's easy. Be the one to make the first step. He did it after he found out and made you move in with him, and I think you kind of enjoy that demanding side of him." Her voice raises slightly. "It's now your turn."

A deep breath is my answer. "You're probably right."

———

STONE HAS DARKER hair than his little brother. He's also extremely kind to me, which is a surprise. I kind of expected him to be wary, considering I never informed Vaughn he was going to be a dad. Instead, Stone showed up with flowers for me and a giant stuffed monkey and a few wooden toys for when Nora is older.

He's holding her now as we sit outside on the patio with snacks on the table.

"For sure she has my brother's eyes," he states.

I smile. "Thought so." I side-eye Vaughn, confirming that I'm right.

"Geez, the jury has spoken." Vaughn grins.

"What are you going to do when Vaughn starts traveling?" Stone wonders.

Vaughn and I look at one another because we still have so much to talk about.

"I still have maternity leave for a little while, then hopefully I can find a part-time nanny or something. Daycare seems a bit too early for Nora. Plus, a friend's mother said she could watch Nora one day a week, and I trust her with my life," I explain.

"We have options. Money isn't an issue," Vaughn adds. No, it's not. Vaughn won't let me pay for anything, and it's frustrating at times.

Stone looks down at Nora as she waves her arms. "I'm not a babysitter, unless it gets me the attention of the ladies in this town," he jokes. "But I'm in the process of moving to Lake Spark soon for more inspiration."

"I still can't believe you're going to write a book," I say.

"Well, nobody is supposed to know. It's not every day you expect some retired hockey jock to write."

"A smart one at that," Vaughn adds.

"Anyway, I also have a writing retreat happening here soon. My publisher is sending some romance writer to this retreat, and I'm confident she doesn't even write her own stories. I'm not at all looking forward to it, so I may need to escape to this house."

I laugh and grab some crackers. "She's your best chance at any excitement. Pretty much all the women in this town are taken."

"I feared you would say that. It's breaking my heart," he says, playing along.

Vaughn rubs his face due to his brother's humor. "Or you could just deadbolt her in."

"Oh, like you two did." Stone glances down at Nora then back up to us.

Vaughn and I both awkwardly look at one another.

"Cheese plate?" Vaughn offers to his brother to divert the conversation.

"Nope, I'm good. What I meant to say is I'm happy to check in when my brother is out handling the attitudes of his hockey players. But what's the deal going forward? Just going to live together under one roof?" Stone isn't afraid to be bold.

Vaughn gives his brother a warning glare. "Stone, maybe focus on the kid."

"Yikes. Did I just trigger a conversation between you two later? My bad." Stone isn't the least bit sorry.

Clearing my throat, I decide to keep us moving. "You two are close. Kind of like me and my brother."

"Yep, which is why I watch out for him." For the first time since he arrived, Stone looks at me seriously.

"Christ, Stone, chill it for a bit." Vaughn's eyes shoot another caution to his brother.

I smile shyly and adjust my shirt. "I get it, I would do the same."

A silence around us breezes in.

"She's the chillest baby. Doesn't really cry much and always seems calm," Vaughn attempts to break the quiet, and his brother just smiles softly.

Taking this opportunity, I decide to escape this confronting day. "I think it's Nora's feeding time, she must be getting hungry." I stand to take her out of Stone's arms.

"Is that why her little fingers are getting grabby at my chest."

"Exactly. It'll give you some time alone with Vaughn."

"You probably won't see him when you come back down," Vaughn mentions. "Either my brother hits the road or I'll be throwing him in the lake."

I grin. "Probably go with option one."

Walking away and closing the sliding door behind me, I still manage to hear the beginning of their conversation.

"Isla seems like a great mom, I don't think you need to worry," Stone tells his brother.

"When it comes to that, I never did," Vaughn replies.

The smile forming on my lips is as natural as can be.

———

A WHILE LATER, I return down the stairs and into the kitchen where Vaughn is placing snacks back into their containers. I stop his arm so I can grab another nibble of the cheese cubes.

"Sorry, I'm like a famished monster." I hold the cube up.

His lips tilt up. "I've noticed."

He continues his quest to clean up, and then we're stuck in a long gaze.

Blowing a breath through my pursed lips, I go for it. "Look, I think we are both aware that the underlying tension—"

"Attraction," he corrects me.

Now my own grin begins to form. "Attraction," I repeat. "It's bringing a debate inside our heads. As much as I want to discuss the..." My finger twirls in the air. "What..." It drags out.

Vaughn smirks before he stands closer to me with purpose and confidence. "The not-parent part of our equation is what you're trying to say."

I suppress my laugh and instead smile tightly. "Yep, that. I just can't think clearly right now. I'm adjusting to this mother thing, and I literally get excited when she blinks."

"I get it, me too." He steps closer, and my heart rate picks up.

"Can we maybe just wait a bit to talk about everything? You know, the living situation, childcare, your traveling, my work, when to start solid foods, or should it be eggs or toaster waffles for breakfast," I ramble. "*Everything*."

Vaughn is so ridiculously amused. His finger hooks under

my chin to tip my face up so I have no escape. "The thing between us is what you're trying to say." He drags his thumb across my bottom lip.

"Uh-huh." I do my best to look away, but my eyes only find his as my destination.

"You're cute when you're flustered." His eyes are lust-filled, I see it.

"For heaven's sakes, Vaughn." I'm only half annoyed. "Can you keep us on track?"

He chuckles, with zero issue that his sultry gaze is sending us down a hole. "Relax, I'm well aware that you need to recover for a few weeks, and we need to establish boundaries. But can't I enjoy looking at you?"

"No. Nope. Uh-uh," I clearly state. "We have a child sleeping between us, and she's now officially our barrier between crossing borders."

"We suck at limits." His sexy look falls to a hopeless one.

"Yeah, exactly why we should take some time to clear out our adrenaline of our life change and then address stuff." My hands pretend to shovel the air, him included.

Vaughn removes his finger from under my chin, and the excitement from his touch lessens slightly because it can now be tamed.

He kisses my forehead. "Agreed but not forgotten," he promises before he walks away.

21

VAUGHN

Isla is standing behind the boards with her jaw hanging low as she watches, unsure if this is a good idea. But Nora is now a few weeks old and loves her carrier wrap.

I'm on my skates with Nora bound tightly to me as I skate slowly around the rink. She's bundled warmly against my chest, and this is her first taste of life on the ice. I love it.

I decided my break between meetings should be this, and since we only have summer training camp happening, it's a little easy on the ice with the players. The person from the marketing team taking a video can't be helped, but the world already knows that I'm a dad. The team posted a congratulations photo on their social media channels. Naming the mom? It made a lot of fans go crazy in the good type of way. The whole "sister of the hockey player falling for another hockey player" has an angle that people seem to eat up.

Except we're not officially together, and nobody has corrected the public either. It doesn't matter, right now my focus is on being Daddy Vaughn.

I'm well aware that Nora has no clue what's going on

while we skate, nor will she remember this, but her nervous mom on the other hand most definitely will.

"Just don't fall," Isla mentions when I pass.

"Relax, I'm a pro at this," I assure her.

"Yeah, and I'll beat him to a pulp if he does," Briggs pipes up as he skates by me, enjoying his time off but still hitting the ice.

I sigh because there is no escaping Isla's brother before he leaves for Seattle next season, but he has been tamer around me, and occasionally he backtracks.

"Supportive as always," I call out sarcastically.

Skating some more, I look down and notice that my daughter is slowly closing her eyes. "Uhm, you're supposed to be wide awake for this. It's your big ice debut." I tease my little girl who has no clue what I'm saying, especially as her eyes shut. I guess this is relaxing for her.

I notice that Briggs has stopped up ahead near the goal post, with his eyes skeptical as he stares at me. Approaching him, I decide to extend an olive branch, but he beats me to the punch.

"My sister seems happy. She was meant to be a mom, even if by accident."

I smile softly to myself. "Does it matter how it happened, as long as she's okay?"

Briggs swipes a hand across his jaw. "About that… as much as I hate this, I want us to have a man-to-man talk."

My posture straightens in surprise. "Probably a good idea. I was waiting for you to cool off from everything, but I also want to talk, so let's do it now."

We both glance at Isla who is far enough away that she can't hear; instead, she studies us warily.

Briggs starts. "You have to take care of her when I'm not here. She may appear to be strong, but I can guarantee that she's more scared than you can imagine when it comes to having a family. If she ever says she can do it alone, then it's a lie; she would be brokenhearted for Nora if you are not involved."

Inside I'm in complete agreement. I understand more than Briggs will ever know.

"If you're giving me a warning, then you don't need to. I wouldn't do that to Isla or Nora. I will always be involved." More than my old man ever was.

Briggs seems to grasp my sincerity. "Good. Because I've been the one to watch her, but now I won't be here all the time. I need to know she's okay. I also don't want to break any laws if I find out she's in pain, especially if it's by you."

I pinch the bridge of my nose, trying not to get aggravated, but I could repeat myself a thousand times. "Briggs, you have my word. We can agree on one thing and that's Isla and Nora."

He scoffs a laugh. "You do realize I am only talking about the parenting factor. Whatever the hell you two do on the relationship factor, then that deserves a whole other discussion. I'm not sure what in the world you two got up to the last months before Nora entered our lives, but I sure as hell hope that my sister doesn't end up upset. It's no longer fun and games, you know."

Licking my lips, I'm not sure that I should be having this conversation with Briggs. It's far too close to home, it's a topic that I have to tread carefully around. I'm an equal partner in the Isla-and-me equation. She has the same power as me to bring disaster, as far as our non-parenting relationship is concerned.

"Again, stating the obvious. What would you like me to do to prove to you that you don't need to worry? Do I look like a man who is going to play a game with my chance at a family?"

Briggs looks at me intently, almost with a profound empathy. He even tips his nose slightly up, as if he is whiffing out my intentions in order to approve. "She no longer likes ice cream sandwiches. It's cherry cobbler, with vanilla bean ice cream."

I smile wryly at the advice he just gave me. Almost as if I should sway her. Did the world stop turning?

He begins to skate off, but I call out his name. "Briggs." His attention returns to me. "I'm also counting on you. Summer is by no means easy on the schedule for me, but it is for you. I need you to take care of her when I'm not there, be the extra support we probably need."

Briggs nods in agreement before he skates away.

I can't process fast enough what just happened as my daughter grabs my attention, sleeping peacefully without a care in the world. Completely unaware that her parents need to figure out some things.

———

Isla and I go for a walk around the neighborhood, with me pushing the baby stroller.

"What should we do about the childcare situation?" I ask. The weeks are quickly passing.

Isla exhales with dread. "I'm trying not to think about it. I still have a little more time on maternity leave, as Ford gave me extra. They also said I can work part-time if I want going forward. It's just…"

I gently touch her back while my other hand continues to push Nora. "It doesn't excite you in the same way."

Her shoulder slants. "Exactly. Also… I don't want to feel like I'm leaving her too much. That's what…"

"Your mom did." I fill in her sentence, and we stop in our stride.

"Yeah." I hear the sadness in her voice.

I wrap my arm around her from the side from instinct. "We're not our parents."

"We'll do it better." She doesn't sound enthused. "Motto of our lives."

"It can be true."

She leans over to touch Nora's belly; our daughter is the lightness we need when things get too real. "But to answer your question, I just don't think I'm ready to head back to work, but I should."

"You don't have to rush, Isla. You don't need to work at all if that's what you want. I want to take care of you both. If you feel it's better for yourself or Nora, then we're lucky enough that it's not an issue financially." I'm offering because I mean it when I say that I want to take care of her.

"I couldn't let you do that," she's quick to protest.

I chuckle to myself and wet my lips. "Remember, I can get a little insistent. Don't be surprised if I hand in your resignation," I joke with her.

Her brows raise. "Oh, I know you would. But we're just adding to our list of things that we should establish, in parenting or with us. Because what you just offered is more than a kind gesture that doesn't necessarily involve Nora."

"And? I'm not worried about it. Nothing about you scares me," I admit. I'm drawn to her like water in a tide, unable to go in the opposite direction.

Isla seems to let my revelation sink in. "Maybe you should be. I kept a secret from you. You never once doubted my irresponsible birth control accident, or asked if she was really yours. You went in headfirst without question."

I bite the corner of my mouth. "It's because I do trust you. Even though you didn't tell me and it hurt, I slowly understand your reasoning."

"I never slept with anyone else after the hurricane or even the months before, in case you're wondering."

"Ditto for me."

Now she seems shocked. "What? You really didn't sleep with anyone else?"

I shake my head.

"We're having this conversation a little late," she one-tones.

I begin to grin. "Sounds about right."

We both look down at our daughter whose eyes are big and curious.

"I want her to know she's number one," Isla mentions.

"That's not even negotiable for either of us," I agree.

Isla leans her head against my shoulder as we continue to watch our daughter lying there with the world moving around her. "We got lucky with her."

"Yeah, we did," I nearly whisper.

I got lucky with you too.

We continue to walk slowly back to our house.

"Vaughn, I'm happy we can talk openly about this stuff. Well, the parenting stuff. It makes one aspect easier."

"Me too."

We're still avoiding the us factor like the plague, but it makes sense for now. I'm just tiptoeing us into the inevitable conversation. This is probably the tables turning. She was the one afraid to tell me about the pregnancy for all those months; now I'm the one afraid to share how I feel. More empathy hits me for the whole situation of the last months since November.

I'm going to take the easy road out right now.

"Want to go grab some cherry cobbler with vanilla bean ice cream?"

Isla's face turns appreciative, as if I uncovered the key to her soul. "Ooh, someone just gained points."

I snort a laugh. "If only this was all as easy as a hockey game."

Because I only ever do my best to win, and I'm scared that I may lose all of this.

22

ISLA

Standing at the front door, I take the cow that plays nursery rhymes in one continuous loop and throw it outside. However, the toy nearly hits Vaughn as he walks up the front path. He even ducks and looks at me preciously.

"What did the cow do to you?" His lips slant to the side, entertained.

I growl a sound as I hold a wooden spoon in my other hand as if I'm a crazed woman. "I was playing with Nora, and that stupid thing wouldn't stop playing 'Merry Had a Little Lamb.' Even the off button won't solve the problem, and the batteries won't come out."

Vaughn continues his approach to me. "And the wooden spoon?"

"I thought maybe if I hit it enough that it would stop, but it's possessed and out to give me a headache." I realize how ridiculous I must sound.

He takes the spoon from my hand before we both assess the damage of a plastic singing cow lying in the plants, although miraculously now quiet.

"Let me guess, Connor and Hadley gave us that gift," he comments.

"Or Stone. We have options. Yeah, it's all of their life's mission to give our child annoying toys." I'm still a little salty that a toy put me in a foul mood.

Following Vaughn into the house and closing the door behind me, I'm happy he's back. He came home early, as he said he would try.

The last month has been hectic. Nora grows, Vaughn has meetings, and I'm trying to keep on top of laundry.

Vaughn heads straight to our princess in her bouncy chair. "Hey, sunshine, is Mommy acting a little strange today?" He tickles her belly, and Nora's response is a bubble popping out of her mouth. Vaughn glances back at me with his eyes wide before returning his focus on our daughter. "Your mom says it's because of a poor cow, but I think it's because tonight is the night that you are getting evicted and trying out your big room."

That *is* why I'm not in the best of moods today.

I grumble a sound, as if he isn't right, even though he is. Vaughn stands and heads back in my direction, and despite being sleep deprived, he still has swagger.

"We agreed that it's for the best. If she continues to sleep near us, then she may never sleep alone for the years to come. Hell, she may even sleep better."

An upset feeling swirls inside of me. "I know, especially with her feeding schedule slightly better and also having a bit of formula. A better night of sleep for all does sound appealing." I hold my palm up. "But she's a baby, *my* baby."

Vaughn gently touches my elbows. "*Our* baby, and this is what we both agreed. Plus, you said you tried putting her in her room a few times for her naps during the day and she loved it, slept totally fine."

I stay silent and awkwardly tighten my lips.

He cocks his head to the side. "You did let her nap in there a few times, right?"

My eyes flutter. "I may have… tried… but she generally sleeps in her stroller or in the baby wrap attached to me like a koala."

He gently shakes his head, with his sexy grin staying put. "Okay, now I understand why this might be a big step. Look, it's up to you, but I think you want a little bit of routine, and this way it will be easier to have babysitters."

I sigh and growl. "You're right."

And two hours later, we find ourselves staring at Nora's closed nursery door, with her already sound asleep on the other side. Vaughn is holding the baby monitor like a walkie-talkie, and I'm checking to ensure the app is correctly installed on my phone so I can check on the video feed at any time.

Vaughn and I glance at each other, clearly more affected then either of us care to admit. "She has her dreamcatcher, she's safe."

I give him a dumbfounded look. "Oh, now you want to believe in my superstition."

My feet begin to nearly stomp away in the direction of my room, but the clearing of a throat behind me draws my attention back to Vaughn.

"Where are you going?"

"My room," I inform him like he's crazy.

"Why?"

"Why not? Nora is now in her own bed, and I need to get used to waking in the night and going to her room if she wakes," I explain, as though he has forgotten our plan.

Vaughn steps closer to me, our breaths now mingling as

the tips of his fingers brush down my arm to my wrists. "You're not leaving my room."

Oh… *oh.*

I nervously chortle. "There is no longer a baby lying between us. The baby vacates your room, then that kind of means so do I. I was there because of the baby."

The pads of his fingertips draw back up my arms, causing a quiver in my body. "Do you really want to move back into your old room? In the end, you were only there a few nights," he whispers as our eyes latch onto a moment.

No words form from my side.

We've carefully treaded around the topic of Nora moving to her own room. As in, we've purposely avoided the puzzle of where I might sleep. But leave it to Vaughn to take the step.

My head retreats back slightly, attempting to wrap my thoughts around what he is trying to translate.

"Isla, you're not moving back to your old room." His voice is nearly taunting but so damn delicious and amorous.

"Am I not?" I play clueless… but really, I kind of am. What *is* happening?

Vaughn brings his finger to my cheek before skimming the line of my jaw in a tantalizing move, with his eyes firmly open. "No. You don't want to go, and you don't need to."

I snicker at this turn of events. "Vaugh, I'm not sure—"

His finger lands on my lips to shush me. "You're staying in my room." He is so damn inflexible.

I blow his finger away, determined to challenge him, except I can't. "Horrible idea." I smile.

"All the more reason to do it." He grins.

My finger points to him. "We're sleeping," I warn.

"I'm a gentleman," he counters.

I laugh once as I turn away from him to walk to the devil's den. "Hardly."

This is what continues to happen around him. He gets cocky, and a powerful force within me eagerly follows.

It's a few minutes later when I'm lying on my side in Vaughn's bed, staring at him as he is in the same position, that I know this is the beginning of a road that may lead to a destination that I'm not quite sure of.

Luckily, I'm not sure I'm ready to open business down below yet. The doctor gave the all-clear a few weeks ago, but mentally, I'm just not there. I believe Vaughn is aware, which is why it confuses me even more that his look is soft. He wants me here, in his bed, only to sleep, without our daughter present.

My head rests on my hands under my cheek. "Our wall is gone."

"Kind of the point." Vaughn brings his hand to my hair to stroke once in a comforting kind of way.

"What are we doing, Vaughn?" I hate this elatedness that must be showing on my face.

His eyes are tense yet delicate, and it feels as though he is admiring me in this moment. "Nothing. I just think it's ridiculous for you to sleep in your own room."

"Really?" I'm doubting him.

"Nah, I would have you thrown over my lap in no time to spank you if I could. However, we accidentally made a child who is amazing, which means we have to skirt the lines of caution. Which we can do in bed… to sleep."

I giggle at his word choice. "Hmm, we could end up in murky waters."

"Or it could be the start of the conversation that we've been avoiding."

I nuzzle into his palm near my ear. "It's kind of, I don't know… We're good at the physical stuff, and we have a connection, but we've never actually, you know… dated."

Vaughn sits up in a flash, as though I hit a nerve, but I'm confused why his soft look is anything but scared. "You're right. I didn't really think about it like that."

Now I join him when I slide my upper body up to lean against the headboard. "It's because you were never one to date, I think. Not for anyone. Our ability to connect so easily was also due to distance. We never had to confront the explanation of what we were doing. It was easy to just be… friends with benefits?" My voice sounds uneven, as I'm not sure my word choice is correct.

"A good way to examine it. However, all of that went out the window when you got pregnant. Kind of bound for life now."

Glancing at the monitor on the side table, I see that Nora is still sound asleep. She's also the reminder of a simple fact, which makes me whip my head right back in Vaughn's direction. "I don't think forcing something because we share a child is the right approach." As much as I want everything for our daughter, Nora seeing her parents together because they felt an obligation isn't the best solution either.

A tickle down by fingers resting on the duvet causes my sight to take in the view of Vaughn interlacing our fingers in a way that feels far too natural.

"We agree on a lot of things, Isla. Which is why I wouldn't even be attempting to try anything if I felt it was just for Nora's sake. But it is because of her that we both get to reassess things. You're right, distance made it easier before. Now it just gives us a reason to confront it."

I can't read him right now, but my face tips up in caution. "Did you just say you're attempting something?"

Vaughn's lips roll in before popping out. "You know the thoughts in our head that we've both acknowledged yet haven't said out loud? It's something like that." The man is almost bashful, I'm not sure I've seen this side of him.

This time, I interlink our fingers. "So, I guess this is the beginning of us attempting to address the elephant in the room."

"Maybe. But the elephant is right there." He indicates with his head behind me.

Quickly I look then laugh when I see a stuffed animal on the floor.

"Smartass." I turn to Vaughn and playfully swat his arm. It only triggers us to enter a scuffle of tickling, that ends with me nearly squealing in delight, right before he pins me to the mattress, dragging my arms up over my head. Our laughter fades but our tilted smirks stay put.

It would be so easy if he leaned down to kiss me, yet the dimples on his cheeks tell me that he is about to impress me instead.

"What you said earlier, about how we never dated."

"Mmmhmm." I wait patiently for him to continue.

He looks up then back to my lips. "Let me change that. We'll go on a date."

I nearly bug out in a wonderful way. "You didn't exactly ask, you just stated." We have banter, and it's great.

"Now who's being clever? Besides, I already know your answer, so I'm saving you the consideration in your head." He doesn't let my pinned arms go.

My body curves up to him, and it's far more sensual than what I intended. We should just end our misery of feeding into our magnetism but neither one of us dares to.

"Are you going to let my wrists go so I can sleep?" I raise my brows.

He releases me. "For now, yes."

That earns him my back, because I need to roll away from him to avoid his sweltering stare, and my body feels alive in the way that's eager for me to ignore that my first time since becoming a mom will be different. Then again, it *will* be different with Vaughn, because we are on the other side of a life change.

The feeling of a warm body swooping in behind me doesn't surprise me. However, Vaughn's cuddly nature kind of does.

I've seen him with Nora, but that's fatherhood. When we all shared a bed, sure, I would tuck my body against Vaughn's while one of us held our baby. But now?

I snort a laugh. "We suck at boundaries. Our new motto."

"Totally right, but that's why we can knock them down," he confirms but only wraps his arms tighter around me.

———

A FEW DAYS LATER, I'm taking note of when Nora's next check-up is with the doctor on the shared calendar with Vaughn, when I notice that in two weeks, he will be away for pre-season games. I focus on that a little longer than I should because the thought is a little daunting.

Vaughn arrives home just as I connect my cell to my charger.

"Get dressed," he insists.

I give myself the once-over, and I'm in my usual skinny jeans and tank top. "What's wrong with this?"

He leans against the counter like a man who doesn't know anything else but swaggered stances. "Relax, it wasn't an insult. We both need to change, as we're going out."

"Oh, I should probably go pack the diaper bag." I'm

about to go to my task when Vaughn grabs my wrist in record time.

He has a grimace which is slightly unnerving. "She isn't coming with."

"Huh?"

"You know, normally you don't bring kids on your first date." He watches me while everything registers. An unrecognizable sound rumbles at the back of my throat. "Remember? Date. You and me," he clarifies.

Before I can answer, the doorbell rings, and I decide answering it is the distraction I need. Only, I answer to find Connor. Now I'm confused again.

Vaughn arrives behind me to greet our guest. "Nice, the babysitter is here."

My head whizzes straight to Vaughn. "What?" I nearly spit out with great disapproval on the babysitter choice.

Connor strides in and raises his hands up. "Relax. We all know that I'm not capable of handling itty-bitty humans."

"Oh really?" I'm cynical. "Had you pegged as babysitter of the year."

"Yikes, someone is frosty today," Connor highlights to Vaughn.

He just grins at his friend before placing his hands on my shoulders from the side. "Ignore her. I caught her off guard with the date-night surprise. Perhaps now is the time to tell her the plan regarding our daughter."

Connor stands before me, casual as can be. "Yeah, sure." He throws a thumb over his shoulder. "Hadley and my mom are in my car trying to install the car seat, they're responsible tonight for your little result of procreation."

Relief hits me in whoosh. No way would I have left my little girl with Connor alone.

"Great. That's clarified." Vaughn is guiding me toward

the stairs. "Now go get ready, Isla. You have twenty minutes," he calls out, slightly coaxing me up the stairs.

By the time I'm searching for clothes in my closet and settle on a black dress that will fit and do wonders, then it nearly overthrows my balance; I'm going on a real date with Vaughn.

23

VAUGHN

I t isn't because of our daughter.

That isn't the reason why we're walking up the stairs to the roof of the Dizzy Duck Inn. I have a romantic night planned because I owe it to us to see if we have any future.

This is out of my realm, the whole dating-because-it-matters thing. Then again, so was becoming a dad, and I now believe I was always meant for that.

Maybe I'm also meant to be a better man. One that commits their life to someone.

Isla gasps when we arrive on the roof, her eyes instantly observing the scene. There is a small table with a few candles, and hanging lights border the roof. Most of all, we have the view of Lake Spark and the pines surrounding the water that are outlined by the full moon. The water has specks of a few boats with their lights on, anchored in the middle of the lake.

And we're all alone.

She pivots on her heel to face me. "You arranged this?"

I smirk as my hands rest in my jeans pockets, and my

eyes lower because I've never been one to surprise a woman in this manner. "Yeah, Declan mentioned it, and I put the wheels in motion. The staff seem receptive to bribes and people who play hockey," I joke. "Figured this arrangement is a well-kept secret, and private too."

Her bright smile is pure affection. "I love it."

I tip my head in the direction of the table as I walk there. "You'll like this." I lift the cover on a tray to reveal a bunch of appetizer options, and best of all, a desserts section, with small pots of chocolate mousse, but most of all, fancy cheese with berry compote to complement. "A cheese plate for dessert is very European of us."

Isla comes to join me at the table. "It's also very us. I have to say that our periodic cheese discussion is the last thing I thought would have been the key to getting me interested in our attraction, but bravo that you did it."

We both laugh before we sit down. I hold up the wine from the ice bucket, checking if she wants a glass.

"Please. I can have a glass, it will be fine. I pumped before we left, and mama can let loose, as there is plenty of milk in the freezer. I might be a little buzzed , though, as it's been a while."

I grin as I pour her a glass. "That's okay. You might be kind of fun tipsy. Plus, I know where you live to ensure you get home safely."

Her smile widens. "Ah yes, because someone at this table put my house onto the rental market in a gutsy move."

Leaning back in my chair, I'm confident with my actions. "And? It seems to have worked out."

She playfully offers me a look of doubt. "We'll see."

I bring my glass out to clink hers. "To… a perfect daughter and a good night?" I say, questioning if that's the right toast to give.

Isla ensures our wine glasses touch. "Cheers."

It's a few seconds of silence, kind of in disbelief that this is where we find ourselves. Nearly a year ago, we were just a flirtation at a wedding brunch, with no possibility in sight. Now? We're way more than we ever imagined, our lives intertwined.

"What are you thinking?" I ask.

Her mouth twists to the side while she sets her drink down. "I think, maybe I'm a little nervous about the fact that I'm *not* nervous to be here with you."

I take one more sip then also set my wine aside. "That's encouraging for me."

She crosses her arms on the table. "Okay, so first-date questions. Let me see…"

"Work?"

"Kind of already know that. Uhm, food?"

"You change depending on mood. Currently on hummus and pretzels," I answer.

"And you love a chicken burger with a side of honey mustard sauce, but it has to be in those little dish things and never from a packet."

I chuckle. "Hmm, it seems we already know a few things about one another."

She raises her finger in the air. "I got it. Travel. Where do you want to go? It can't be any place where hockey games take place."

"Huh, that makes it kind of difficult. I love it up in Calgary and near Banff, but warm weather wins every single time. I'm kind of sad to have left Florida simply for that, but summer here is the right temperature. So I think anywhere in Mexico or the Caribbean—wait, actually, I've never been to Italy."

Excitement hits her. "Yes, the Amalfi coast or more up

north near Cinque de Terre. I bet the food is amazing. I actually went to France, and that's the only place I've been in Europe. Briggs and I were planning an Iceland trip, but well… he found a girlfriend, and I became occupied with a tiny human."

I bite my bottom lip, appreciating that we align on interests, but I have to ask. "How did your brother take the news when you told him?"

Isla scoffs a laugh. "Surprisingly well. He wanted to know who to kill, but I told him not to ask, so he didn't. Instead, he supported me in every single way, no questions asked. We are kind of one another's ride-or-die, ya know?"

"Yeah, I know. Stone is the same way for me."

She grabs a piece of fresh baguette. "Your brother seems really sweet. Funny and kind too."

My eyes grow large. "Uh-oh, are you doubting if you picked the right brother?" I tease.

Isla throws a piece of bread at me. "Nah, he doesn't have dimples like you."

Bringing my long finger to slide along my chin, I point out something. "We didn't grow up in big families, in fact we lacked the essential parents in some ways. However, maybe all it takes is one person to be your family, just like we had our brothers."

Her eyes dart to the candle while she gets lost in thought. "I believe that, but it's extra special when you can create, I don't know… more family."

I nod in understanding and agreement. "We established our proven theory."

Her soft smile returns. "We have. Now tell me something else… what is your ideal Saturday? Ours have been kind of scheduled around a certain person. Wait… I already know your answer, actually."

"What? I enjoy grabbing a coffee then a walk. In the evening, go out for a drink or concert. The whole club scene is done, now that I'm past my prime. It's the same for you, no?" My fingers trace the edge of the table while I listen intently.

"Exactly. Coffee, leisurely walks. Concerts are great. We have a summer festival in Lake Spark, and they get quite a few good acts visiting."

It sounds quaint and calm. It's appealing, if I'm being honest.

"We should go."

"We missed it, but there is a big market next weekend."

"Ah, that's why I've seen signs everywhere, and Declan mentioned something about maple syrup as a sponsor or something." I grab a few fried pieces of eggplant while I hear Isla laugh.

It's a solid hearty laugh too. "Vaughn, how can you have forgotten? First..." She holds up one finger. "Everyone in town has been talking about our weekend events; didn't any of the old ladies from the knitting club stop you on the street to remind you of their bake sale? And two..." She adds a finger. "Declan's family owns Grizzly Dash, you know that maple syrup with a dancing bear on it. That's one of the reasons he has more money than we can count. His parents sponsor almost all Lake Spark events. Did you forget about his syrup connection?"

I scratch the back of my neck because I'm playing her completely as, of course, I'm familiar with my team owner's family brand. "Sorry if I've been distracted. Those coffees from Jolly Joe's, with the jellybeans, might have distracted me. Who the hell adds a jellybean to coffee?" I humorously sound frustrated.

"The wizard of happiness, that's who. It's supposed to

bring luck," she states matter-of-factly before her demeanor changes to a hint of seriousness. "Admit it, Lake Spark has grown on you, even if your job wasn't in the picture."

You've grown on me.

"You completely caught me. I'm now a man who abides to signs of deer and duck crossings and patiently waits for the fresh eggs to arrive at the general store," I say in jest. Yet, I owe her an honest truth. "But you're right, I do like it here."

Isla gets comfortable on her chair, holding the wine glass close to her chest. The candlelight highlights her jubilant face and a twinkle in her eyes. "Uhm, you know, I'm kind of aware that the whole hockey-life thing means that eventually you could end up at a different location. I know you have a four-year contract, but I just want you to know that it is in my head, and that if things… flow between us." Her crooked look is priceless. "Then I'm aware that we would kind of follow you, for Nora… and me."

My jaw flexes side to side, grateful that she simply understands, and it doesn't feel like a big issue in terms of logistics, but it's colossal step when it comes to a promising future. "I guess thinking that far into the future is a bright start to this first date. You're totally going fast." I'm completely joking with her. "But I think it's a safe thought to have."

She nervously gulps a sip of wine. "Okay, I should tuck into some food. It looks delicious."

We each pile our plates with some cuisine and get settled into our meal.

"We could have had three courses, but I kind of felt that this would lead to less disruption."

Her eyes flick up at me with a sultry look. "Why? In case you want to take me here on the roof?"

"Nah, I would wait until we're in the car." I love the banter that just flows with us.

She chortles a laugh at the memory and the fact that we had an escapade in my car all those months ago.

"I'm not sure anyone has ever done something this romantic for me, this dinner and location. Sure, I've dated, but it was always simple dinners or beer at the bar. Don't get me wrong, I don't need to have fancy stuff. It's just you put a lot of thought into this."

"You deserve it, plus I only bring my A-game." I take a bite of food.

Isla sets her fork down. "It's definitely worthy of praise."

"Yeah?" I lean back, taking in the boost to my ego. "I have it in me to impress? I mean, I knew that, but you're kind of a different type of judge." *The only one who matters.*

She points her fork at me. "And I approve."

"Besides, the next two weeks are our opportunity to have these kind of nights and alone time. Game season will be sneaking in time, between games and travel… that is, if we continue on this path." I don't want to be presumptuous.

"Where is your cocky demand? You sound unsure." She's completely entertained that she's throwing me off my axis.

We need to change this up, as we keep circling back to a what-if. Action is the best step, not conversation.

I abruptly stand up and offer her my hand. "Come on?"

"Someone sounds like he has a trick up his sleeve." She accepts my hand with ease.

I pull her out of seat, and we walk a few steps until I yank her to me to ensure our bodies are close. She yelps from the surprise move but seems pleased. Clasping our hands together, my other arm snakes around her middle to lead us in a dance.

"Oh my, Vaughn Madden is dancing with me in a romantic setting underneath the stars. Violins are playing for the women in this world whose image of you as the broody playboy is broken."

I spin us around and tip her back. "Isla, they had a damn orchestra the moment the world learned on social media that you and I have a child together. The heart emoji now officially makes me sick from overuse."

"The comments did get ridiculous but in a positive kind of way. I'm just thankful that we only let them see a photo of a little hand."

"You don't mind dancing without music?"

"It kind of makes it better. You might actually hear the thumping in my chest from excitement." She squeezes my hand.

We continue to sway side to side. "I don't need to hear it, I feel it, Isla. Just like I have since you've been sleeping in my bed in my arms."

Her mouth parts open, trying not to read my eyes that are glued to hers. "I think this date is going well, don't you?"

"It's going more than alright." I tip her back.

The sound of distant thunder doesn't deter us. We continue our dance, and I inhale the scent of her hair while I bring her hand to my chest. This is nothing like I imagined a real committed date would be; it's a thousand times better.

Lightning far away, followed a few counts later by thunder only makes this more unique.

She rests her head near my shoulder, and a relaxing breath hits her. "A stormfront is coming our way. It will bring warmer temperatures this week."

I snort a laugh. "That's what's bringing the warm temperatures?" There is an underlying inappropriate meaning in my question. I swear I can hear her smile.

"Are hotels your kink?" She's witty today.

"No, it's just Lake Spark only has so many spots," I rebuff.

"This whole thing started because you showed up at my hotel during a hurricane. Here we are on a date on top of a hotel with a storm approaching."

My hand falls to her lower back to press her closer to me, which is a very dangerous move, because I just want to get lost in her. "I think this will be our start for getting it all right."

A roll of thunder is stronger than a minute ago. It breaks our moment, and we both study the clouds covering the moon and the purple-blue hue of flashes of light.

Isla backs away. "We should probably head inside."

A hand finds my heart. "I failed at my date planning and forgot to check the weather."

It causes her to grin at my humor as she saunters back to the table. "I assure you that you did great, because I'm going to say that I don't want this to end." Her head cocks to the side as I take in the news.

"Well then, I should ask them to bag this all up so we can enjoy this at home."

I stride straight to her and capture her chin between my thumb and long finger, tipping her gaze up to enable my mouth to lower. My lips mold against hers for a kiss that feels far too overwhelming because this is us kissing for all the right reasons. Everything before was attraction and sex. Now emotions are involved, and if I'm honest with myself, a big load of hopefulness too.

Isla whimpers into my mouth when she brings her tongue to mine and swirls. Her fingers find the nape of my neck and curl into my hair. We both kiss a non-respectable first-date kiss because this is far too deep, with no end in sight.

I'm so tempted to lift her up and push everything off the

table to lay her down. But I'm well aware that we have to go slow, and I'm not sure she's ready, even though I know her doctor said I could worship Isla's body. Maybe not in those exact words, but I was there, as they also checked on Nora.

The point is, I can't give into lust right now. Only sink into this kiss and then angle my lips to take in another. This is long, hard then soft, and the parting of our lips is a brush of skin that zaps along my spine straight to my groin, waving to my chest in the process. It's all stirring inside of me.

Our possibilities.

Which is why when we return home and enjoy snacking on food until Hadley returns Nora—because there is no way Isla would allow an overnight—then we fall into a different kind of night.

When Isla and I climb into bed, we find one another with her leg hooking over my hip and my hand resting on her side, before our giddy looks lead us into a make-out session.

"You had to leave your shirt off? A new habit that you formed when it became only you and I in bed," she nearly pants.

A cocky grin hits my lips. "It's effective, isn't it."

She scoffs a sound before kissing me again. This is all we're going to do tonight, until she falls asleep in my arms with her head against my chest. She flicks her eyes up to study my face.

"When is the second date?" she asks.

That's promising.

24

ISLA

I watch as Vaughn speaks to the man sitting next to him at the table as we enjoy a dinner for the management team of the Spinners at Catch 22 here in Lake Spark. They rented the whole restaurant for privacy. The subtle feeling of Vaughn's fingertips on my bare thigh under the table can't be ignored, which is why a wry smile has been fixed on my mouth for the last few minutes.

My focus on the wine glass is broken when Violet touches my shoulder in passing and leans down. "Going to the ladies' room if you want to freshen up?"

"Sounds like a plan." I can use a little break and to check in.

I'm still wondering if I could be so lucky. The past week since Vaughn's and my date, a shift has happened between us. The kind of change that I welcome. We don't tiptoe around the obvious and easily enjoy our time with Nora, but we also enjoy one another through the chances of late-night dinners while she sleeps and a hell of a lot of roaming hands. But the nights that we sit outside on the patio and admire the night are my favorite. We talk about our days and things that we can plan. It was an easy yes when he asked if I would accompany him for his team dinner.

Violet and I make it to the ladies' room and are alone. We head straight to the mirror to freshen our makeup and adjust our dresses.

"This isn't too boring for you, I hope." Violet swipes on a new coat of mahogany lipstick to her lips.

I grab my blush from my bag and begin to apply. "Actually, not at all. It's kind of hot to see Vaughn in his element, plus I'm used to all of this hockey talk."

Violet lifts her brows and turns to lean against the counter next to the sink. "Let's rewind a second, the whole hot-Vaughn mention. How is that going, beyond the parenting thing?"

My cheeks raise because I am happy. "We're seeing where things go, but it feels promising. It was kind of odd doing the whole date thing, considering our past encounters, but it was just right."

She throws a knowing smirk in my direction. "Thought so. I caught wind of those occasional glances with one another and his constant need to keep his hand glued to you. Were you two whispering? Because I'm sure I saw that before you giggled like a woman possessed by a man."

I laugh and stay focused on my blush. "You and Declan are the same."

She feigns doubt with a sound. "He is my husband, but we also started as a purely physical fling. However, normally when something like that carries on, it's because there are deep underlying feelings."

I blow out a breath and turn to accompany her in leaning against the counter. "You're right. We're just both kind of scared that we might be blinded by the cloud of bliss that a new child brings. It would be the wrong reason to be together just because we felt an obligation, but then he said something…"

She pretends to clap her hands together and seems invested in my explanation. "Do tell."

I bite my inner cheek because Vaughn said something poignant, and he wasn't even trying. "He mentioned that maybe Nora is what brought us together to realize what we should be."

Violet gushes for me before she gently touches my arm. "That is more than promising, that's commitment. Sounds like he's there, you just need to accept it and decide if you're ready to jump in."

I chortle a laugh and turn my body back to the mirror to assess myself, and I feel and appear more radiant than I have in a long time. "Vaughn is a guy who won't relent, yet he has been patient. I'm beginning to see that it's me holding us back."

Violet side-glances to me. "If that's clear to you, then you just have to be the one to take action."

My head tilts as I stew in her words for a few seconds. "Maybe you're right."

"Do it in your time and be sure, but it's your turn."

I nod once in understanding, and she offers me her lipstick, and I hand her my blush. "This is a nice evening. It kind of feels as though the team is not just a team but a sort of community and family."

"For sure. Declan wanted it that way. I do my best not to get too close to the wives of the players, except Hadley, of course. Players come and go, but the management team is slightly more stable."

"That makes sense."

We both put our makeup back in our purses. "Enough

relationship talk. We need to praise our kids with the latest photos."

A proud smile hits me as we both open the screens of our phones and begin our few minutes of child talk.

By the time I'm back at the table, Vaughn seems to be nearly done with his wine. I place my hand on his shoulder right before he leans in.

"You were gone for a while, I was nearly scared you ran away." He winks at me, and those damn dimples are going to cause a flood between my thighs.

"Never," I rasp, and I wonder if he heard me, as someone attempts to grab his attention.

I don't mind being his plus-one and not getting much alone time with Vaugh. It allows me the opportunity to explore my deep thoughts that have been floating in me lately. Except it's not a thought; it's truly a feeling that we can be more.

Vaughn brings his gaze back to me as the person went onto a new topic with someone else. "You okay? You seem a little out of it." His subtle smirk informs me that he must be aware that I'm contemplating.

My eyes flutter, as if I'm slipping out of a daze. "Oh yeah, totally." I reach for my wine to take a sip.

He chuckles under his breath. "Won't be much longer—"

Declan slaps a hand on Vaughn's shoulder. "This man here is who we need to keep everyone in line. Hope you're ready for me to steal him away for the season."

"I'm sure I'll behave in his absence," I retort, and both men laugh in response.

"Enjoy the last few days together before preseason games," Declan mentions.

"She will." Vaughn stares at me intensely, and I'm curious what dirty thoughts are running through his head right now.

Declan grins as he walks away, because Vaughn and I are locked into facing one another with understanding eyes.

"Come on, let's get out of your way." He stands and offers me his hand.

I gladly take it but want to double-check. "Are you sure it isn't too early?"

"I'm sure. We should get home."

Home.

I never get tired of him saying that.

———

THE DRIVE back to our house is quiet, as Vaughn and I sit in the back of the car since we have a driver tonight provided by the team. It's the kind of silence that heightens the tension in the best possible way. A mix of revelation and passion.

Even when we say goodbye to April, as she watched her adopted niece, and head upstairs to check on Nora sound asleep, Vaughn and I can't seem to shake the air between us, with a feeling that something is about to snap.

He quickly says he'll be right back, and I walk to our room. The moment I begin to slip off my dress, the answer feels clear.

I smile to myself before I plant myself in a spot on the middle of the bed in only a bra and black lace panties. I shake my head to loosen my hair and look down to see that my cleavage is out of control, but that doesn't matter.

Vaughn unknowingly walks into our room and stops in his tracks when he catches the view.

His brows raise from the unexpected, yet approval shades his face.

"We only have a few days left before the schedule goes

haywire. Better make the most of it," I say in a sultry voice that I make an effort to speak.

He begins to unbutton his dress shirt. "Oh really? Are you sure you want to do this, considering I have about a hundred ways that I could ravish you?" He throws his shirt to the side, and it lands somewhere on the floor. Doesn't matter, as he's slowly walking toward the bed.

I move to all fours and slowly crawl toward the edge of the bed, doing my best to make it as sexy as can be. "Well, we have a problem then, as I also have a hundred ways— well, eighty, but who's counting," I tease.

Vaughn stands next to the edge, reaching out to slide his hand along my back to my ass that he squeezes, and his breath turns to a hiss. "Isla, you're so fucking beautiful."

"You've mentioned before." I push up onto my knees and peer up as I begin to work on his belt. "There is only one thing I'm craving right now."

He combs his fingers through my hair softly before they increase to a more clawing nature to keep a hold on me. "I won't deny you, that's for sure."

I feel a bashfulness take over me because something does freak me out, thanks to our daughter in the other room. "As excited as I am for this, this does kind of feel like losing my virginity again, except this time I know what I'm doing."

Vaughn chortles a sound. "Ah, yeah… I can imagine this is kind of a new realm."

I swallow. "Exactly."

"Well then, I guess I'm lucky to be the guy that you lose it for."

My mouth parts open, and I run the tip of my tongue along my bottom lip to the corner, showing him that I'm eager for a taste. The sound of his zipper that my fingers undo notifies me that I can have what I want now. Sliding his boxer briefs down, I flatten my tongue to show him right before I lean down to lick his hard cock.

He moans the moment my tongue traces his length. "Isla, you do a lot of things to me, but taking my cock like a good girl is hands down second best to being inside of you."

Taking him deeper into my watering mouth, I only want to please him. The last time we were like this was before everything changed. Still, I refuse to cement us with only vanilla transgressions. That's just not us, never has been.

My tongue continues to glide along his length while he groans a sound, with his eyes hooding closed before glancing down at my actions. I need to hold his hips as I take him deeper and don't want to lose my balance. Bobbing my head, the palm of his hand on the back of my head pushes me forward slightly to ensure he hits the back of my throat.

I make a sound from the force and breathe through my nose, as it's by no means a gentle lick of his tip. Yet I wouldn't trade this for anything else.

"Such a good girl you've always been." His hand sneaks behind to slap my ass once before he hooks his fingers under the waistband of my thong to snap once. I love his hand cascading up my spine until both his hands cradle my head. "As much as I want every last drop rolling down your throat, I need to come inside of you more. On your back."

His demanding tone has returned, but it only makes me smirk. I begin to slide backward up the mattress on my hands, purposely taking my time and letting my foot slither up his thigh as Vaughn follows me by slowly crawling to hover over me. My head raises to ensure our lips can meet for a kiss, and he takes the opportunity of space behind me to unhook my bra.

Lying back down, I get comfortable with my head on the pillow. His mouth trails down my neck by skimming his lips then ghosting around my nipple. "Your tits have been driving me crazy." His tongue darts out to lick a circle around my hard bud. I nearly whimper from the overwhelming sensitivity of it all. "I wish I could worship these more."

I sputter a laugh and bring my hand to cover my face. "Yeah, it might get a little messy if you suck. My breasts are aching, but I think this time it's all because of you, the good kind of aching."

Vaughn nuzzles his face between my breasts then gives attention to the other breast, and his journey continues down my body, tracing around my belly button.

My body is a little different than before, but for the most part, I still feel sexy. I gasp a moan when he strips off my panties.

"We might have to go slow," I whisper. Okay, I might be slightly petrified of what's about to happen. I kind of refuse to look down there, and I can't even imagine what this might all feel like.

That mouth of his, with a little evening stubble, brushes along my thighs, and he encourages my legs to open wide. He retreats his head back slightly to get a view.

"Trust me, this is nothing to be scared about. You're glistening and soaking, and I desperately need a taste," he assures me, so much that it sounds like he's being honest. It eases me a little more.

The swiping of his tongue sinks me into a moment of ecstasy. Vaughn has always been a giver, especially when licking my pussy is involved. He knows where to point his tongue and swirls in the right places until my body coils against his mouth, with my moans becoming a string of slurs.

Then my eyes shoot open the second he dips a finger inside of me. It feels different. I feel tight, but everything feels ten times better than before. I'm not sure that I've ever been this sensitive inside of me, a new kind of magic.

"Christ, Isla, you feel amazing."

A sound cracks out of me as I soak in this feeling. "I'll feel better when your cock is inside of me, please," I beg.

Vaugh kisses my thigh once more before he adjusts my legs to ensure he has space to be between them, with his cock finding home and slowly pumping in.

The instant connection causes me to gasp and Vaughn to groan in pleasure. "I'm not going to last."

"Mmhmm. Me neither."

Our mouths meet for a kiss to ride out his length driving deeper inside of me. Our breaths become one as the intensity is too overwhelming.

"You okay?" he whispers near my ear.

"Totally," I promise.

The fingers on our one hand interlink, and he draws my arm up and over my head as my pussy wraps around him, and he drags in and out until he feels comfortable enough to move faster.

I can't get enough, and I raise my thighs higher then wrap around his waist, with my toes digging into the muscles of his ass.

Our lips continue to dance around one another as we both begin to pant.

"You're heaven, you know that?" he grits out as he continues to keep us connected.

"You're just meant to live inside of me it seems."

His response is to kiss my neck with a slight nip of my skin between his teeth.

We simmer like this for a little while, and then it happens. Our eyes connect, and we slow down for a second.

The confirmation between us that we both feel this pull is

by far more than we imagined. It only leads us to chase our release.

"You'll need to…" I remind him.

"Maybe a good thing, because if I come inside of you, I'll be completely gone."

A drowsy smile hits my lips. And it doesn't leave until I'm trembling around him, and he pulls out to come on my thigh.

He collapses onto his back after he cleans my thigh with his boxers and throws them to the floor, and then I tuck into him, when he kisses the top of my head and drags the duvet over us. Kissing his chest, I bring my nails to draw lazy patterns on his bare skin.

"So, was this like our second date? Because if it is, then I think I'm becoming too easy," I joke.

Vaughn ignores it and wraps me closer, tucking my head under her chin. "Nah, we always seem to be a few steps ahead."

Maybe I was, and now we can focus on our solidified relationship status.

25

VAUGHN

I shake a stuffed turtle over Nora where she's lying in her stroller while we walk along the stalls of the Saturday market in town. I'm well aware that I'm going to miss her like crazy. Every day she does something different. She's already holding her head up.

"Gosh, should we be concerned that she really doesn't cry much and just seems to be happy all the time?" I ask Isla, smiling widely at our daughter.

Isla glances sideways and throws me a humorous glare. "Don't jinx the crying part, and this all means that she is happy."

"True. We're lucky."

"I promise that I'll send you photos and videos every day," Isla mentions as she sips from her to-go cup filled with tea.

"I know you will, but it's just not the same."

"Before you know it, you'll be back. Your moments with her will be extra special."

My lips quirk out from her comment, but I have to believe she's right. "I guess we'll do an hour more here, then head home before it gets too noisy here." I have the afternoon free as everyone prepares for our first team flight tomorrow for a preseason game up in Toronto.

"We also have those noise-canceling headphones for babies that you were adamant we get so she can attend the first home game of the season." Isla twists the corners of lips, clearly finding it all amusing.

"Safety first," I defend.

She sighs as we continue our stroll. "I fear the day when Briggs will play against the Spinners. My alliance feels questioned." She's half serious.

I indicate to the free bench up near the oak tree. We both find ourselves a seat there and continue on from her statement.

I nudge her shoulder with mine. "What if I tell you that I'll let you have a pass for that game. You don't need to choose the boyfriend-slash-baby daddy over your brother."

She scoffs a laugh and brings her eyes to meet mine. "That's very kind of you. Is that what your new title is? Boyfriend-slash-baby daddy?"

My arm now rests on the back of the bench behind her in a sort of claim to the outside world that we're together. Trust me, in no part of my past was I this sweet with a woman. "We may need to work on that."

"Uh, but your offer is… I don't want you to think that I don't have loyalty to you."

I brush it off. "I know you do. But I also know how much you love your brother. So feel free to secretly support him while wearing my shirt. But only one game." I give her a sheepish look.

Her hand comes to rest on my thigh, her touch already making me untamed. Since we started upgrading our sleep time—and the shower—activities, we've both been kind of avid. Before we were orbiting around one another in a peculiar way. Now everything is on the table. We can be parents, lovers, and two people who care deeply for one another.

"Vaughn…"

I'm broken from my spell of thoughts. "Yes, Isla." I grin because her delicate tone informs me that she has a meaningful question about to hit us.

"We can be something real, you and me, right?"

My eyes widen at her. "How do you do that?"

"What?"

"Read my mind as if you knew exactly what I was thinking."

She shrugs her shoulders. "Coincidence?"

"No, it's not a coincidence." It only takes a beat to state the truth. "Yeah, Isla. We can be something real going forward. It's more than a chance too." I hear the vulnerability in my voice.

Her face lightens with that gentle smile of hers. "I was hoping you would say that."

"You shouldn't be relying on me to lead the way, although I do love it. It's just… don't be afraid to say what you want."

Isla straightens her posture and ceremoniously takes my hand in hers. "I always thought you would be the one hesitating, but I guess it's me. Except now I'm clear about what I want, and it's you."

An emotion overcomes me that feels raw, unfamiliar, but exhilarating.

It gravitates my lips straight to hers for a warm kiss. I can't get enough of this, all of this. Her.

Isla gave me a gift twice over. A daughter and a relationship with her that I never intended or expected. I'm one lucky man.

"Careful," I warn her as I murmur against her lips. "I

might have to end this outing and take you right home to bed. Screw that, we can do a memory-lane session in the front seat."

Her head falls back with hysterical laughter that can't not make anyone within our radius smile. "Vaugh, please, oh please, explain how that will happen with a child in a car seat in the back."

"Solid point." Disappointment floods me. "Let's just buy a bottle of wine, and we have options. I can take you on the patio table, or we can go traditional and use a bed."

She dives in for another kiss, her finger tipping my chin. "I'm completely on board with that plan."

Which is why we walk to the general store to stock up on wine and pick up some takeout on the way home. We enjoy some tummy time with our daughter on the living room floor before I take her to the shower where I sit on the floor holding her. It's our moment that we share. She gets plenty with Isla.

"Your mom is finally being less stubborn. Seeing the light when it comes to me and her," I tell Nora, and she coos in response. "I know, right? Why the hesitation? It's me, I'm the man of her dreams, I'm sure. Her own version of Prince Charming," I lightheartedly explain to my daughter. "Go easy on her while I'm away. I'm not here to relax her in a way that she and I enjoy."

"Jesus, Vaughn, must you already traumatize our child?" Isla arrives holding a towel, ready for me to hand over the goods.

"Hey, never interrupt our serious conversations." This playfulness around our child is good for the soul. I'm not sure how anyone could turn away from this. It leaves a sour feeling in the pit of my stomach considering my upbringing, something I missed. Or how at first when I was blindsided by the news of Isla's pregnancy, I wasn't sure for a brief moment.

Isla opens the shower door, and I hand off Nora. "Be quick with the bedtime routine, we have a long night ahead of us."

"Yeah, yeah, yeah. Let me just feed her, which could be a while. She loves my chest as much as her daddy."

I grin at her. "We both know a good thing." Well, minus the milk aspect. Admittedly, I tried a little in a cup because one of the guys on the team said it's extra protein or vitamins, which is why he adds it to his coffee. *Yeah*, not going forward with that plan. Not my style.

"Don't fall asleep. I plan on coming to bed naked tonight," Isla casually mentions as she shimmies away to the nursery.

I rub my face, trying to keep myself in check, so I don't rub one out in the shower due to impatience.

I must hold out, though, because we have to make it somewhat special tonight. To reconfirm what we spoke about and to have an excellent parting before I leave. There is a lot on the line tonight.

By the time I'm lying on the bed waiting on my side, I'm nearly going out of my mind. But then my little vixen struts into the room, slowly untying the flimsy fabric of her satin robe. The robe falls in a swoosh down her skin to pool at her feet.

"I believe someone was waiting for me." Isla comes to me and is quick to push me to my back and swing one leg over to straddle me.

"This is heaven." I rest my hands behind my head.

She smirks and leans down to press a kiss on my chest then sits back up with her breasts perked out and her fingers tangling in her hair, giving me a view. I plant my hands firmly on her waist.

"I really want to watch you touch yourself before you ride me the way you want." My voice is thick with desire.

Isla takes my hands and brings them to her breasts to cup. I'm careful not to get carried away but still allow the pads of my thumbs to circle her nipples.

"I just need you in me."

I sit up and drive my thumb up to her bottom lip to drag across. "Then do it. Remember, just say what you want."

Her hips move in a wave over my cock, creating friction.

"Fill me up and show me that you meant what you said earlier." Her arms hook around my neck to ensure my lips stay close to hers.

Her pussy finds its way to welcome my shaft inside, and I slowly drive up into her.

"I meant every word," I promise and place a kiss on the curve of her shoulder. "I meant every word," I repeat and press a kiss to her collarbone. I don't stop until I'm back at her mouth.

Isla's lips grow into a satisfied smirk against my mouth. "Me too."

Then we tangle into one another, not sure where our limbs start or end. We crumble in one another's arms, forgetting that we should have been more careful, but it's a chance worth taking if it means I don't need to leave her warmth.

I stay inside, and I drop back onto the mattress, keeping Isla flush to my body.

"Shit, I wish I didn't have to leave."

She shushes my mouth with her long finger. "Stop it. Hockey is who you are, and we'll be here when you get back. Plus, Declan already said that we can join you on his plane; the perks of being an owner, I guess."

I didn't realize how much I needed her to say all of this. It's true, a lot of the times, I won't be flying with the team or coach so Declan and I can talk freely.

Inside my brain I'm figuring out what flowers to send or what our next outing will be, ignoring that our phones will become our main method of communication. A beacon of light hits me when I imagine Isla at the home games, there to support me.

It's only positive things ahead, especially since she reassures me that she'll be waiting for me.

How the hell did I miss it all those months ago that Isla was going to be more than a friend with benefits? I believe, though, that this is how it was all supposed to be.

I'm fairly confident that even though I never found the one before, I do not need to look further, as she is standing right before me. For the first time, I'm beginning to realize what this is.

She's a gamechanger.

I just don't tell her and instead kiss her with full force, catching her off guard.

But in my head, I'm beginning to be certain that this is what love is.

ISLA

With a baby wrapped around my middle, I'm sitting up near the owner's box where I float between the box and stands to watch the late-afternoon early-season home game. I can't control the complete contentment inside of me. Everything seems to have fallen into place in life. A far cry from a few months ago when my life seemed to have been unpredictable about what path I would end up on.

The past few weeks since Vaughn and I have made it clear that we want to do it all when it comes to us, a relief I didn't know I needed hit me. Now our days are filled with texts, occasional nights, and if he isn't in the owner's box, then I get to stare at him where he's sitting behind the team on occasion, focused on the game.

"Getting used to the new routine?" Hadley asks as she sits by my side, watching her husband like a hawk.

"Completely. So far, it's easier than I expected. Probably because I seem to subconsciously work around Vaughn's schedule."

"That's how hockey wives tend to do it. So, you've been

officially upgraded to girlfriend status, but do you think one day you will get an even better title?" She casually throws that in.

I scoff a laugh. "That's probably not on our minds any time soon. I'm thankful it never once came up during the whole pregnancy and having a baby. Vaughn never went all 'we must get married because it's the right thing to do.'"

"No, he just forced you to move out of your home and to sleep in his bed which you thoroughly enjoy, I'm sure." She gives me a straight-laced look before she flashes her eyes at me.

My head lolls to the side from her humor. "We are sticking to our pace, okay? Besides, not all happy couples see marriage as the be all and end all."

"That is also true. However, I don't know… you both seem to be bringing out this different side that I've never seen from either one of you. You both seem to be surprising all of us."

I bite my inner cheek from the remark because it's overtly true. "I can't deny it. We found our road, and now we're just enjoying the ride, no need to speed."

We both look down at our men, Connor racing down the ice and Vaughn standing near the coaching staff in a suit. I'm confident I've always enjoyed hockey because of the men in suits before and after games.

Occasionally he glances back to search for us and then winks. It's subtle and nearly a secret message. Kind of cute too.

"I'm relieved this is the last pre-season game and now we get a tiny break before the season kicks off," I mention.

Hadley gently touches the top of Nora's head who is tucked away. "I bet. Family time and alone time. We cherish these moments even more. It will be good for you and

Vaughn. You're supportive of him, and right now it might feel like his needs are more important, but the sports mindset is a species in itself. He wants everything to go positively for the team."

I lean back to take a sip from my water bottle. "I completely get that, and I'm prepared as well. As much as I hate to admit it, our house is kind of turning traditional, and I don't seem to mind. You know, I keep thinking about returning to work, even though Vaughn said I don't need to. I never agreed, nor have we spoken about it since. However, I'm thinking of only helping with select projects on a freelance basis and the rest of the time being at home with Nora. I kind of get why so many wives of the hockey team run the house."

It feels that everything I worked for in life is no longer relevant when it comes to the professional world. However, I realize that the only goal in life I think I had was forming a family, and here I am. I'm not going to be shy about admitting that. Everyone can do it their own way, both in motherhood or not being a mother at all.

"You're thinking clearly, I can see it. It's great that Vaughn is supportive."

"Exactly, which is why I want to make it easier for him. Who knew laundry would be so fun," I quip.

Hadley snorts a laugh. "You're joking, right?"

"Totally. Vaughn has a dry cleaner he uses." I interlace my arm with Hadley's as we focus on the game. "Who would have thought, Hadley, that a year after your wedding this is where I would have ended up."

"You didn't even need to catch the bouquet and you still had better luck than the now ex-girlfriend of the goalie who caught it."

We both shake our heads in entertainment at this conversation then squinch our faces when we see two defensemen crash into the boards.

"I am relieved that Vaughn's new hockey career doesn't involve injuries," I note.

"Tell me about it. The only thing he has to worry about is stress and unbalanced chakras or something like that." Hadley tilts her head to study the scuffle down on the ice.

"Which is why I don't plan on causing that," I swear.

After the game, Vaughn quickly comes to see us before he heads to a team meeting. Those stolen moments are the best, even if a camera is most likely in the vicinity. He normally whispers something in my ear before looking down at our daughter with a glint in his eyes of pure cherishing. Tonight, it was murmuring into my ear how I should wait up for him. And I will.

———

HENCE, why I am standing in the kitchen barefoot and in his shirt while I load the dishwasher. It's a bit after ten when Vaughn returns home. The moment his foot steps onto the kitchen tile, we head straight to one another.

I grip his loose tie and wrap it around my hand, pulling him closer. "Every time that I see you in this outfit, I'm exceptionally wet."

His smug grin appears before his velvety raspy voice hits me. "My money is on the fact that right now you're not even wearing anything under my shirt." His brows raise.

I yank him to me for a kiss, and he brings his hands to my middle, groaning a sound in the process before he lifts me. The feeling of one hand traveling to my bare ass is heavenly but short-lived because he drops me onto the counter, parts my knees, and traps himself between my thighs.

"Did someone come home all bossy?" my voice rhapsodizes as his gleam meets my eyes.

"Isla, that's the only way I'll be coming home to you."

Letting his tie go, I opt to link my arms around his neck to play with his hair and rest my elbows against his shoulders. "Except you're kind of a softie. You sent me flowers while you were away. I wasn't expecting that."

"Then I asked you to send me a nude selfie," he deadpans, because he hates when I highlight the other side of him. The opposite of the playboy persona that used to follow him.

I hum a sound as our lips begin to dance then fuse together again, his tongue seeking entrance, which I give. Vaughn begins to guide me back, and I can hear the clink of his buckle coming undone.

I'm more than compliant to follow his lead, and I use my forearms for support as I lie back then watch him. "And you are such an excellent provider when it comes to your tongue on my pussy too," I coyly mention to maintain my list of his qualities.

He laughs sinisterly as he drags my body to the edge. "That's because I need you wet and ready so I can fuck you the way I want."

I gape my mouth open right before he dives down and licks me, my body writhing and my moan a little loud, as we are downstairs.

Time and distance do this to us. We don't hesitate, we just give into the moment when opportunity arises. Which is why he works me into a frenzy before I slide off the counter to turn over so Vaughn can take me from behind. I don't even bother taking off my shirt, and his pants are hanging around his knees. But a carnal need possesses us every single time. Slow goes out the window when we have kitchen sex.

It's becoming tradition after we've finished for him to

throw me over his shoulder and walk us to the sofa where he pulls a throw blanket over us and turns on the fireplace with the flick of a button.

We should both be seeking sleep, but we can't. Our time is scarce.

Leaning against his chest, our fingers trace one another's.

"The Spinners should have a great season," I note. "They played better than last season from what I could see."

"Yeah, we managed some good trades and draft picks. The team is almost completely altered now. But I don't need to talk hockey. How was it this evening here?"

I half smile because sometimes it feels as though this homelife is his refuge. "Normal day. Bath time, milk time, white noise for sleeping, and night light. She has a good life."

Vaughn kisses my head then brings his lips near my ear, his breath hitting a sensitive spot below my lobe. "And you?" he whispers.

"Watched the highlights from Briggs's game with a bowl of soup, took a bath, then debated which shirt of yours I should wear. I'm running out of options since I seem to wear them when you're away."

"Hmm, guess that might mean you'll be sleeping naked and sending a few pics and videos." His long finger skims down my arm.

Playfully, I pinch him. "By the way, your new luggage arrived. Marketing made sure to have the team logo everywhere… Wait, sorry, no hockey talk."

"I guess it's hard. So far you're staying strong for this professional life of mine."

"It's fine. Ooh, we have the team Halloween party coming up which should be fun." I'm rambling and only stop when Vaughn captures my chin to guide my gaze up to him, as he is looking down at me.

"You're amazing, you know that?" I blush from his apparent sentimental proclamation. "I haven't decided if that makes it easier or harder when I'm away. I have a good thing happening here."

"Don't worry, all is well. Besides, you will be distracted, and I'll be distracted for different reasons, which only means our focus is there when we see one another," I promise.

Vaughn holds me closer and lets a deep breath escape as we both focus on the fire. "Tomorrow morning, I get an extra hour, so let's enjoy breakfast together before we start this routine all over again."

"Sounds perfect." I pause for a second then attempt to study his face in the glow from the fire. "You're happy with your job, right?"

"I am. Doesn't mean I can't complain about the logistics of it."

"Okay, just checking." It is a hard situation that we're in, purely from external factors. We're a new family, and throw in hockey and it's an extra layer.

"We should get some sleep." He's already dozing off, and it makes me smile.

I slip off the couch to offer him my hand. "Come on, our bed will be far more comfortable."

"As long as it has you," he laments.

"Always," I say softly, realizing I'm thinking long-term. "And that was a very cheesy line, but I'll let it go." He chuckles as he follows me along.

SITTING around the breakfast table with the bright morning sun flooding in through the floor-to-ceiling windows and only a few leaves on the trees beginning to change color, I watch

Vaughn sip from his coffee cup in one hand while his fingers on his other hand wiggle to Nora who is in the newborn insert of the highchair so she's at our level.

My knee is propped up against my chest as I eat some cut-up fruit off my fork. This is heart-melting, all of this. The nights, the morning, him, her, us.

Everything was foggy before, but now it's clear skies for us. I breathe differently.

I smile at Vaughn who gives Nora her toy keys, and then he grabs a piece of toast for himself.

"I'm sorry about last night," he begins.

Lines form on my forehead, as I'm slightly confused. "For what? You took me in a flash on the counter. What am I missing?"

Vaughn's head lolls to the side slightly as he bites his lower lip, debating his words. "Maybe I sounded a little down or out of sorts."

"You're stressed for this season, I get it. I don't see it as a big deal."

He nods once, not quite believing me, even though he should.

But I begin to have a change inside of me, and I can't shake a peculiar instinct hitting me.

A suave smile begins to appear on his face, and he eases in his mood when he looks at Nora blowing a bubble. "I can't believe I ever doubted when you told me about the pregnancy that this maybe wasn't for me. The pregnancy and family thing. It's exactly where I should be."

It was that instinct. A strike hits somewhere near my heart, and an emotion begins to roar inside of me. "What do you mean you doubted the pregnancy?" We never really talked about this because for the most part he jumped right in, it seemed.

"You know, the first thought with the news was if I want to do this or not. There was an option to walk away." His off-the-cuff tone isn't helping this situation.

I sit up and try to wrap my head around his words, but I can't seem to do that fast enough. "You only ever said that you needed time to think and absorb the news. But really you wanted to walk away? You didn't want this pregnancy?" Now I recognize it, that fear that I thought faded is again boiling up inside of me.

"Isla, I was blindsided about the pregnancy, of course my mind went in all directions and options." Vaughn doesn't seem to get the magnitude of what he just said. Nor did I realize how an underlying fear has been lurking still.

I stand up and look at our daughter, which only sets off the tears burning my eyes, desperate to come out. "You thought she might not be something you wanted. I mean, did you think our daughter was just a mistake? I know I gave you an option to walk away, and maybe I feared it my whole pregnancy, but the moment you walked into that room, I realized I didn't mean any of that."

The gravity of my thoughts seems to hit him, and instantly his hand comes out to signal for me to calm down. "Isla, you're taking this all wrong. It's only fair to acknowledge that I was in a position where I had just discovered the truth, and for a millisecond, an absolute millisecond, I thought about an out."

The tear that I've been holding in falls down my cheek. I ignore Vaughn's gaze and begin to unbuckle the safety belt around Nora to get her out. Right now, I don't want to be here in the moment. I need to process and think, most of all shake this shudder inside of me.

"It's still a millisecond, which means eventually you can

return to that thought and consider it an option." I sadly point out.

Vaughn stands up. "Isla, you're taking this out of context. I thought we were over this." I begin to walk away from the table, with aggravation filling me just as his phone sounds an alarm that he swipes off. "Shit, I have to get to the airport." He rakes his hands through his hair then drags his hand to the back of his neck to rub.

"You jumped right in or so I thought. But at first you really had doubts and thought of the out I offered?" I wonder.

His facial expression indicates *really?* "Because I see it as a non-issue, especially as this is exactly what I want."

"I never once thought of an out when it comes to her," I state blankly.

"Maybe because you knew from the start and had time to process in a normal way," he replies. But it's a scornful reminder of what I did, and remorse seems to hit us both. Him with his choice of words and me for a secret that I kept all those months. "Isla, this conversation is just sinking me into a bigger hole, when it really is a non-issue. It should be clear what I want, and I'm not going anywhere."

Vaughn walks to me, kisses Nora goodbye, then caresses my cheek with the back of his hand. "We already proved we are good parents. Sometimes we have to let go of wounds to be happy."

Then he leaves.

This is our first big disagreement since what I thought was our new reality. Or is it just an agreement? Either way, it hurts all the same.

But even I know it only takes a split second for someone's mind to change. And what happens when Vaughn does that?

VAUGHN

This is not good. Not in the slightest.

Isla is not in a great place now. It's been two days since I left, only because I had to go to Seattle for the team. Since then, it's been basic messages about Nora. I thought the best thing to do is give a little space.

The last thing I wanted was to upset her, but I'm not going to hide the truth either.

Which is why I'm sitting next to my brother in the hotel bar, thankful he was in Seattle for book research, whatever the hell that means.

With whiskey in hand, I sigh again. "I have to turn this around."

"You will. She's going to realize that this is something you both can move on from," Stone assures me.

I rub my forehead in frustration. "We better. This is making me lose focus and setting Isla and me back. Most of all, I can't find it in me to apologize over a thought I once had, because I can't change it. She also needs to allow some understanding to consider how this all came to be."

"Didn't you move on from the whole pregnancy secret?"

I nod to confirm that he is right.

"It's got to be different for her, and you're going to have to meet her halfway to end this lovers' tiff." He lifts his glass to me before taking a sip of his whiskey.

I give him an unamused look for his choice of words. "We are a bit more than lovers, you ass."

Stone smirks. "Yeah, which is all the more reason that you both need to accept that couples have disagreements."

"Should I feel guilty for a thought I once had?" I wonder, because I keep questioning it.

"No, like you said, it can't be changed. A lot of guys may be the same way when an accidental pregnancy happens, let alone finding out late. Even a woman can think it. But like I said, you got over that detail. Give her space. Focus on your daughter, and eventually everything will fade away."

My lips quirk out. "Nah, its more than that. I know it is."

I know a sleepless night is ahead, which isn't great, as tomorrow is game day.

"Okay, then what is your plan of action?"

I nearly groan. "I'm in Seattle. Who plays for Seattle?" I give him a hint.

Stone's voice rumbles a deep laugh. "No way, you're going to talk to *her brother*?"

"Hopefully I come out alive."

"Damn, the guy hates you."

I wince at the thought. "It eased to only dislike lately. Desperate times, desperate measures."

"When is this showdown happening?" Stone inquires.

"I asked him to come here in a little bit. Figured a public place is the best solution, plus tomorrow after the game we head off right away."

Stone grins. "Can I sit in the corner to watch the show?"

I shake my head. "Don't be an ass. Why are you here again?"

"Research," he simply states.

My face turns puzzled. "What the hell could that be?"

His head tips the side slightly. "A woman, actually."

I stifle a laugh. "Since when?"

"Since she pushed me because I threw an apple onto the ground, and she got concerned for a deer."

"Well, that's kind of weird."

He proudly grins. "*Yeah*, but here I am, because she has a book signing. She doesn't know I'm here, but I figured the element of surprise and a basketful of apples to piss her off will do the trick."

For the first time in two days, I have to smile at that ridiculous move. "I can't even process that right now."

Stone grips my shoulder. "That's good, because your murderer just arrived." He tips his head in the direction of Briggs who is standing at the other end of the bar with his shoulders puffed out.

I groan, and my jaw ticks as I prepare myself.

"Going to head to my room." Stone stands.

"No, you're not."

His grin is making me ready to push him like we did when we were kids and he stole my Ninja Turtle. "You're completely right."

By the time he is gone and Briggs fills his seat with a steely look, I feel like I might be regretting my move.

"Okay, Vaughn, you get ten minutes to tell me why I shouldn't beat your ass. Isla didn't tell me what happened, only grumbled some sounds which I feel like were not in your favor." Briggs crosses his arms.

"Hello to you too." I scratch my cheek.

"Spit it out." His tone is stern.

"Your sister is pissed because I mentioned when I found out about the pregnancy that for a split second, I wasn't sure if fatherhood was for me, but a thousand thoughts were in my head, as I was in shock." Honesty is the only way that he will give me the insight I need.

He snickers his disapproval. "Why the hell would you admit that?"

"Does nobody appreciate that I'm being open?" I sigh, slightly irritated.

He looks at me with strong discontent. "Not with Isla. You have no idea, do you?"

"Did I not immediately stay with her when I found out?"

Briggs shakes his head. "Do you know how much Isla wanted everything? The second she told me she was pregnant, she was already more than in. From moment one, she never had a single doubt. So, for her to hear that the father of her child might not have felt the same, then it only adds a hole into the fear she's always carried. She may have been petrified to tell you during her pregnancy about the baby, but she always had hope. As soon as she saw you, she realized her error and wanted only one thing. Then you hopped on the train and now it feels like false hope to her."

I stare at him, waiting for him to explain further, my eyes intent on taking in his knowledge.

"Vaughn, she holds onto the wound of our dad never playing a role. He was around the first two years of my life then completely bailed on our mom when she was pregnant and left before Isla was born. Her biggest fear is that history will repeat with her own child. So yeah, the tiniest bit of doubt will send her over the rails."

My eyes close as realization hits me. How could I not see it? Dots connect of why she may have felt panic as her first instinct.

"Why are you being this open with me?"

Briggs shakes his head. "You may have been the guy I hated on the ice, but you won't be the guy who leaves her. I fucking hate to admit that I see that. But it's also what Isla deserves."

"I'm not sure what to do to ensure she shakes that fear that seems to chase her."

"That's relationship 101. You have to prove to her that you are committed for life. Why the hell am I even pointing out the obvious to you?" He looks at me as though I'm an idiot, and maybe I am.

I roll my eyes to the side and let out a deep breath. "Because your sister isn't anyone. I haven't been in this situation before, and I want to get it right."

"Damn well you will." We stare at one another blankly, then Briggs sighs. "Look, maybe she overreacted. Hell, if I found out when a baby is about to pop that I'm going to be a dad, then yeah, a hell of a lot of thoughts would be in my head too. But just let her win this one and ease her."

Briggs stands and gives me a glare. "Do you love her?"

I think for a second with a realization sinking in. I nod. "Yeah, I do."

"Then tell her, that's a start."

"Thanks, Briggs." I mean it sincerely.

For once, he gives me a sympathetic yet agreeing look. "Fix this." He walks away but not before he stops and turns back to me. "By the way, I have every intention to crush your team tomorrow, even if it's the one I used to play on."

"Figured," I confirm.

"Oh, and our general manager is better, he at least smiles when under pressure. You look like hell."

I tighten my wry smile and hold my two fingers up in the air to wave him off. "A pleasure, as always," I call out.

It only takes a few seconds before I hear a slow clap and turn my head to find my brother casually sitting in the corner on a burgundy leather couch with drink in hand.

I shake my head, not amused. "Of course, you witnessed all of that."

Stone stands and strolls my way before sliding onto a seat at the bar. "Hell yeah, event of the year."

"Great. Add it to the memory pool for future Christmas dinners."

"He made some solid points. We also have some abandonment issues. You completely understand where Isla's mind is, and you know it."

It hurts in me that I now feel her pain. "I do, which makes this all worse."

"When is the next time you see her?"

"In two days."

"Then you have two days to figure out how you will show her that you can relate and comfort her," he reminds me.

My lips purse out with a breath. "You're right."

"And you are also better than the man who let us down. I don't need to tell you that. You love her. It's so obvious but maybe not to her."

I now look at him peculiarly. "Where the hell did you get the basis of this pep talk?"

He grins and awkwardly scratches his cheek. "Apple lady is a romance writer. Might have read a few of her books to prove her wrong and show her that her books are sappy bull that doesn't happen in real life."

"Yet here you are using her wise knowledge."

Stone's face drops. "Shit."

"I'll let you know how it goes."

"Yeah, you will. I would hate to hear that Isla kicks you to the curb or throws you into that lake."

A glimmer of subtle smile hits me. "She won't. I'm not going to let her walk away from everything I will do to assure her."

Hadley walks next to me as I lead an aimless path through the grocery store. She has Nora in the carrier against her chest.

"*So,* what are we doing here exactly?" she asks with caution.

"Diapers, bananas, hope," I list with my voice, fatigued. My energy is a little low since the other day when Vaughn and I had what I wouldn't say was a fight but a discussion that caught me off guard and cracked a little bit of my heart. Disappointment flooded me, and now I'm not sure what's happening.

Hadley takes hold of the bar on the cart to stop our slow stroll. We're alone in the cereal aisle, which is kind of off course for what I needed, but that's beside the point.

"Isla, I think… you need to put yourself in his shoes."

My face floods with disbelief at the audacity of my close friend taking Vaughn's side. "What? How can you say that?"

"Because, well, given the circumstances, then maybe he deserves a little slack? Shock does a lot of things to people, and since then, he has only proven that he wants to be a dad and be there for you." She's delicate in tone but seems assertive with her theory.

"What is to say that he won't change his mind? After all, he thought once that maybe he shouldn't be involved." My reasoning has to make sense to anyone who listens.

Hadley purses her lips out then rolls them in before she tips her head to the side slightly. "Isla, do you really believe that one day he will wake up and leave? You truly believe that?"

A few ticks go by while I search within me. "Most of me believes he is fully involved for our family. I just… can't shake that tiny piece of fear."

She examines a box of bran flakes, giving us a moment to let my admission float in the air between us.

"When is he back?"

I swallow due to the logistics of time. "Tonight."

Hadley taps the cereal box with her nail. "You're not the only human to have a wound inside of them."

I sigh and look down at my daughter, feeling the crack in my throat as tears threaten to break out. "How could he even think…"

She touches my elbow to comfort me. "He doesn't think it. You know, my dad and I, we had our own issues," she begins. I've never known what they are, but I'm hoping Hadley can give insight. "Things are not always clear, and you might discover something from a time now passed. But sometimes it makes us stronger, the bond between people stronger. We also have to remember that we won't always do things the way our parents did. You have to see that. I know you do because you are the proven fact. We can be better."

Hot damn, she makes that tear fall. "I'm beginning to feel

like I overreacted, and now I'm not sure what to do when I see him."

Now a warm smile slants on her mouth. "Maybe you don't need to say anything, just listen."

I nod in understanding but still take a deep breath for courage. "Am I being unreasonable?" I need to double-check.

Hadley's face turns crooked and her demeanor changes. "Okay, Isla, real talk for a second. I'm not going to sugar coat this. Yes." She throws the box of cereal into the cart. "Maybe you are overstretching, but I respect that everyone has a right to feel the way they do. I'm completely team Vaughn because he hasn't done anything wrong. He stepped up within minutes of finding out. I mean, come on, the guy literally saw you nearly about to deliver a baby and still went into action mode… one that gives you everything you've been waiting for. You get everything if you just let go a little. Now, enjoy your bran cereal," she huffs, and my daughter just coos as if she is giving her input.

As much as I'm taken aback by Hadley's abrupt disposition, I can't help but soften inside. I'm not completely ignoring what she said. It's food for thought.

I grab the box of cereal and place it back on the shelf. "Geez, Hadley, at least pick Cheerios if you're going to go on a tangent."

She scoffs a laugh and smiles at me with reassurance. For the first time in days, I feel a light beginning to brighten.

I'M SITTING on the living room floor while Nora lies on her back, attempting to reach for the hanging wooden toys on her baby gym while I have a video call with my brother. Pointing the camera at his niece, of course.

"She's smart."

I have to chuckle. "She's reaching for a bell, I'm not sure that's rocket science."

"And? Intelligence starts somewhere."

I shake my head and switch to selfie mode so we talk.

"You called? I saw your game. You kind of annihilated the Spinners. I feel bad saying that, but Vaughn said I'm allowed to quietly cheer you on when you play against them."

Briggs goes quiet, and it isn't often that he doesn't have anything to say. He licks his lips while he looks to his side then back at me.

"What's going on? You don't seem like a man who just won."

"Uhm, I saw Vaughn."

My shoulders slant up to my ears. "And? You were at the same game, it's kind of bound to happen."

His cheeks tighten and he scratches his chin, appearing to get comfortable with whatever he is about to say. "It wasn't at the game."

"Oh." Now I understand why he called.

"We met at his hotel bar, man to man," he explains.

I bite my bottom lip, curious yet scared about what he is about to say. A part of me is petrified that Vaughn sent my brother to deliver heartbreaking news. Even though it makes no sense.

"You should give him a chance."

Immediately, I do a double take. "Wait, what?"

Briggs grins at the camera. "You heard me. Don't make me utter the words again."

"Are you seriously defending him right now? As in, did something happen last night, aliens landing perhaps?" I'm quite frankly astonished.

"Nah, we have to communicate since he is the father of my niece. Most of all, he's the guy who is crazy about you."

A smile tugs on my lips, as it feels extra sentimental that my brother confirms what I've been feeling the last weeks when Vaughn is around. "Yeah… I may have noticed."

"He isn't going anywhere. Don't let tiny things prevent you from moving toward something better."

Now my eyes bug out. "You're giving me a pep talk? Really, is there something in the Seattle water?"

He laughs and leans back on his couch. "Isla. I'm stating the fucking obvious."

I huff yet again today and drop my shoulders. "I'm hearing that a lot lately."

"Listen, I may need to roast him in the wedding speeches if you ever get married. But Vaughn… I don't know… I hate him when it comes to hockey, but he is bearable when it comes to you and my niece. This isn't even about Nora, and you know it. You were just looking for a crack to justify that everything is within your grasp, the whole nine yards." He rolls a shoulder back and dips his eyes as if he wants to downplay his confession. "So yeah, maybe he is a little more bearable than I thought… he'll fight for you."

"Yeah, I will."

The sound of Vaughn's voice from behind me catches me off guard, and my head whips in his direction. I didn't hear him come in. But he's now leaning against the wall with his hands in his pockets and his feet crossed, his face stoic.

I quickly glance back at my phone.

"I guess that's my cue to hang up. Didn't plan this timing, but I don't particularly want to watch this go down." He drags out his words then speeds up. "Bye, Sis." And my screen shows me that the call ended.

Which means that I need to turn back to the scene of

Vaughn who has returned and is ready to pick up right where he left off. This time he is calmer, poised, and making my heart thump in a new sort of way.

"I wasn't expecting you this early." I slowly manage to form a sentence.

A glimmer of a faint smirk appears on his lips. "The element of surprise is something we have experience in." Vaughn uncrosses his feet and strides toward us with a bit of swagger that just comes naturally to him.

The moment he enters my bubble, a ripple spreads across my skin. It's anticipation for what is about to come.

He leans down to greet our daughter, an instant smile appearing on both their faces. "Hey there, kiddo, you're growing a little too much for my liking. Slow it down, will ya? You're rolling over and reaching for things. Next thing I know we'll need to baby-proof the fu-… fudge out of this place."

The view of them together thaws my mixed emotions slightly.

Vaughn glances at me. "Let's get her down for a nap and then we can talk. I'll do it." He's already swooping Nora up into his arms before I can answer.

It makes sense, as the revelations that are floating around us shouldn't have little ears present, however, it doesn't help my shooting nerves. I pace a few times around the living room, debating if I should grab a glass of wine, because I need to feel a little more serene if I don't want to be an emotional mess.

By the time Vaughn re-appears, we take a moment to get lost in a gaze. I'm debating if sitting down is a good start to keep the next moments flowing. He doesn't let me decide as he walks straight to me and frames my face in the palms of his hands. His eyes stare straight into mine, ensuring I can't escape from the shackles of his fortitude in this moment.

"I'm not going anywhere, Isla," he whispers. My mouth parts open but barely a sound escapes. "I understand. Really, I do. I can't apologize for expressing the truth," he informs me.

"You kind of threw it back in my face that I never told you," I begin to rehash the other morning, but I keep my tone weak while I blink a few times.

His thumb starts to draw a circle on my cheek. "Not my intention. We can't change the facts, but we can move on from it. I promise I have. I got to see Nora born, and that's what really matters as far as your pregnancy is concerned. You get that, right?" He gently presses his palms tighter against the outline of my face.

I swallow, as this is one aspect that I believe we can both let go of. "I do. We can agree on one thing."

Vaughn steps closer which only heightens the beating in my chest. "We can agree on a lot of things. Hell, we want the same things."

"Maybe I've overreacted, okay, I probably did. But you said that once you thought—"

He cuts me right off. "Shh, Isla. I was honest, but it also takes a millisecond for things to be clear. I had a brief speck of doubt, only for extreme certainty to follow. A commitment that I'm never going to break."

Geez, can these tears stop appearing. Do I even have any left? Because water pools at the bottom of my eyes.

"I'm scared."

Vaughn presses his lips against my forehead and releases his hold on my face, only to wrap his arms around my back to pull me close to his chest. "Fear only makes us do better."

Through my tears, I snort a laugh. "Is that something from your hockey career?"

"It's the truth, though." His voice sounds eased. He holds me tighter, as if he will never let go. "This isn't about our daughter at all. Because we have something to celebrate, as we are the type of parents we hoped to be. I think you are confronted by the fact that we were probably two broken people who were missing something. But now we fit together, and it fixes everything. I believe we are one and the same. Our hope was always lingering. Now we are two people who connect on a different level than we ever expected. It's scary, but it's us."

My mouth begins to quiver. "It sounds so poetic the way you said it, even if it's the truth."

He begins to half grin, with his head tilting to the side. "I may have practiced my speech with Stone on the phone, and he gave a few tips."

I have to laugh at that.

"Stop trying to believe that it's impossible to be this happy. Just accept it."

I nod because he completely peeled away the writings inside my heart. "I don't want you to walk away one day," I whisper, a mumble against his chest where the fabric is now wet from my tears.

"You don't need to want something that you already have. I'm here to stay," he guarantees.

Peeking up to search his eyes, I only see honesty. Especially when his eyes dip down to capture my seeking plea.

With one hand wrapped around my middle, his other slides up to weave his fingers through my hair. "It's like this, Isla. My whole life I've been playing a game. But it turns out the one game that I want is the family card with a woman that I love. I've been waiting for you, and I didn't even know it. I've only ever played to win, and that's the point. Once you win, it's cemented as fact, and you can't go back to change it.

Which is perfectly fitting, because this family is the win for the game I've been waiting to play."

His words touch me deep within, even reaching the dark abyss that holds every apprehension and dot of sadness. My mouth slants up slowly. "I think… I needed to hear that… Wait…" It dawns on me. "Did you say the woman that you love?" My head perks to the side as I try to digest a revelation.

That sweltering grin appears again, this time with a fixed sentiment. "You heard that right. I love you, Isla."

Now I can't help but smile through fucking tears. "Is this really happening?"

"We already happened." His voice is neutral as I soak in his words.

I raise onto the balls of my feet to wrap my arms around Vaughn's neck. "I'm sorry for the way I acted."

"Don't apologize. It's how you feel."

"We can really be something… real and raw and the dream that's now fact… especially since I love you too." I say it and realize that this proclamation has been building for months. I never wanted to let the feeling bubble up inside of me. Feeling it wouldn't be wise to assess the overpowering wave happening right now. Because I refuse to let a child be the reason for moving forward if it isn't right.

But this *is* right.

Vaughn kisses me in response, his bottom lips nuzzling my own, preparing me for the passionate kiss that ensues, then sewing in a tenderness that feels as though we are confirming we can move forward. His tongue delves into my mouth, and a dizziness hits me because suddenly my last few days of gray have been replaced with a confidence that every-thing has fallen into place.

I murmur, and it encourages his mouth to cover mine,

ensuring our breath becomes one. I'm going weak from the overabundance of relief and his tantalizing lips. My head falls back which doesn't help, as he immediately brushes his lips down my neck, sending a ripple of sensitivity down to my toes.

"Getting you to bed will have to wait." He nips my skin then drags his bottom lip down before retracing his line back up.

We barely part, his fingers combing a few strands of my hair behind my ear. "We should talk all night. We're on the same page, but we should go over it a thousand times. If you want to have extra reassurance, then we'll put your name on this house. I can draw papers up to ensure you know that you and Nora will always be taken care of. I'm sticking around, but I'll do whatever you need."

I plant my finger over his lips to stop talking. "I trust you. Which means your word is enough."

He pecks a kiss on my fingertip before my hand drops. "Don't hide what scares you, because most likely I share it too. All the more reason we'll work hard to have the best damn family and relationship there is."

I nod and smile as I lick a tear from the corner of my mouth. "You're saying all the right things, I believe every single syllable… but I can't get these ridiculous tears to stop. It's like full-on waterfall, hormones, or the vitamin powder in my morning shake making me produce enough water for the lake," I joke.

We both let out a stunted laugh, accepting that the hard part of our conversation is over.

"It's been a crazy few months. Let it go. If you're still like this at Christmas then I'll grab a bucket so we can start a reservoir," he teases.

A quick kiss happens before we whisper again our I-love-yous.

The next hour we sit on the sofa with the fireplace on and recap our months ahead until end of season; we don't go past that in the calendar. We're both okay with going slow or fast, we're seeing where our relationship takes us.

Inside of me I'm celebrating because it's going to be everything we always wanted.

We already are.

Vaughn looks at our daughter blankly. "What in the world is that?"

I give Nora an extra squeeze. "It's a snowman unicorn onesie. See? The horn has a little snowflake on it."

He blinks his eyes several times. "I'm just going to roll with this."

I chortle a sound. "Hadley's mom got her a unicorn-themed outfit for every holiday. Fear Easter with all your might," I warn.

Vaughn's face finally breaks, and he can't help but laugh.

I just arrived at the team's family holiday party. First, lunch with Santa, then ice skating—with safety because there are going to be a lot of kids around.

Vaughn takes our little girl from my arms to make our way into one of the rooms used for gatherings. It's nothing too fancy, a buffet and decorations. I'm fairly confident the two odd-looking gingerbread men were made by two rookies, and now we all have to vote who decorated which. One is missing an eye or possibly a mouth, I can't tell. It's also noisy, with a lot of aws and ohs.

It's been a few months since Vaughn and I solidified our direction, which is why everything feels like an easy breeze. We still have his hectic schedule, which means moments are sparce until the end of season, but despite our frantic lives, everything feels as stable as can be.

"Let's go take a seat over there." Vaughn indicates to Violet, Declan, and their kids. I follow, taking note that Nora is making little noises as she responds to us now, with eyes more magical.

Vaughn mutters to me when I reach his side. "We won't stay too long. I'm eager to see you in your naughty elf costume."

I shake my head, because under no circumstances am I bringing holiday characters into the bedroom… stockings and lace inspired by winter colors, sure.

We settle at the table, with a camera instantly hitting our peripheral view, which tends to happen at team events. They know they need to angle to keep Nora's face out of view; maybe we'll change our minds later. At games, she's so bundled up that I'm not sure they could even get a clear view.

"What are you two up to for the three token days off at Christmas?" Violet asks while Declan talks to someone at his side.

Vaughn brings an arm around my shoulders and, being the talented man he is, holds the baby in his other arm. "Taking it easy. My brother will join us for dinner, and my favorite brother-in-law is back in town." Vaughn smiles tightly.

I playfully turn my head to pretend to bite his arm. "He loves it. They're becoming fast friends," I say, because their relationship is nearly a 180 to a year ago. Meh, let's settle on a 90-degree angle.

"I forgot to ask. Didn't you two have an anniversary not

so long ago?" Violet wonders as she hands her toddler a cucumber slice.

Vaughn and I look to one another with affection, then it twists into a goofy grin.

"You mean, do we celebrate our anniversary on the date of a hurricane?" I ask, trying to hide my smile.

"Well…" Violet shrugs. "We all kind of know the creation date of your little angel. Just assuming that's the date that you chose for your anniversary. One year is a little milestone."

"It is, which is why Isla flew out with Nora to our away game," Vaughn explains.

Violet looks at us, unamused. "Boo. Who wants to celebrate an anniversary with a baby? Albeit they are cute, but alas, a baby. Seriously, go find some alone time."

I roll my lips in, attempting to keep my tongue in check. "We do find time together, don't worry."

"Oh, I think it's our turn with Santa," Vaughn lies and stands up in record time. I play along and follow him in the direction of a dressed reindeer.

"She was a little too blunt," he states.

I wave him off. "It's okay, we're friends. Our playdates for the kids mean we don't need to hold back, plus those playdates might entail breaking out a bottle of wine around three o'clock."

"Moms who wine, sounds about right."

We approach the deer, and then it happens. At first a tiny squeak and then the quiver of Nora's little mouth before a high-pitched cry hits our ears.

Oh fudge, someone doesn't like the costumes descending upon us.

"Well, no cute first Christmas photo for us." Vaughn begins to bounce Nora in his arms.

"Was this ever going to go as planned? Last year I found

out I was pregnant, this year I discover our child hates people in costumes, except when she's wearing one herself," I casually mention.

Vaughn side-eyes me before quickly kissing my cheek. "Sounds like your year only got better."

"Yeah… yeah, it did," I lament.

———

SNAP.

"There is the golden shot," Stone says as he examines his screen, as he just took a photo. It's fun having him around. He moved to Lake Spark like he said he would, which also means he stops by even when Vaughn isn't around. Believe it or not, he is a baby whisperer too.

It's Christmas Day, and we just managed to get a calm baby to comply with our photos by the tree.

"The party is here," Briggs announces, as he must have come in through the back. He's holding up a six-pack, which is kind of hilarious considering this house is anything but simple.

Briggs sets the beer on the counter then strolls right into the living area to drop onto the sofa on the other end from Stone.

"Where's your girlfriend?" I ask.

"Ivy will be here in a bit. Her casserole needed a little more time in the oven, and I wanted to be sure that I get enough time with my niece since I have to fly out tomorrow," Briggs explains.

Vaughn and I stand but leave Nora on the rug so she can admire the wrapping paper that catches her interest.

Stone tips his nose up at Briggs. "Just remember that the better uncle arrived on time."

Briggs gawks at Stone. "I'll prove to you that I can out-uncle you…" He snaps his fingers. "In a minute flat."

Vaughn shakes his head, almost annoyed. "Let's leave the Hunger Games for another day. What are the chances you can show me your teamwork skills to watch your niece for a few minutes?" Vaughn requests from both.

They both have a stiff look and raise their posture. It's utterly ridiculous, but they'll soften the moment they see Nora roll over or shriek in delight.

"On it," Briggs announces.

Vaughn and I both smile as we walk down the hall where we grab our coats and boots then walk through the garage to the back patio where a fire was already started a little while ago. Vaughn thought we should have options for where we sit today, and he wanted to deep fry a turkey with Stone, which honestly, I don't see it being a success.

He sits down then pulls me onto his lap. "We get a few minutes alone." He flashes his eyes at me.

The snow on the ground isn't light, but still the lake looks breathtaking, even with ice on the shallow water.

"Only if you keep me warm," I purr into his ear and link my arm around his.

"Are you happy?" he asks, and I notice a glint in his eyes.

My own eyes squint for a second. "Very. Are you even questioning it?"

"Not at all. It's been a great day, plus we even have a special cheese plate for snacks," he jokes.

I stifle a sound. "Remember how this all came to be? A ridiculous cheese conversation and your flirting skills."

"Ah, so I charmed you from second one."

"Absolutely."

We both sigh as we sync our breathing and stare out to the

view. This is peaceful and quiet, yet completely intimate in a way, as it's us.

"We're going at the right pace? You and me?" Vaughn asks.

"Geez, what's with the interrogation? Are you okay?" Now I look at him with worry.

His smirk appearing means trouble. He has a trick up his sleeve, I feel it in my bones. "May I just throw an option out on the table?"

"Why do I feel like this isn't our usual 'catch-up and take a moment to be with one another' chat?" I lean back slightly to examine him more, as if I'm trying to solve a riddle. Then I notice Stone and Briggs standing by the window, pretending that they're not observing. It seems Briggs won the battle of who gets to hold the niece.

Vaughn grabs my attention when he breaks my daze with a kiss to draw me back to him. A long kiss, and I can feel his hand rummaging around our middle, as if he is adjusting his coat.

Our lips part, but I just want to dive in for another kiss. Yet I can't because his eyes have locked with mine.

"I'm giving us a few options for when you're ready, but I think our slow ship has sailed." His gaze lowers then pops back up.

It was a sign for me to search, and when I follow the line of his coat zipper down to his hand, I gasp.

A ring.

A big ring.

A ring that signals commitment.

A forever type of ring.

Forever.

We're not fast, we're not slow. We're exactly on track.

Bliss hits me in a swoosh, and I throw my arms around his neck again. "Yes."

"Uh, I didn't even ask. It could be a promise ring for all you know."

"Oh, shut up, you know you want to lock me in for the future."

His suave grin appears while he begins to grab my finger. "Marry me, Isla. We can wait or not, but just know that I want the longest game there is… with you."

The moment the ring slips onto my finger, my life changes yet again.

Crap, tears again. Happy tears, yet still tears.

We're going to need to start that reservoir.

EPILOGUE: VAUGHN

6 MONTHS LATER

The sun is holding out on us, yet the dark clouds to the west should be concerning.

I'm confident Illinois June weather will hold out for us a little longer. Enough time to seal this deal, anyway.

Standing at the end of the aisle in dark jeans and a white linen shirt with the lake behind me, I wait impatiently for the next moments of this day.

I glance to my side and my face still puzzles. Who the hell knew that Briggs would go this far for his sister, that he would be the guy to marry us, since he got ordained somewhere between scoring goals.

"Remember, I'm not retired yet, which means my physical strength may be strong in the event it is ever needed," Briggs informs me in a low voice so only I can hear, but then he pats my shoulder, and a beaming smile hits him.

My eyes travel to the front row where Hadley is sitting with Connor who winks at me, and Declan and Violet smile as they wait for the big show. My brother gives me a thumbs-up from where he sits at the end of the row.

Isla and I decided that we would do simple. Casual yet elegant were her words. A buffet is waiting for us inside, with a hell of a lot of champagne, cheese, and cobbler.

My instinct has me search the aisle until the end, and there she is.

We acknowledge one another with soft smiles in a perfect image that will be imprinted in my brain and heart. Isla's in a thin-strapped white gown that looks like a second skin and has a plunging line along her breasts. She's radiant, especially as one hand holds a small bouquet, and her other arm is carrying our daughter who is in a puffy dress with a headband bow that I didn't quite agree with.

Everyone stands as Isla begins to walk down the aisle, every step feeling too slow.

Halfway down, with everyone admiring her beauty, she stops. But I don't stress. Nora is reaching her arms out for me and squeaking "Dada," which earns an *aww* from the guests. Isla laughs then decides to set Nora down who immediately starts her speeding crawl following the ribboned cloth and heading straight to me.

She steals the show, and I kneel down to pick her up.

Then we continue on with the wedding schedule.

When Isla reaches me, we can't break away from our smiles.

"Should we hand her to someone in the front row?" Isla asks, with her eyes going wide.

I turn to my future brother-in-law. "This is going to be quick, right? We requested the speedy version."

"Relax, I listened," Briggs assures us.

"Then she stays with us," I confirm.

And that's how we do it. We get married holding our

daughter. The fastest ten-minute service of our lives, which is good, as storm clouds are rolling in.

I have no choice but to hand Nora to my brother because when Briggs tells me I can kiss the bride, I do just that. I tip Isla back and kiss the hell out of her. We're not going to start our life as husband and wife with a chaste kiss, uh-uh, not in my book.

The guests clap and cheer as sprinkles of rain begin to fall. Thunder in the distance breaks our kiss.

"It's going to storm," I tell my wife.

She wraps her arms around my neck. "Storms are my favorite when they're with you," she hums.

"I'm aware, which is why I paid someone up there to arrange it, assuming it makes our wedding night even better," I joke.

Isla giggles right before I pick her up and twirl her around.

"Set me down, Husband. How am I going to get inside?"

I dip my mouth down while she's in my arms and kiss her real quick. "I'll carry you, I always will."

We take a second to soak in this moment between us, with her lips gently tugging into a sentimental smile right before I carry her back down the aisle.

TOASTS WERE DONE, first dance complete, cake cut, bouquet thrown, and our daughter crashed from a sugar rush since we let her have two spoonfuls of cake.

Declan, Connor, and my brother are sitting outside on the terrace while they drink their whiskey. Luckily, the storm went to the south. I join them since Isla is with Hadley and

Violet freshening up, which means she'll be a solid twenty minutes.

Someone offers me a glass of champagne, as they have an entire bottle sitting on the side table.

Connor tips his glass up. "A toast."

Declan reaches into his blazer's inner pocket to pull out some cigars and passes one to each of us before we all hold up our glasses.

"To locking down your wife in the most unconventional story that will be awkward as fuck to explain to your daughter one day." *Okay*, so that's Connor's speech.

It causes all of us to glance at one another.

"Listen, kid, you accidentally got married in Vegas," Declan points out to Connor. "And you really want to call Vaughn's road to marriage unconventional?"

"Says the guy who used the Dizzy Duck Inn for his secret escapades with my aunt before my dad found out," Connor counters.

Christ, we're going down a rabbit hole.

Declan points his glass to Connor. "Hey, first off, the Dizzy Duck is sacred ground in Lake Spark. I hope the new owners keep it that way. Secondly, Violet and I are married not by accident or due to a hurricane baby."

My brother looks between all of us. "Holy hell, what does this town do to people?"

Declan relaxes. "Normally hockey and finding the love of your life. Haven't you discovered that yet?" With his tone flippant, he directs his question to Stone.

"That's clear. And by the way, one of the new owners is also a retired athlete. We used to attend a few charity events together," Stone mentions, which causes me to half smile, because truthfully, he invested as a silent partner with the new owner.

"If he changes the name of this fine hotel then the town will riot," Declan points out. Stone tries to keep his face neutral as he listens.

"Aren't we supposed to be having a speech now?" I attempt to get us back on track.

My brother snickers, then his jaw ticks while his cheeks tighten.

"Something you'd care to share?" I poke.

We give up on a proper speech for a toast and all clink our glasses before taking a sip, but my focus snaps back to Stone.

He takes another gulp. "Actually, I'm kind of in a predicament with someone, a writer…"

"Apple lady?" I ask, my voice one-toned.

"Yeah, something like that… a bit more complicated, though…"

www.ingramcontent.com/pod-product-compliance
Lightning Source LLC
Chambersburg PA
CBHW071416300726
48976CB00006B/2118